F
Rey

16087

Reynolds, Marilyn.

No more sad goodbyes.

DATE DUE			
DEC 1 '08	SEP 21 '10	FEB 8 '12	
DEC 2 '08	OCT 8 '10	FEB 22 '12	
DEC 8 '08	NOV 30 '10	APR 17 '12	
SEP 11 '09	FEB 18 '11	MAY 21 '12	
SEP 28 '09	APR 11 '11	OCT 18 '12	
OCT 26 '09	SEP 14 '11	NOV 7 '12	
NOV 10 '09	SEP 29 '11	OCT 22 '13	
DEC 18 '09	OCT 27 '11	JAN 27 '14	
JAN 14 '10	DEC 12 '11	FEB 22 '14	
APR 9 '10	DEC 16 '11	MAR 71 '14	
7 '10	JAN 25 '12		

Praise for the Hamilton High Series from Teen Readers

"I read *No More Sad Goodbyes* non-stop! I liked that it showed that everybody makes mistakes, and we are not alone."

Monique, Roanoke-Benson High School

"Out of all the books I've read (and trust me, I've read tons of books), yours have impacted me the most. They are filled with reality and hope and strength, and make me feel stronger."

Gillian (email)

"I have just finished reading *Detour for Emmy*. I wanted you to know that in all my years of school that book is the first book that I have honestly read from cover to cover. I have never in my life read a book, and I can't wait to read more of yours."

Amy, North Toole County High School

"I want to tell you that I find your books very interesting and reading them has helped me get through a lot in my life. Thank you."

Julie, La Puente High School

"Before I read *If You Loved Me* I had never bothered to check out a book at a library, but now I can't stop reading. Thank you for changing the way I lived my life."

Maria, Bell Gardens High School

"Your books have led me into the world of reading. Thank you."

Paola Torres, San Luis High School

"Your book [*But What About Me*] touched me because it felt like I was the only one going through these things, but when I read your book I knew that I wasn't alone."

Praise from Professionals

After a tragedy leaves Autumn with no living relatives, this teen must decide whether to abort, keep, or give up the baby growing inside after a one-time mistake with her best friend's heartthrob. Readers will feel Autumn's grief, anxiety, confusion, and relief throughout her decision-making process as she strives to follow her father's mantra to "be part of the solution." Reynolds has outdone herself in developing both an awesome character and a captivating story that will stay with readers long after the book ends. This is a must read for adolescent girls and interested adults.

Joan F. Kaywell, PhD, University of South Florida,
Editor of Dear Author: Letters of Hope

In *No More Sad GoodByes*, Autumn thinks she has a plan, but life spirals out of orbit and she has to face the inevitable — she's going to have a baby. Her father's advice "to be part of the solution, not the problem," seems impossible. Who will help her? Read Autumn's story and feel your heart break for a teenager facing one of life's biggest challenges alone. Anyone who judges a pregnant teen needs to read this book.

Deb Young, Librarian, Roanoke-Benson High School

As always, Reynolds breathes life into important social issues with likable, believable characters who elevate this [*Love Rules*] beyond a "problem" novel.

Booklist, Debbie Carton

The writing is superb and the realistic tone sets this book [*But What About Me*] alongside the best of the genre.

School Library Journal, Robyn Ryan Vandenbroek

The seventh title [*If You Loved Me*: True-to-Life Series from Hamilton High] is characteristically informative and insightful, exploring difficult teen issues with honesty and a multifaceted perspective. Reynolds' treatment of youth and their challenges, from sexual abstinence to mixed-race parentage is compassionate, never condescending; the dialogue, situations, emotions, and behavior of the well-defined teen characters ring true. An engaging, thought-provoking read . . .

Booklist, Shelle Rosenfeld

No More Sad Goodbyes

Other titles in the
True-to-Life Series from Hamilton High
by Marilyn Reynolds

Love Rules

If You Loved Me

Baby Help

Too Soon For Jeff

Detour for Emmy

Telling

Beyond Dreams

But What About Me?

Also by Marilyn Reynolds

I Won't Read and You Can't Make Me:
Reaching Reluctant Teen Readers

No More
Sad Goodbyes

True-to-Life Series
from Hamilton High

By Marilyn Reynolds

Morning
Glory
Press

Buena Park, California

No More Sad Goodbyes

Copyright © 2008 by Marilyn Reynolds

All Rights Reserved

No part of this publication may be adapted, reproduced,
stored in a retrieval system, or transmitted in any form
or by any means, electronic, mechanical, photocopying,
recording, or otherwise
without permission from the publisher.

Library of Congress Cataloging-in-Publication Data
available upon request.

ISBN 978-1-932538-72-4 (hdbk); 978-1-932538-71-7 (pap)

MORNING GLORY PRESS, INC.
6595 San Haroldo Way   Buena Park, CA 90620-3748
714.828.1998, 1.888.612.8254   FAX 714.828.2049
e-mail: info@morningglorypress.com
Web site: www.morningglorypress.com
Printed and bound in the United States of America

Finally, when our stomachs ache from laughing and we're on the last of the champagne, Jason gets all serious.

"Look at that sky. Look at those stars. Maybe there really are whole other worlds out there, like in that old "Lightning Strike" story from *Weird World*.

"Maybe," I say. "I don't know."

"But there's got to be more than just us," Jason says. "I mean, we can't be the most highly intelligent forms of life in the whole universe. In this whole universe? That would be stupid . . . I don't think God's that wasteful, to make this whole, huge universe just for us."

"Do you think God made everything in six days?"

"No. That's just a metaphor."

Sometimes I don't get Jason when he talks like that, but right now, under the stars, feeling the glow of champagne, he's making sense. And when he leans over and kisses me, that makes sense, too. And when we do exactly what he wanted to do for his birthday, well, that seems right at the time, too.

No More Sad Goodbyes

ACKNOWLEDGMENTS

For help along the way —

For careful readings, shared insights, and reality checks,
I thank:

Dale Dodson, Kathy Harvey, Karen Kasaba, Judy Laird, Karyn
Mazo, Michael Reynolds, Kyle Sarton, Jeannie Ward, the
UUSS "Write-to-Life" group, Jennifer Harmon and her Adoles-
cent Parent Program students, and Deb Young and her Roanoke
Benson High School library readers.

For the gift of solitary writing quarters, I am ever grateful to
Barbara Gardner and Jeanne Lindsay.

No More Sad Goodbyes

To

Lena Reynolds Kyle

and Mika Genevieve Reynolds

No More Sad Goodbyes

CHAPTER

1

It's the last day of our junior year at Hamilton High School and my best-friend-almost-sister-Danni and I are sitting side by side at the Spruce Juice counter. Her real name's Dannielle, but no one calls her that except her mother.

She's poking her straw around the bottom of her Mega-Mango smoothie, trying to get one last taste.

"Can you believe we're going to be seniors next year?" Danni says.

"I can't believe you are," I say. "I thought you'd never make it."

Danni throws her wadded up napkin at me.

"Very funny," she says. "So funny . . . "

". . . I forgot to laugh," I say, finishing the sentence with her.

That gets us both laughing.

"So funny I forgot to laugh" was Danni's favorite slogan when we were in the fourth grade and we had this teacher, Mr. Westly, who was always making totally lame jokes. Danni's constant "So funny I forgot to laugh" remarks irritated Westly so much his face would get all red and blotchy, which was funnier than the joke and

. . . well . . . even though it doesn't sound so funny now, it still cracks us up. In fact, we're laughing so hard the man sitting next to me at the counter picks up his newspaper and moves down to the other end, which makes us laugh even more. Not to be rude or anything, it's just that we're both happy about summer. There'll be lots of days at the beach, and a two week volleyball camp, and . . .

"What's up?" Jason says, sliding onto the stool the newspaper guy just left.

"The sky," Danni says — another of her fourth-grade witticisms.

The counter guy asks Jason what he wants and when Jason says he just stopped in to say hi, the guy gives Jason a wave, reminding him of the "no buy, bye-bye" rule.

"No problem," Jason says, getting off the stool.

"So Autumn," he says to me, "6:30 tomorrow night?"

"Okay," I say, avoiding what I know is Danni's piercing look.

Jason's barely out the door when she asks, "What's that about?"

"What?" I say, all innocent.

"6:30 tomorrow night! That!"

"It's Jason's birthday."

"So?"

"So . . . his Dad won a gift certificate for two to this really great restaurant over in Hollywood, and he gave it to Jason for his birthday and . . ."

"You're going on a date with Jason?"

"It's not exactly a date," I tell her.

"Dinner at a really nice restaurant in Hollywood is a date!"

Danni spins off the stool and rushes outside so fast I don't even know she's leaving until she's gone. I hurry after her but she's already in the car with the doors locked. I pound on the window but she won't even look at me. She starts the engine and I move away. I don't think Danni'd run over me. Right now I'm not sure, though.

I watch her drive out of the parking lot and down the street, hoping she'll come back for me. She doesn't. It's not like I'm trying to steal her boyfriend away. He's just her fantasy boyfriend. And I don't even like him, except as a friend. I knew she'd be mad, though, which is why I kept hoping she wouldn't find out.

I could call my dad to come get me, but it's not quite five o'clock and he works until seven tonight. Or Jason. He'd come get me in a heartbeat, but why complicate matters even more? I take my cell phone from my jeans pocket and call Grams to tell her I'll be a little late. Then I start walking. It's nice, once I get started. There's a light breeze, not much smog, and if I didn't feel so bad about Danni I might even enjoy it.

Just two blocks away from the shopping center I'm walking in a neighborhood with nice houses and lots of trees. When Dad decided he had enough money to buy a house for us, I wanted him to find one over here. He just laughed.

"I haven't found that pot of gold yet," he said.

We've been looking on the other side of Hamilton Heights, not far from the high school. That's cool. All I really care about is that I get my own room, and that the place has more than one bathroom.

I guess I'm thinking about houses because I don't want to think about Danni.

Jason and Danni and I have been tight since the third grade when he first moved to Hamilton Heights. The three of us ended up doing this cool project on Native Americans, complete with a village built to scale. Really, Jason was the brains behind the project. Ours took first place over all the other third grade projects, which sort of cemented our friendship. That plus our shared interest in those weird supermarket newspaper stories. We had some favorites that we read over and over again. There was the "Danger in Organic Honey" story about a guy up in Alaska who sneezed a swarm of bees out his nose and got so many stings he had to be airlifted to a hospital.

Then there was "LIGHTNING STRIKE SPURS MEMORY OF LIFE AT EDGE OF UNIVERSE" about these four married couples in Nebraska who were kidnapped by space aliens and taken to their planet to be studied as primitive life forms. After a year, the Nebraskans were brought back to their beds in the middle of the night. Their friends and family had been looking all over for them, and so had the police and the FBI. But the funny thing was, they didn't even know they'd been gone.

"I can't believe how Johnnie's just shot up overnight," one woman said when her surprised thirteen-year-old found her fixing breakfast the morning of their return.

Five years later, one of the guys was struck by lightning. It was like a miracle that he lived, but the really strange thing was that when he was revived he had total recall of everything that had happened in the alien world. Of course no one believed him, not even the others who'd been taken away with him, even though they all knew something weird had happened to them.

The guy who'd regained his memory kept trying so hard to convince people of what had happened that everyone thought he was crazy. Then he got this idea, "like it just came at me from outer space," he said.

He put one of those invisible electrical boundaries across his backyard and cranked it up to the highest power. Then he told his wife he'd noticed her favorite rose bush was full of aphids. She went rushing out the back door to check her roses, but when she got to the invisible fence she was knocked flat on her butt. Sure enough, though, she remembered being in that other planet world. She didn't remember as much as her husband, maybe because the shock of the fence wasn't as strong as the shock of lightning. Anyway, we loved that story. Since it was in Jason's paper, he was the one who got to use it for our current event assignment.

He'd stood in front of our class, his eyes twinkling with the excitement of telling everyone about this great story. But when the teacher saw what newspaper it was from, she told him he couldn't use it.

"That's not an appropriate source for a school current event," she'd said.

"What's more of a current event than being struck by lightning?" he'd argued. "It's about what current can do. Get it?"

Jason was given a time out for being disrespectful to the teacher, but at recess everyone gathered around him and he told the whole story. Jason's really smart, but not in a way that's usually noticeable. I noticed it on that day, though, because he remembered all of the details from that story.

I guess teachers finally noticed how smart he was, too, because they skipped him from fourth to sixth grade. But even when we were in different grades, the three of us still stayed tight.

I get good grades, but I'm not smart the way Jason is. I work hard for my A's and he only has to work a little for his A's. Danni only works a little, too, for her C's. I study hard before every test, and Danni prays. I once told her that her grades disproved the power of prayer, but she claimed it was just the opposite.

"Without my prayers I'd be failing every single class!" she'd said.

My dad says that with the combination of Jason's brains, Danni's exuberance, and my common sense, we form a terrific triumvirate. I don't know about that. I think our friendship is kind of like that butter substitute, a "Perfect Balance." At least that's how it seemed until about a year ago when Danni suddenly decided that Jason was the man of her dreams and things started getting weird.

The three of us had been hanging out at Danni's house while she babysat her little sister, Hannah. Danni has to babysit pretty often because her mother, Carole, goes to a lot of meetings at their church.

Anyway, we'd been playing Scrabble, or at least trying to. Hannah, who is five, kept poking around in the bag and pulling out the letters for "cat" and "dog," and "Hannah." And since there are only two "H"s in the whole game, it took her a long time to find what she wanted. I mean, Scrabble's not exactly a fast moving game anyway, and with Hannah playing it was so slow you could take a nap between turns. On this day we were reading from an old *Weird World* whenever it was Hannah's turn.

"Check this out," Jason says. "A cow born in Wisconsin with two heads!"

"You're not supposed to be reading that!" Hannah said.

"Chill out, and take your turn," Danni said.

"Jesus doesn't like it," Hannah said, sullenly.

Jason got up from the floor where we'd been playing and said he was going out for burritos, and did we want any.

"You can't go yet," Danni said. "We haven't even finished the game."

"I'll be back before it's my turn."

"Where are you going?" I asked.

"Señor Rick's."

That got a laugh, since Señor Rick's is this place clear up in Pasadena, and it would take him at least an hour to get there and back, even if he called our order in ahead of time.

"Trust me, I'll be back in time for my next turn. If I'm not, let Hannah take my turn for me. Okay, Hannah Banana?"

"Okay. What word do you want me to make?" she said, all serious.

"Do supercalifragilisticexpialidocious or cat. You choose."

Jason tossed Hannah a nickel for her work, then left.

"He's such a hottie," Danni said.

I just looked at her, stunned.

"Oh, don't tell me you haven't noticed!"

"Jason Garcia? A hottie?? No way! He's just Jason!"

Danni grabbed one of Hannah's "h"s and spelled out "hottie" on the board.

I added "not" in front of "hottie." Then Danni went on a word frenzy, rearranging the words on the board to spell "dimples" and "fine" and "smile" and "eyes" and "sexy," until there was nothing left of the game we'd been playing. By the time we heard Jason pull into the driveway the board was filled with Danni's praises of Jason. She quick jumbled up all of the letters, except for "cat," which Hannah protected.

"Hey, what happened to the game?" Jason said, putting a bag of burritos on the coffee table.

"They weren't playing right," Hannah said.

"Oops. Forgot the drinks," Jason said, heading back outside.

Danni watched him leave, then connected "butt" to cat.

"I'm telling!" Hannah said, scrunching her eyes up the way she does when she's angry. "That's a bad word!"

Danni picked up the letters, laughing.

"I'm telling anyway! And I'm telling you've been reading about bad stuff again, too," Hannah said, grabbing the paper.

"No, you're not, because if you tell we're not playing Clue."

Hannah ran off to get Clue while Danni and I got all the letters into the bag and folded up the Scrabble game.

It wasn't until later that night, after Jason had gone home and Hannah was asleep, that Danni told me she was seriously crushing on Jason.

"I can't stop thinking about him," she'd said. "He's just so . . . so . . . right."

"When did you, like, lose your mind?"

"I didn't lose my mind. I found it. Yesterday, when we were at the mall, and he came out of the game shop with that guy, Carter?"

I nodded my head.

"Well, I just, like, noticed Jason for the first time. Not like a third grader, or a sixth grader, like the old days, but like . . . like a man."

That totally cracked me up, but by the time I stopped laughing I realized Danni was serious.

"You've got to help me," Danni said.

"How?"

"Just say good things about me whenever you see him, like how cute I am, and how half the guys at Hamilton High think I'm sexy . . ."

"Half the guys think you're sexy??? That one guy, Steve, kind of likes you, and that other guy, Austin, sort of hangs around, but that's hardly half the guys at Hamilton High."

"Yeah, but Jason doesn't know that. He's been in that Catholic boys school since the seventh grade."

"So you want me to lie to Jason? Our lifelong friend?"

"Not lie, exactly. Just stretch the truth. Guys like girls that other guys like. Just help me out here."

"I don't know," I told her.

"I'm desperate! I've named my pillow Jason and I'm kissing and cuddling him all night long. You've got to help me get the real thing," she said.

2

Halfway home and I haven't even noticed any of the houses I've passed, or the streets I've crossed, like I've been on cruise control, stressing out about Danni, and Jason, and me. Now, walking past our old elementary school, I think how much easier things were back when we were at Palm Avenue, back before we got older and life got complicated.

After that Scrabble game, Danni had bugged and begged until I finally told her I'd try to help her out with Jason. His dad owns the market where my dad's the manager, and Jason and I both help stock shelves there sometimes. Whenever we worked together I'd tell him about how Austin was always hanging around Danni and wanting to sit next to her at lunch. I told him I thought Danni was one of the nicest, funniest people I knew, which was mostly true. And then I'd report back to Danni.

"What'd he say when you told him about Austin?"

"Well . . . I think he asked me to hand him the box cutter."

"Okay. So then tell him I've only got six months to live. Guys really go for that tragedy stuff."

The closest I could come with that one was to tell Jason that Danni'd been sick. I mean, really, what kind of bad luck is that asking for, to pretend someone only has six months to live?

Anyway, that's how things went for a few months or so, me giving Jason some stretched out version of the truth, then reporting back to Danni, then getting my next truth-stretching assignment. All of this — interspersed with Danni's agonies of love.

Then things got over-the-top weird. I got this email from Jason telling me how he'd loved me for a long time. He was too shy to tell me in person, but he could no longer keep his feelings all bottled up inside.

I read the email over and over about ten times, not believing my eyes. Then I emailed him back, telling him how important he was to me, as a friend, and that I wanted us to stay friends. He emailed me back that he would be patient. I was worth waiting for, and he was sure I'd change my mind about him.

Until then, Danni and I had always told each other everything. But I couldn't bring myself to tell her about Jason's confession of love for me. Our whole junior year, besides playing on a champion volleyball team, and running track, and me working my head off to get good grades, and Danni barely working to get mediocre grades, and us laughing our heads off over any silly thing, Danni kept feeding me lines to say to Jason to get him to like her. And I kept getting emails from Jason, declaring his love for me, to which I constantly responded "only friends." The longer it went on the guiltier I felt, even though I wasn't doing anything wrong.

I kept hoping Danni'd start liking Austin and forget about Jason. She did go out with Austin a few times, but that was only because she hoped it would make Jason jealous. But Jason hardly even noticed, even though I told him about it.

The other hope I had was that Jason would forget about me, but he keeps telling me he loves me, and he knows I'm going to change my mind any day now. Well . . . he doesn't exactly tell me any of that. He emails me. We never, ever, talk about how we feel, or don't feel about each other. We only email on that subject.

"Hey, Autumn!"

Coach Nicholson, Nikki, leaning out the window of her silver Subaru, waving and calling my name in her loudest coach-voice, jolts me back to now.

"Need a ride?"

"Sure," I say, climbing into the passenger seat as Nikki tosses team rosters and notebooks into the back.

"Going home?"

"Yeah, thanks."

Nikki starts talking about how great it is that so many girls from our volleyball team are going to camp this year.

"I think we've got an excellent chance at state. You and Danni and Krystal are already fantastic, and Stacy's getting really good, too, plus there's . . . "

When Coach talks about volleyball she gets so enthused no one else needs to say a word. It's not that I stop listening. It's just that I keep thinking about Danni being mad at me.

"This is your street, right?" Coach says, turning onto Camellia Street.

"Yeah. The house with the yellow submarine mailbox."

Coach laughs and pulls into our driveway.

"That always gets me — your dad and his yellow submarine fetish."

"He's sort of normal otherwise," I say, getting out of the car.

"Hey, I'm not complaining," Nikki says. "I wish all of our parents were as supportive as your dad. Your grandmother, too."

"Thanks for the ride," I say, slamming the Subaru door closed.

She backs out the driveway and stops at the curb. Lowering the window and leaning out she flashes her big Coach Nicholson smile.

"Have a great time at camp! Have a great summer!"

"You, too," I call back to her.

She takes off down the street in the same direction we just came from and I realize she went out of her way to give me a ride. But that's just how she is. We're lucky. The volleyball coach at Wilson is a total witch. It's a good team, but I don't think they have much fun.

Inside I go straight to my email. One from Jason, the usual, and one from Danni.

"You could at least have told me," she wrote.

I email back that I'm sorry, and remind her that Jason and I are only friends.

"It's just that I love him so much," she sent back to me.

It would be lots easier to talk on the phone, but Danni's parents are super strict and she's only allowed one personal call a day, which I happen to know she already used this morning because she called to ask what I was wearing to school.

I want to tell her to get over Jason — find someone she's got a chance with. But she's so into her Jason fantasy, she can't possibly listen to reason.

What Jason told me when he invited me to dinner was that he wanted more than anything to celebrate his eighteenth birthday with me, his longtime best friend.

"What about Danni?" I asked. "You know, the Three Musketeers and all?"

"Yeah, well, that's how it used to be, when we were kids, but Danni and I aren't that close anymore."

"Really?"

"Yeah, really. I mean, she's still ditzy in that funny kind of way, but she's changed a lot this past year or so. Don't you think?"

"We've all changed," I tell him. "We're in our late teens. We're supposed to change."

"Yeah, well, I still like her and all, but I guess I've sort of outgrown her."

That was one conversation I didn't report back on.

"Anyway, the deal is dinner for two, not dinner for three."

It's not a date, he told me, just two best friends going out to dinner to celebrate a very big birthday. I could hardly say no to that. We are best friends and eighteen is incredible!

Because we're going to such a nice restaurant, I decide to wear the white silk dress I got when I went to a very fancy tea wedding for someone from my dad's work. It's got spaghetti straps and a sort of scoop neck, and a matching jacket. Grams helped me choose the outfit.

I guess it sounds funny to be taking fashion advice from an old blind woman, but she knows a lot about clothes. We don't do this for casual stuff, but for special clothes she always goes with me. She runs her hands over both sides of the fabric, checks all the seams, then, if the dress, or blouse, or whatever, meets her standards, she and I and Casper, Gram's guide dog, crowd into a dressing room where she checks the fit, and how it drapes, and the evenness of the hem. Finally, if we all like it, she pays for it with her Braille Visa and we celebrate our successful shopping trip with peppermint chip double ice cream cones and an extra cone for Casper.

Anyway . . . that's what I'm wearing to dinner. My dad's eyes get all shiny when he sees me.

"Awesome Autumn," he says. Then he goes on and on about what a beautiful young woman I've become, and how much I look like my mother.

"You've got her exact same hair — that light gold color that glows in the sun."

I was only five when my mother died, so I don't exactly remember what she looked like — I only know how she looks in pictures. And I know my dad gets all sentimental sometimes when the way I look, or something I do, or say, reminds him of her.

It's lucky Jason shows up in time for me to get out of there before Dad goes totally sappy. I mean, it's sweet and all that, but it's sort of embarrassing, too.

Jason's dad let him borrow his very cool Lexus and we drive over to the Hollywood Hills with the moon roof open and the stereo blasting. Not blasting like rappers do, but loud enough to feel surrounded by the music.

Walking from the parking lot to the restaurant, Jason runs his hand lightly, quickly, over my hair.

"You should always wear your hair down," he says.

I laugh.

"Too much trouble. Besides it gets in my eyes when I play volleyball. Sometimes I think I should get it all chopped off — like Krystal's."

Jason groans.

"That's what my dad says, too."

"Smart man."

The restaurant has crisp white tablecloths and silverware that's really silver. The waiters wear tuxedos and are polite but not exactly friendly. These are not the kind of waiters who sit down next to you and say "Hi, I'm Jimmy and I'll be taking care of you this evening."

I'm shocked by the prices on the menu. You could buy a month's worth of double cheeseburgers with fries and a drink at McDonald's for the cost of the cheapest dinner here.

In an old fashioned way, though, the whole thing is sort of glamorous, like in one of those old movies where people are always dressed up and sipping drinks from fancy glasses and smoking cigarettes.

After dinner the waiter brings us two wedges of chocolate cake, one with a candle in it.

"We didn't order dessert," Jason says.

"Your mother called ahead," the waiter says. "Happy Birthday."

I give Jason his present, a book of poetry by this guy, Luis Rodriguez, who Jason really admires. Jason says he's going to be a writer. All the other guys I know want to be basketball stars, or pilots, or lawyers. But Jason's different. He's been accepted to some school in Iowa that's famous for its writing program. He's already got plans for graduate school. I guess he's really dedicated. I mean Iowa? From California? But he's all jazzed about it. He's leaving in August, which is sad in a way. But at least I won't have to be delivering any more of Danni's "stretched truth" messages once he's gone.

A lot of the poems in the new book are about life in East Los Angeles, which is where Jason used to live. He took me and Danni down there once, just after he got his driver's license. He drove us past his old school and the house he used to live in. It looked way different than Hamilton Heights.

The title of the book, *My Nature Is Hunger*, makes us laugh, since we're definitely not hungry after our tricolore salad, hand cut pappardelle with meat ragu, and chocolate cake.

After dinner we drive up to the planetarium. Jason wants to see the new "Brightest Stars of the Universe" show, but it turns out we need reservations, which we don't have. A volunteer hands us a slick brochure and we take the elevator back down to the parking lot.

"We don't need no stinkin' planetarium," Jason says, laughing. "We'll go look at real stars."

We drive out past lights and traffic and park at the edge of a dirt road with a "no trespassing" sign posted. Jason opens the moon roof and we look up into the night sky from our reclined leather seats.

"Sure beats the planetarium show," Jason says.

A very bright falling star streaks across the sky, as if to prove Jason's point that the real thing is best.

"You're supposed to make a wish," I tell him.

"Okay," he says, looking at me for too long.

"You're supposed to close your eyes when you make your wish."

"You too," he says.

We squinch our eyes closed for a few seconds and I wish for a volleyball scholarship to Cal Poly.

"What'd you wish?" Jason asks.

"If you tell, your wish won't come true," I say.

"It's just a game. It probably won't come true, anyway."

"Mine might," I say, but really, I know it will take more than wishing. It will take a lot of hard work and discipline. Which is okay by me.

After a while, Jason picks up the book I gave him, turns on the map light, and reads one of the poems to me. It's about people who have to scramble just to get food for their kids, and who live with violence every day.

"That's so sad," I tell him. "I wish I'd bought you a happier book."

"Nah. This is the book I wanted. You gave me exactly what I wanted," he says. Then he adds, "Well . . . almost exactly what I wanted."

I pretend not to even hear that part about almost exactly. I know from all of his emails exactly what he wants. He wants me to do the sex thing with him but that's never going to happen.

Jason reaches behind the seat and takes one of those little bottles of champagne from an ice cooler. He opens one and hands it to me.

"I never drink alcohol," I tell him. "You know that!"

"Yeah, but this is really good. Just taste it, for my birthday," he says, opening another bottle for himself.

"Come on, here's to eighteen," he says, clicking his bottle against mine and taking a sip.

I'm a serious athlete and besides, parties where people binge and get stupid and then throw up all over everything aren't exactly my idea of fun. But a sip of champagne for Jason's birthday? No big deal. And he's right — it tastes pretty good. We sit sipping champagne and reminiscing and watching for more shooting stars.

Jason points to the planetarium brochure on the floor beside my feet.

"Hey, remember when we were in the fourth grade, and Mr. Westly brought us all up there on that field trip?"

"And Danni kept telling her mom we were going to see the stars at the sanitarium?"

Jason starts laughing. "And her mom got mad because she thought it was rude to put sick movie stars on display?"

"Rude and sinful," I remind him, which makes us laugh more.

"It's the Eleventh Commandment," Jason gasps out, "Thou shalt not look at sick movie stars."

I'm laughing so hard I snort champagne out my nose.

"Watch out for the bees," Jason yells and puts his hand over my nose, pretending to be terrified. Then he jerks his hand away, looks at it in disgust, and wipes it carefully on the carpeted floor mat beneath the driver's seat.

By that time even if a swarm of bees did fill the car we could only have laughed harder. If I'd been with a real boyfriend instead of Jason, I'd have been embarrassed to death about spewing champagne from my nose. That would have been horrible, but with Jason it's just soooo funny.

Finally, when our stomachs ache from laughing and we're on the last of the champagne, Jason gets all serious.

"Look at that sky. Look at those stars. Maybe there really are whole other worlds out there, like in that old "Lightning Strike" story from *Weird World*.

"Maybe," I say. "I don't know."

"But there's got to be more than just us," Jason says. "I mean, we can't be the most highly intelligent forms of life in the whole

universe. In this whole universe? That would be stupid . . . I don't
think God's that wasteful, to make this whole, huge universe just
for us."

"Do you think God made everything in six days?"

"No. That's just a metaphor."

Sometimes I don't get Jason when he talks like that, but right
now, under the stars, feeling the glow of champagne, he's making
sense. And when he leans over and kisses me, that makes sense,
too. And when we do exactly what he wanted to do for his birthday,
well, that seems right at the time, too.

CHAPTER

3

I'm on the floor in the living room, stretching my quads and hamstrings, which is part of the routine Nikki bangs into our heads every day at the end of practice. To be fair, all of the coaches at last summer's volleyball camp were stretch fanatics.

At the end of each day's practice, Nikki yells, "Morning and night! Stretch 'em out, stretch 'em out, wayyyy out!" This is her own variation of Hamilton High's favorite defensive football cheer to "Push 'em back, push 'em back, wayyyy back."

With her drill sergeant voice and volume, she really gets into our heads. I could be ten thousand miles away from Hamilton Heights, but if I even think about skipping my morning stretches, Nikki's voice comes screaming into my brain.

"Hey, Kid," Dad says, walking over my outstretched legs on his way to the kitchen.

My mom named me Autumn. Autumn Elena Grant. The Elena's after my other grandmother, but she died a long time ago, too. Everyone else calls me Autumn, but my dad calls me Kid. Except sometimes, after a really good volleyball game, or a really good report card, or when he's getting all sentimental, then he calls me

Awesome Autumn. And there are other times when he calls me Fall. Autumn? Fall? Get it? My dad, the comedian.

Mostly, though, I'm Autumn, after my mom's favorite season. She loved seeing the bright reds and yellows and oranges when the leaves change color in October. At least that's what my dad and Grams tell me. Like I said before, I hardly even remember her. I think I remember that she laughed a lot, and sang me to sleep, but maybe I only know that because of what Dad and Grams tell me. They want to keep her memory alive for me, so I'll know how much she loved me, but it's hard to really feel the love of a dead mother.

I breathe out slowly, releasing the stiffness in my left upper thigh, pushing the stretch a bit farther.

"Firing up the griddle," Dad announces from the kitchen.

"I'll be done in a sec," I say.

Moving on to hip flexor stretches and spine twists, I'm hoping there's still a chance to twist a little something loose and finally get my period. Well . . . more than my period, since it's been over four months since I've had a period and no matter how many times I lock myself in the bathroom and pee on a little plastic strip, it always turns pink and says I'm pregnant. Absolutely no one else knows, not even Danni. Especially not Danni, considering the circumstances of my pregnancy, and my plan for abortion. Well . . . the counselor at Planned Parenthood knows, but that's all.

I read somewhere that a huge percentage of teen pregnancies end before the first trimester, so I've been hoping all along it would just go away. Hoping, and doing jumping jacks, and torturous stretches, and painfully hot baths, but nothing happened.

Well . . . things have been happening, just not what I want to have happen. The first thing that happened was that all I wanted to do was sleep. It took every ounce of strength I had just to drag myself out of bed. And the only thing I could eat without hurling was plain crackers with Coca Cola. Since everyone knows I'm a total health nut, my sudden switch to a diet of soda and crackers was hard to explain. And what's happening now that the queasy stomach thing is over is I'm getting these butterfly-tickle feelings in my stomach. I guess it's the . . . you know . . . the embryo moving around. And it's getting harder and harder to get my jeans zipped up. Any day now someone's sure to notice it's more than bloat that's enlarging my belly. But . . . just four more days and it's over. Four more days.

I know some people say abortion is murder — a sin against God. That's what Carole says, and Danni agrees with her mother on this one. I don't see things that way. I mean, we're talking about a lump of cells here. It's not like it has a brain yet, or feelings. Besides, I've got lots better things to do with my life right now than to have a baby.

T wo summers ago I went up to Northern California for a four-week internship at the Guide Dog Training Facility — the place where Grams got Casper. I stayed with another intern and her family, and I actually got to work with the dogs. It was so cool! Ever since that time, I've known I want to be a trainer. But to be the kind of trainer I want to be takes a college degree.

Last year these college recruiters came to our school and watched some of our games. The guy from Cal Poly and the woman from Stockton both talked with Nikki about me and Danni and Krystal. She says if we play as well as we did last year, we're sure to get scholarships. That'd be so cool! No way can I have a baby!

E very morning on the way to school, our bus goes past the corner where this girl, Sarah, and her baby wait for the van to take them to some special school for teen parents. I remember Sarah from last year, in our ceramics class. She came up with some of the best pots in the class. Mine were always lopsided, but hers were perfect, like something you'd have to pay a lot of money for in a store. She was always laughing and joking around, too. Now she waits on that corner looking tired, and bored, and depressed. I always try to wave to her, but she never even looks up. That's not for me.

Besides, if Jason found out I was pregnant, I know he'd want to get married and raise a little junior Jason Garcia. How lame would that be?

I was sooooo stupid to get in this mess, but I'm not going to pile more and more stupid things one on top of another, like giving up college and marrying Jason, and whatever else would go with a baby. No way! I don't care what Danni thinks. Or, I do care what she thinks, which is why I'm keeping my secret to myself. And why I never even told her what happened on Jason's birthday.

Danni called me that next morning after I'd been out with Jason. I was still groggy and maybe sort of hung over, but I dragged myself out of bed to answer the phone.

"How was the birthday dinner?" she asked, still sounding mad.

"Okay," I said, my head swirling with images of what I wished hadn't happened.

"That's all? Just okay?"

"Yeah . . . well . . . the food was good."

Danni waited for more details, but what was I going to say? Jason wears boxers? Champagne had a strange effect on me? I gave it up to the love of your life? I don't think so. So one secret led to another and another, until the only thing I feel safe talking to Danni about is school and volleyball.

At least Jason is in Iowa now. Danni's not quite so obsessed with him out of her line of vision. I'm super relieved that he's gone. No matter what I tell him, Jason's convinced that one stupid night meant I was truly in love with him. All that night really meant was that I drank champagne when I shouldn't have. And life got very complicated. Four more days, though. That's all. Then I can go back to being just a regular high school senior with nothing to hide.

Crossing one leg behind the other, I lean forward, stretching the weight-bearing ankle, holding the stretch for ten seconds, then switching sides.

The clatter of pans accompanies my dad's off-key breakfast-making rendition of "We All Live in a Yellow Submarine." Dad was a kid in the sixties, and he's a total Beatles freak. He probably knows all the words to every song they ever recorded.

Grams and Casper make their way slowly through the living room. Usually Grams doesn't need to use Casper at home because she knows where everything is. Right now, though, all of the rooms are cluttered with boxes because we're moving to a new house next week, so she's depending on Casper to lead her around the boxes and into the kitchen.

If I weren't all worried about the pregnancy thing, I'd be totally excited about the game tonight. We've got a really good chance to go to State, which definitely would improve my scholarship chances. And I'd be all excited about the move, too. It's the first house we're actually buying, and my new bedroom is about twice as big as the one I have now. And there are two and a half bathrooms, which means I can take as long as I want without having to hear about anyone's elimination emergencies. And it's only a few blocks from Hamilton High, so I won't have to depend on the bus anymore. But it's not easy to be excited about the good stuff with this big worry hanging over my head . . . or in my belly.

I wait for Grams to get settled at the kitchen table, Casper lying close beside her chair with his nose resting on his front paws, then I go in to warm the syrup and set the table. I move flower catalogs and paint samples from the table to make room for plates. For weeks now, Dad's been reading about roses, trying to decide what kind to plant at our new house. He's looking for deep color, a long blooming season and, for Grams, a strong fragrance.

Dad stands at the counter, mixing the pancake batter and singing, " . . . And our friends are all aboard, many more of them live next door, and the band begins to play . . ."

Here Grams does the horn sounds, her hands curled around an imaginary trumpet.

I join in on the "We all live in a yellow submarine, yellow submarine, yellow submarine" chorus. It's not that I love to sing, it's the price I have to pay for pancakes. No singing, no pancakes. That's Dad's rule. I go along with it 'cause my dad's pancakes are amazing.

They're so happy, my dad, and Grams, singing and playing pretend instruments and goofing around, that whenever I even think of confessing to them that their good little girl hasn't been so good after all I get this thick, heavy lump in my chest.

I reach into my pocket and touch the heart-shaped stone I always keep with me — the one my dad gave me on the day I got my first period. He was all sentimental that day, talking about how I was becoming a woman and blah, blah, blah. He said the time was coming when I would be doing more and more on my own, beyond his protection.

He said I would make mistakes along the way, because everyone does.

"One thing I know for certain, though, whatever mistakes you make, you'll always figure out how to be part of the solution, not part of the problem."

That's a major theme with my dad. According to him, if everyone on the whole earth worked in whatever way, big or small, to be part of the solution, and not to make problems, the whole world would live in peace and harmony.

When he finished his "you're becoming a woman" talk, he handed me a little heart-shaped rock, about the size of a penny, only thicker.

"This is just a reminder that I will always, always love you with all of my heart, no matter what. And I know for sure you will grow up to be a part of the solution for this problem-filled world."

I took the rock and held it to the light, catching glimpses of glittering sparkles of green and gold, not thinking about mistakes I might make, or problems, or solutions.

Now, feeling the smooth surface of the rock that's been tucked into my backpack, or pocket, or purse, for over five years, I'm sure my dad still means what he said that day. But I've done this really big, stupid thing, and I know if he found out, he would be horribly disappointed, and hurt, and even if he still loved me, everything would change. Grams, too. She's pretty opinionated about girls who get pregnant before they get married. She definitely sees pregnant teens as part of the problem. Love me or not, she'd have a big shift of opinion about her granddaughter.

But . . . four more days and they'll never have to find out.

"Any dreams last night?" Dad asks, pouring four circles of pancake batter onto the sizzling griddle.

Grams starts.

"I was in the garden at the old house, planting petunias back in that little patch we had behind the garage. Purple, pink, red . . . they were so beautiful."

She pauses, smiling, like maybe she's remembering colors.

"Then what?" Dad asks.

This is what we do every single morning. Not the pancakes

part, because weekday mornings are so rushed, but the dream part. "Dream Routine," we call it. Dad's usually pretty mellow, but the dream thing is like an absolutely unbreakable rule. Come in late after curfew? He's reasonable. Get a "D" in geometry? Not the end of the world. But skip the morning dream routine? He gets all red faced and yells and screams and stomps around. It has to do with honoring my mother's memory, which, as I mentioned earlier, is a very big deal to my dad.

Back when I was thirteen or so and thought my family was the weirdest, I skipped out on dream routine every morning for three days in a row. The third day my dad told me I was pissing on my mother's grave! That really got me. My dad never uses words like that. He says it shows a lack of imagination.

When I was younger, excited about every new bad word I heard, Dad would play the "trade a letter" game with me, sort of like on that old Scrabble TV show. So when he heard me showing off to Danni by calling some girl a bitch, he traded me a "w" for a "b" and from then on it was witch. I got a long vowel for a short one to say "shite." It worked the same way, long for short in the "f" word. "Foke" you!" I told Danni once when she demanded I let her borrow my favorite jeans. This wasn't just Dad's idea for how his little girl should talk. He used the same substitute system for himself.

With all of the effort Dad put into keeping our mouths clean, I was completely shocked to hear him say "pissing" instead of "wissing." And then I got this gross, ugly picture in my mind, of me squatting over my mother's grave and letting go with a torrent of yellow pee, and seeing it flood down into the ground and seep into my poor mom's casket. That was three years ago, and I haven't skipped morning dream routine once since then.

Anyway, here's the way the dream thing got started. A long time ago my mom read about some tribe deep in the jungle of New Guinea that had this practice of telling each other their dreams every single morning, before they did anything else. And there was no such thing as mental illness or unhappiness with anyone, ever, in that tribe. So from then on, Dad and my mom told their dreams first thing in the morning. Then when I came along, and learned to talk, I got in on it, too. Later, when Grams came to live with us, Dad asked her to do the morning dream routine with us, too.

Mom claimed our dream routine worked because no one in our family ever went crazy. The other side of that proof is that Dad does go crazy when we don't tell our dreams.

I take the orange juice from the refrigerator and pour out three small glasses while Grams continues telling her dream.

"When I looked up there was a giant balloon flying over the garage, and that actress, what's her name? Used to be in all of those musicals?"

"Mary Martin?" Dad asks.

"No, that other one."

"Mitzi Gaynor?"

"No, the other one," Grams says. "The really famous one who drank too much."

"Judy Garland?" I say.

"Yes, that's the one . . ."

I don't know much about old musicals, but I have seen "The Wizard of Oz" about a zillion times.

". . . and I think the balloon was taking her over the rainbow . . . That's all I remember, but the flowers, just plain old petunias, they were beautiful . . ."

My grams always says that even though she's blind, she hasn't lost her sight. She still sees pictures in her dreams.

"First pancake for you, Kid," Dad says, handing me a plate with a perfectly round golden brown pancake.

"Test it. If you live the rest of us will eat pancakes, too."

I slather on butter, pour on warm maple syrup and take the first delicious bite. Weekdays it's a protein bar and juice for me, and quick dream talk with Dad and Grams. I'm out the door by six-thirty to make a zero period class, so I can devote more afternoon time to volleyball. That just makes me love weekend pancakes all the more.

Dad brings a pancake-stacked plate to the table and sits down.

"You want another one, Mom?" he says to Grams.

"One's already too many," she says, sopping up the last of the syrup on her plate.

My grams is hecka worried because she can barely get the zipper up on her favorite wool pants anymore.

Just the other day Dad asked Grams, "What do you care if your pants are too tight? You can't see them."

"I have a way of seeing tight pants," she'd said, reaching for his belt and giving it a tug.

We all laughed at that because Dad's put on a little weight recently, and it's funny my blind grandmother would notice. Scary to me though, because what if she's noticing my waistband, too.

Dad finishes a giant bite of pancake, then starts telling about his dream.

"The Kid was on the volleyball court, but it wasn't really a volleyball court. It was a deep, murky lake and the girls were playing at the bottom . . ."

On it goes, and then I tell mine. All I can remember is that I was supposed to be taking a test, something that would get me into college if I did well, but would keep me out if I blew it. In my dream, I kept going to the wrong room and I woke up tense and worried.

The way things are now, I'd be afraid to tell my dreams if we analyzed them, like maybe a dream would reveal something I want to keep hidden. But we don't analyze them. We just tell them. That's all the tribe in New Guinea did and it worked for them.

When we were in the seventh grade, Danni always used to just happen by at breakfast time on Saturday mornings. I don't know how she managed to time it so right, because sometimes we'd be having breakfast at eight and other times not until eleven. Somehow, though, every Saturday morning, she'd show up just in time for breakfast. She'd probably have done the same thing on Sunday mornings, too, but the Hopkins family all went to church every single Sunday morning, no matter what. They still do.

Anyway, Dad was never more than halfway through the first "Yellow Submarine" verse when Danni'd open the back door a crack and Dad would invite her in for pancakes. It was soooo embarrassing! My dad singing totally off key and my blind grandma playing the pretend trumpet, and then the bizarre dream routine.

"Your family's so cool!" Danni would say.

"No, they're not! They're weird," I'd tell her. "Why can't they just be normal, like your family?"

"Normal's boring!"

Back then we always wanted to trade families. She wanted to be an only child and not have to put up with her little sister, and I wanted a little sister. Hannah was so cute and she totally idolized me. Who wouldn't want that? Plus I wanted a mom.

Danni never went so far as to say she wished her mom was dead. She just said not having a mom could offer certain desirable advantages.

Now that we're both over being bratty seventh graders, we're pretty much over wanting to trade families. Danni is back to eating boring oatmeal with her own family on Saturday mornings and I'm back to liking my dad's goofy singing and my gram's colorful dreams. We do sort of share families, though, because we spend so much time at each other's houses.

Grams and I wash the dishes, then pack them into one of the many boxes labeled "Kitchen." It's amazing what all Grams can do. She likes to tell people, "I may be blind, but I'm not useless."

After we finish cleaning up, I go in my room, close the door, and do jumping jacks. When I first figured out I was pregnant, I started doing twenty-five jumping jacks a day. Now I'm up to eighty. But really, I guess the only thing that's going to work now is the termination procedure scheduled for next Friday. Four more days.

CHAPTER

4

"**I**'ve got to meet Ron at the escrow office to sign some papers, but we'll be right back," Dad says, pulling into the parking lot outside the Hamilton High gym.

Ron is the real estate guy and it seems like he's constantly calling about loans, or inspections, or some kind of house buying detail.

I grab my gym bag from the backseat next to Casper, who sits tall and straight, scanning the parking lot, noticing other cars, and anyone walking near our car, all while Grams is safe, sitting shoulder to shoulder right next to him. He cracks me up the way he's always on duty.

"We'll be back before the game starts," Dad says. "If this paper signing deal takes longer than fifteen minutes, it'll just have to wait."

Grams laughs. "Since when has any meeting with Ron taken less than an hour?"

"Since now," Dad says. "This is a big game!"

Danni pulls in next to us and lowers the passenger side window.

"Hey, Yellow Sub Guy," she shouts to Dad.

"Hey, Danni. Is this going to be a win tonight?"

"We've got it wrapped up," she says, laughing.

Dad gives us both a thumbs up.

Grams wishes us good luck. As they drive away, Dad calls out to me in an embarrassingly loud voice, "Kick some batt, Awesome Autumn!"

Casper's the only one in the car who doesn't seem interested in this game with Wilson, even though he's seen every game of the season. That should definitely qualify him as a fan.

Shantell joins Danni and me as we walk into the gym.

"Kick some batt?" Shantell says.

"My dad just traded vowels," I say. "You know, an 'a' for a 'u'?"

"Oh, right," she says, smiling and shaking her head. "I wish my dad could be a Mr. Clean. That fucker embarrasses the shit out of me sometimes, the way he talks."

We're still laughing when we get to the locker room. But then Danni gets serious.

"This is going to be a tough game," she says.

"I just heard you say we've got it all wrapped up."

"That's just what you say to parents. It's not necessarily true."

We all know this game is far from "wrapped up." We're unbeaten for the season, but so is the Wilson team. We both beat Marshall, but Wilson beat them by seven points and we had to go into overtime to get our win.

We change into our uniforms and go out onto the court. Latoya and Stacy are already doing warm-ups. Jasmine's talking with Coach Nicholson. Krystal's sitting on the bench, talking on her cell phone. It's kind of a joke, how Krystal's practically married to her cell phone. The first thing she does when class is over is turn on her cell. Even if it's just for a seven minute passing period.

"Shut it off!" Nikki says, motioning to Krystal to stash the phone.

Krystal nods okay and goes right on talking. Coach starts walking toward Krystal, who shuts off the phone and puts it in her gym bag.

The whole team is on the floor thirty minutes before game time and we do some easy warm-up drills. Nothing to show our real strength in front of the Wilson team, though. They're doing the same thing — easy warm up drills.

During a short break, Shantell nods toward the front middle section of the stands and asks, "Where's Casper?"

I glance over at the spot where Dad and Grams and Casper always sit, the Grant section, coach Nicholson calls it, and see that they've not shown up yet.

"My dad had to sign some papers for our new house," I say. "They should be here any time."

"I hope so. I think Casper's our luck!"

At five minutes before game time we sprint back to the locker rooms where Nikki gives us our pre-game pep talk and reminds us how good we are. As we head back out to the court, I get a side view glimpse of myself in the mirror. Gad! It's pretty easy to disguise my belly with tops that hang down over my waist, but suddenly my changing form is pretty obvious in my volleyball jersey. Is it my imagination, or is everyone staring at me?

I start as middle blocker and Danni's to my left as outside hitter. Stacy takes the first serve, low and with a top spin that's tough to return. We take the first point, and then the next one. The Wilson team will figure out soon enough how to deal with Stacy's serve, but it's good to start out in the lead. I finger the smooth stone tucked into my pocket, hoping our luck will hold.

We take a short break after the first game, and I'm surprised to see that the Grant section of the bleachers is still vacant. I guess Grams was right about no meeting with the real estate guy ever taking less than an hour.

Coach starts me again in the second game, next to Danni. We've played together so long we practically read each other's minds. Even so, we're only a few minutes into the game when I miss a dig and lose a point for us. Nikki puts Krystal in my place and motions me to the bench.

"Great job! Take a breather and give Krystal a chance."

Nikki never says anything critical during a game, but she and I both know I'm a little off balance on some of the digs.

Hamilton and Wilson stay within one or two points of each other until the very end, when Stacy delivers three perfect top-spin power serves that win the game for us. We all jump around, high-fiving and shouting. We calm down enough to do a cheer for Wilson and shake hands with all of the players, then we head back to the locker room, laughing and joking around.

I step out of the shower, careful to keep my boobs and belly covered with the towel. Standing close, facing the locker, I quick get into my bra and big, loose sweatshirt. I'm just stepping into my jeans when Nikki walks up beside me.

"As soon as you're finished dressing, come to my office," she says.

My heart gets all fluttery. She's noticed. I know she has.

"We're going to Barb and Edie's," Danni says.

"I'll see you there," I tell her, opening the door to Coach Nicholson's office. "Order me a garbage burger, will you?"

"No problem."

Nikki and two sheriffs, a man and a woman, are standing in the little room, looking grim. Sheriffs? Because I'm pregnant??

"Have a seat," Nikki says, motioning to one of the chairs opposite her desk. She sits down next to me. The sheriffs both lean against Nikki's desk, facing us.

It's totally quiet for what seems like a long time. Then the lady sheriff, Gail Stern according to her name badge, says to me, "There's been a terrible accident."

That's how I've been thinking about my pregnancy all along, a terrible accident, but . . .

"Accident?" I say.

She nods.

"Your father and grandmother . . . " Nikki starts, reaching over and taking my hand.

"What?? WHAT???"

Nikki's eyes fill with tears and both of the sheriffs are looking at the floor. I know before they tell me that this is really, really bad.

The guy sheriff, Daniel Ontiveros, looks up.

"I'm very sorry," he says. He takes a long, deep breath. "Your father's car was hit by a gravel truck at the intersection of Live Oak and Spruce. Your father and grandmother were killed instantly."

I don't know what I'm hearing. The words don't make sense to me.

"Who?"

"Your dad, and your grandmother," Nikki says.

"An accident?"

"A gravel truck lost its brakes," the sheriff says. "Demolished the car."

"My dad and my grandmother?"

The sheriff glances at his clipboard.

"Timothy Edward Grant. Martha May Grant. 1273 North Camellia?"

I don't get it. They were here just a few hours ago. They were supposed to come back. Dad said he'd be back for the game. He never lies to me. He never . . . I hug my arms across my chest and try to get a breath. My words come out choked and whispery.

"You're sure?"

"We're sure."

Nikki puts her arms around me and I lean my face into the crook of her neck, trying to shut out light, and sound, and time. A cold numbness creeps out from my heart, up through my brain and down to my toes. So numb. So cold. Nikki pulls away, gently.

"Autumn . . . Autumn . . . The sheriff needs some information."

I force myself to look up. Sheriff Gail drags Nikki's desk chair around and sits close in front of me.

"We need to notify other next of kin," she says. "Can you help us with that?"

I shake my head. "It's just us," I say, unable to believe what I've just heard — to think that it's now just me.

"Are they in the hospital?" I say.

"They were dead on arrival."

"When?"

"Approximately 5:50 p.m."

God! I played through a whole volleyball game not even knowing my family was dead! And I was worried about being pregnant?

"Did your grandmother have any other children? Or any brothers or sisters?"

"What about Casper?" I ask.

"Casper?" Sheriff Daniel says.

"The grandmother's guide dog," Nikki says.

"Oh, yes. It was killed, too."

The image of Casper on duty, sitting so straight and tall next to Grams in the back seat of the car cuts through the numbness of my mind and reaches my heart. I gasp at the vision, then give in to waves of heaving sobs.

Nikki pulls a bunch of tissue from the box on her desk and hands them to me.

"Autumn, is there anyone we should call to come get you?" she asks.

I shake my head.

"It's just us," I say. "It was just us."

I rub my thumb back and forth across the little coin pocket of my jeans, feeling the outline of my heart-rock.

"No other next of kin?" Sheriff Daniel asks.

"Just us. That's all . . . Are they in the hospital?" I ask again.

Sheriff Gail looks at me with sad eyes. She speaks softly.

"They were taken to the hospital where they were both pronounced dead on arrival. Their bodies are in the hospital morgue for now, until other arrangements are made."

"I want to see them."

"Not a good idea," Sheriff Daniel says.

"But I want to."

"Their bodies are . . . wouldn't recognize them."

"I want to see them anyway." I turn to Nikki, "Will you take me to see them?"

"How old are you?" Sheriff Daniel asks.

"Seventeen."

"You'll need permission from your guardian to view the bodies."

"I don't have a guardian."

"We'll take you to the county home. You can stay there until they find a foster home for you."

"Foster home? Why?" I ask.

"Well, you don't have a guardian, or any other close relatives, and you need a safe place to stay."

"No! I want to go home!"

I close my eyes and lean my head down over my knees.

Sheriff Gail says the county home is a nice place, with nice people. I put my hands over my ears. Nikki leans her face down next to mine and gently pulls my hands away from my ears.

"Come on, Autumn, you can come home with me tonight."

"I'm sorry," Sheriff Gail says. "Without an official guardian, Autumn is now automatically a ward of the court. We have to . . ."

"I'll be Autumn's guardian for now," Nikki says. She pulls a folder from under a messy stack of papers on her desk and shuffles through it.

"Here," she says, handing a paper to Sheriff Gail. "I've got release papers in my file for everyone on the team. In the absence of parents or guardian, I become the acting guardian."

Sheriff Gail reads the form and passes it to Sheriff Daniel.

"The last thing Autumn needs tonight is to be with strangers in a strange place."

Sheriff Daniel hands the form back to Nikki.

"Gail?" he says, motioning for her to follow him. They're back within minutes.

"Autumn, you can go home with your coach tonight, but we'll need to see you at the station before noon tomorrow," Sheriff Daniel says.

He hands Nikki his card. "Anytime between eight in the morning and noon. Okay?"

"Sure," Nikki says.

She guides me out the door and waits for the two sheriffs to follow.

Unhooking the giant ring of school keys from her belt, she locks the door behind them, then speed dials the custodian on her school-issue cell.

"Hey, Mack. There's been an emergency here and I need to leave. Will you double check to be sure everything's locked up? Thanks."

We walk to the parking lot and get into Nikki's Subaru. She takes the car keys from her bag, then fishes around in it some more until she finds her regular cell phone.

"Penny? I'm bringing someone home with me."

"The game? Oh, yeah. It was great! We won by three points, but listen, there's been an accident . . . "

"No, I'm fine . . . No . . . Just listen for a minute. Autumn's coming home with me and she's going to need something to help her get to sleep. Would you call Dr. Phelps and have him call in a prescription? And would you please pick it up so we'll have it when we get home?"

Nikki puts the key in the ignition.

"Yeah. Just tell him it's an emergency. He'll understand."

She starts the car.

"I'll tell you all about it when we get there," she says, driving slowly out of the now empty parking lot.

"I want to see them," I tell Nikki.

"Oh, Autumn. I don't think so."

"They're my family!"

I start crying again.

"Let's wait until morning. They'll still be there."

"I want to see where it happened!"

Nikki sighs, checks her mirrors, and makes a "U" turn. We drive about five miles to the intersection of Live Oak and Spruce. Everything's cleared away, like nothing ever happened.

We turn around and go back the way we came. Twenty minutes later we pull into the driveway of Coach Nicholson's house in San Remo. A woman about Nikki's age, but lots bigger, rushes out the door to meet us.

"Is everyone okay?"

"Penny, this is Autumn Grant."

"Oh, yes," she says, smiling. "I saw you play last Saturday. You were awesome!"

Awesome . . . Awesome Autumn . . . It's like everything in my head is jumbled, echoing. Awesome Autumn. What will those words mean now, without my dad to say them?

Nikki leads me to a chair and sort of eases me into it.

"Is there anything we can do for you?"

I sit there, numb.

"Are you hungry? Can I get you something to eat?" Penny asks.

I shake my head.

"Nikki?"

"Yeah, I'll have a cup of tea. I can fix it though."

"I've already got the kettle on," Penny says.

Nikki and I follow Penny into the kitchen. A big, grey tabby cat is stretched out on the kitchen chair closest to me. Penny gives it a playful poke. "Scoot, you big blob."

The cat jumps down and slinks off into another room.

"That's Elvis," Nikki says.

Penny wipes at the chair with the palm of her hand.

"Sit down, Honey," she says to me.

I sit down, not knowing what else to do.

"Did you call Dr. Phelps?" Nikki asks.

"Right here," Penny says, holding up a prescription bottle.

Nikki takes the bottle and reads the directions.

Penny looks back and forth between me and Nikki, then says softly, "Tell me what happened?"

Nikki pulls her chair up beside me and puts her arm around my shoulder, pulling me close.

"A bad accident," she tells Penny. "Autumn's father and grand-mother . . .'

I cover my ears with my hands, not wanting to hear the news again.

"Oh, no!" Penny says.

She sits next to me, close, on the other side.

"Should we call someone for you?" Penny asks.

I shake my head.

The three of us sit for a long time, not talking.

Finally Nikki asks, "Autumn, would you like a hot bath before you go to bed?"

"I don't think so."

She fills a glass of water.

"Come on, then. Let me show you where you're going to sleep."

I follow Nikki down the hallway.

"I made up the sofa-bed in the den," Penny calls after us.

"Autumn needs a real bed," Nikki says, opening the door at the end of the hall. I go into the room and sit down on the bed, suddenly so tired I can hardly move. Nikki sits beside me.

"Is there anything at all I can do?"

I shake my head.

"I feel so helpless! I'm so, so sorry this happened," she says. "They were such nice people!"

After sitting for a long time in silence, Nikki leaves the room, then comes back with the glass of water and the pills.

"Take one of these," Nikki says. "It won't hurt you and it'll help you get some sleep."

I take a pill from her and wash it down with a big gulp of water. She walks over to the dresser and turns a switch on a little speaker-like thing.

"I'm turning the monitor on so all you have to do is call me if you need anything. I don't care what time it is. If you need me, call. You don't even have to get out of bed. I'll hear you."

She sits down next to me again.

"I'm so sorry," she says. "So, so, sorry . . . Remember, if you need anything at all . . ."

She gestures toward the monitor, then leaves the room.

I take off my shoes and lie back on the bed, thinking how less than six hours ago my dad, and my grams, and Casper, were alive, and now, all of a sudden, they're not. What if we'd talked just two more minutes longer in the parking lot? Would the gravel truck have already gone through?

There's a soft knock on the door.

I know I should say something, but I can't.

Nikki opens the door.

"Here's a big T-shirt for you to sleep in, if you want," she says, putting the folded shirt on the chair near the door.

I turn away from her, back to my thoughts of what if. What if Danni hadn't come up at exactly the time she did? If they'd left a minute earlier, would they have been out of the intersection before the truck came through? I pull the covers over me, over my head, trying to warm the hollow, empty space that used to be me.

CHAPTER

5

I awaken slowly, opening my eyes to sunlight filtered through pink curtains, to teddy bears piled high in a crib on the other side of the room. Framed pictures from Disney movies — "Cinderella," "The Lion King," "Aladdin," "The Little Mermaid," look down on me from every wall. A moment of quiet peace — then shock. Memory and loss pulse through me. They are gone. They are dead. I close my eyes, longing for sleep. I'd take another one of those pills, more maybe, but I see that only the water glass is on the bedside table, no pill bottle.

Voices reach me through that thing on the dresser. What did Nikki call it? A monitor?

"But she's in our baby's room," Penny is saying.

"We don't have a baby, Penny, and it's senseless to keep it set up like some kind of weird shrine."

There's some shuffling around and then I hear Nikki saying, "Shhhh. Don't cry. I'm sorry. Shhhh."

"I just . . . I just need time."

"Shhhh. I know."

"I feel so selfish. That poor girl who's lost everything . . . "

There's more shuffling and the voices fade.

I get up to find the bathroom and when I come back to the bedroom Nikki is waiting for me.

"Did you sleep?"

"Yes."

"How are you doing?"

I shrug my shoulders, not knowing what to say, or how to say it.

"Well . . . Here's a never-been-used toothbrush, and a fresh towel and wash cloth . . ."

Shuffling sounds and then Penny's voice comes over the monitor, "Scoot, you big blob, so I can make the bed."

Nikki looks up, surprised.

"Hmmm. I guess the two-way switch was on," she says, reaching over and turning off the monitor.

"I guess."

Nikki sighs. "Not that you need to hear any sad stories right now, but . . . we thought we were getting a baby. Adopting. This is all Penny's doing," she says, indicating the room with a wide sweep of her arm. "Everything was set and then, at the last minute, things changed and there was no baby. Just the room. Whatever you heard through the monitor . . . that's what it was about."

"It's okay," I say, not that anything will ever be okay again. It's just something to say.

"Come have some breakfast."

"I'm not hungry."

"Just try," Nikki says. "You should at least eat a little something."

I follow her out to the kitchen and Penny hands me a plate with toast and fruit. I take a bite of banana but it turns dry and sawdusty in my mouth and I can barely swallow it. I sit at the table, moving fruit around on the plate, tearing the toast into small pieces, staring at the mess I'm making while Nikki bustles around doing morning stuff — feeding the cat, emptying the dishwasher, taking out the trash.

"Do you want to come sit outside with us for a little while?"

I shake my head.

"Well . . . We've got to do a bit of gardening. It won't take long.

Then I'll take you to the sheriff's station. Okay?"

"Okay."

"It's nice outside," Nikki says, pulling on her gardening gloves.

"Sure you don't want to come out?"

Again, I shake my head.

"Well . . . at least try to eat a little more breakfast," she says, walking out the back door.

I go back to the bedroom and get my cell phone out of my gym bag. There are two messages from Danni, frantic, saying she's heard what happened and doesn't know where to find me. Then there are three more from her just saying to call. There's one from Jason, in Iowa, saying he heard about the accident, saying he'll call again later. Then there's an old message from Dad from two days ago.

"Hey, Kid. I'm bringing home pizza. What kind do you want? Call me, otherwise I'll assume you want pineapple." He gives his maniacal laugh. "Only kidding," he says.

I play the message over and over, wondering how it's possible that I will never again hear his voice, or that laugh, except on an old phone message.

I call Danni and as soon as I hear her voice I start crying.

"Autumn!"

I can tell she's crying, too.

"I can't believe it!" she says.

"It's so . . . so . . ." I can't finish the sentence for crying.

"Where are you? I've been calling everywhere trying to find you."

"I stayed with Nikki last night."

"It's so bizarre," Danni says. "We were all at Barb 'n Edie's and these guys in the booth behind us were talking about some horrible accident down on Live Oak. The conversation with Krystal and Stacy was getting sort of boring and I started listening to what the guys behind us were saying . . . I can't believe . . . ."

Danni takes a deep breath, like she's trying to keep from crying again.

" . . . I was just half-listening, thinking about maybe eating your garbage burger, or half of it anyway, because you were so late, and I heard this one guy say how he saw this awful accident on his way home from work — a big gravel truck hit a little car — I wasn't paying that much attention but then . . . then . . ."

She pauses for another long breath.

"Then he says this big yellow dog came flying through the front windshield and it landed on the street right in front of him and it had one of those special blind dog collars on and . . . I got so scared! I started yelling at him about what color was the car and who was in it and . . . and . . . I knew who it was. I tried to find you everywhere . . ."

"They wouldn't let me come home. They wanted to take me to some foster home place."

"You should have called me," Danni says.

"God, Danni. I couldn't think what to do — I still can't."

"I'll come get you right now. I know Mom'll let me borrow the car. She's really worried about you. Everybody is."

"I've got to go to the sheriff's station pretty soon. Nikki's taking me."

"I'll meet you there . . . I can't believe any of this . . ."

"Me, either," I manage to gasp out.

I shut off my phone and lie back on the bed, pulling the pink comforter up over me. How can this be? Please let it be just a dream I'll soon wake up from. A dream to tell at breakfast. I try to go back to sleep, so I can wake up at home, so the nightmare will be over. It doesn't work.

On our way to the Hamilton Heights Sheriff's Department, Nikki starts talking about volleyball, and how proud she is of our team, how we've got a good chance for State this year, how this will bring in even better scholarship offers for seniors, etc., etc. Maybe she's trying to make me feel better. You know. Like take my mind off things? Or maybe she's just uncomfortable with the silence. It's not like I can think of anything to say.

When she runs out of volleyball talk she starts in on the adoption screw-up.

"It's not easy for two women, you know, like me and Penny, to get approved for adoption. But we did all of the right stuff, had our lives looked at under a microscope for the home study, did biographies and turned over all of our tax information and financial stuff

— three years of jumping through hoops. When we were finally approved we advertised on the Internet and got an interview with this birthmother who seemed perfect — three months pregnant, healthy, smart, all the right stuff. We ran it past our adoption counselor and everything seemed to check out.

"We flew to Phoenix to meet the mother in person. The reason she was giving up her baby was because she was a single mom with two other kids and she was very strapped financially. We visited with her in her apartment, which was tiny and not in a great neighborhood, but it was neat and clean. We took her and her kids to the park. We talked with the mom while the kids climbed play structures and went down the slides. They were great little kids! We could picture ourselves with a kid like that. The mom, Sherry, liked how we were with her kids. We decided we were a match.

"Sherry showed us a prescription from her ob-gyn that she couldn't afford to get refilled. She was also supposed to be taking certain pre-natal vitamins that she hadn't been able to buy yet. We left her with $200 for medicines and vitamins. The minute we got home, we contacted our adoption counselor, signed pre-agreements, and spent the next six months planning for a baby.

"The month after our visit, Sherry called, crying, saying they were about to be evicted because she was behind three months in her rent. We dipped into our savings to pay her back rent of $3,000 and then sent her money to pay her rent through the rest of her pregnancy.

"The baby was due September 13. We knew it was going to be a girl and, as you may have noticed, Penny went crazy with pink. Around the first of September, we heard the baby was going to be a week late. Then it was going to be two weeks late. When we finally started checking things out, we found that it was all a scam. The woman hadn't even been pregnant. We'd been duped."

When Nikki's finished with that story, she starts talking about how things were when she was in high school. By the time we get to the sheriff's station, I've heard her whole high school career. Every detail. Before we get out of the car she reaches over and smoothes my hair, leaving her hand resting at the base of my neck.

"I'm sorry, Autumn. I've just been filling space with words because I don't know what else to say."

"I don't know what to say, either," I tell her. "I just . . . I can't believe they're gone . . ."

Tears start again and Nikki reaches into her glove compartment for a stack of Starbuck's napkins.

It's funny. Not funny LOL but funny strange. I remember that night in the gym, getting the news. I remember everything the sheriffs said, and where they stood, and spending the night at Coach Nicholson's. I remember how her car smelled like volleyballs and nets and girl-sweat. I remember the tabby cat, and sunlight filtered through pink curtains, the too-dry-to-swallow banana, and everything Nikki said in her nervous monologue on the way to the sheriff's station.

I remember walking through the door at the sheriff's station, and Danni and her mom waiting there for me. They rushed to me and put their arms around me and we stood there hugging and crying until a sheriff came to get me. This was someone different from the night before, a woman named Erin Stroud, from the juvenile division.

Only one person could stay with me during "processing," so Carole stayed and Danni left with Coach Nicholson.

We were taken back to a small room with a desk and a few chairs. Sheriff Stroud sat behind the desk and Carole and I sat side by side across from her. Carole kept a tight grip on my hand, the way she used to when we were little and she'd have me on one side and Danni on the other, walking us across the street to the park.

I remember Sheriff Stroud handing me a plastic bag with my dad's wallet, and the "contents of his pockets," and my grandma's purse. I had to go through all of the items and sign a receipt for them.

Gram's purse was super neat, with all kinds of compartments where she could keep her dollars separated, ones in the highest compartment, then fives, tens and twenties. She never carries anything bigger than twenties. Carried. She never carried anything bigger than twenties. There were six ones and two fives and seventy-seven cents in change.

Her talking key chain was attached to an inside key ring and her tin of breath mints was tucked next to her house keys in an outside pocket. I signed the receipt that itemized all that was in Grams' purse, then looked through Dad's stuff. There was $86 in his wallet, plus his driver's license, two credit cards, a picture of me and Mom before she got sick, a picture of me in my volleyball uniform, and a news clipping about last Saturday's game that mentioned me as one of the star players.

From Dad's pockets there was some change — a nickel, two dimes, and six quarters. He always keeps quarters for parking meters. Kept. He always kept quarters for parking meters. Grams never carried any bills higher than a twenty. Kept. Carried. Kept. Carried. The words marched through my head in huge, black, block letters. Kept — Carried — pounded against the back of my eyes and pushed at the top of my head, banging, whirling, until I was so dizzy with kept and carried that I couldn't see the quarters, or the wallet, or anything else on the table in front of me. Then, slowly, the letters lost their shape and ran together. Black became gray and substance became mist, filling my head with a cold, dense, murky fog.

I have no clear memory of anything that happened for more than a month after the fog came in — came in and stayed.

CHAPTER

6

One day at lunch, a tiny crack opens in the curtain of fog. I'm at our regular table with Danni and a bunch of other volleyball players.

Over the noise of the lunchroom, Shannon yells, "Hey, listen to this!"

Somehow, that gets my attention. Then Shannon tells this lame joke about a girl who brings her boyfriend home to meet her parents. The guy's all tattooed and pierced and the mom takes the girl aside and tells her she's worried that the boyfriend doesn't seem like a very nice boy.

The girl says, "Oh, puh-lease, Mother! If he wasn't nice, why would he be doing five hundred hours of community service?"

Lame as it is, I follow. I get it. I smile.

"Hey, look! Autumn's smiling!" Krystal says.

They all look at me as if I've maybe just grown another head. Then they start clapping. I can feel the smile muscles working, breaking through the numb slackness of all these past weeks.

In Government, I actually pay attention to what the teacher is saying. I even take a few notes. English, too.

That evening, standing in the kitchen talking with her mom, Danni tells how I'd smiled at Shannon's joke. Carole stops stirring the spaghetti sauce and turns toward us.

"She smiled?" Carole says.

"She smiled!" Danni says.

"You smiled?"

"I guess I did," I say, smiling.

Carole reaches out, taking each of us by a hand and bowing her head.

"Dear Lord, thank you for answering our prayers, and bringing sweet Autumn back to us. Give her the strength to get through this most difficult time, and guide us all to do thy will. In Jesus' name, Amen."

"Amen," Danni echoes

I say "Amen" too, because I know I'm supposed to. Just like I know I'm supposed to bow my head when Danni's father, Donald, says grace at dinner. I don't know what it means exactly. I just do it to be polite.

During those weeks when I was lost in the fog, everyone says I seemed sort of okay — kind of distant, not so talkative, but . . . okay. All I know about that time is what people tell me. Danni's been filling in the blanks. She told me that when the sheriff said I had to go to the county home until a foster placement could be found, her mom threw a fit. I don't know the details, just that Carole and Donald had to go through the hassle of getting an emergency foster care license so I could stay with their family. Otherwise I'd have been sent to live with strangers.

The week after the accident, Danni and her mom had helped me finish packing all of our stuff — Dad's, Gram's, even Casper's papers and extra harness. Everything. We . . . I . . . had to be out of our old house within a week of the funeral. Because the escrow papers never got signed, there was no new house to go to. So besides being a total orphan, I'm also homeless. Not only that, I'm destitute. My dad had a small insurance policy for me, plus there was money for the down payment on the house, and a savings account. Not a lot, but probably enough for at least a year of college. But it's all being held in a special account that I can't get to until I'm eighteen.

Except for my clothes, my dad's wallet, and my grandma's purse, everything from my old life is in storage now. That's how I feel, too. Like I'm in some kind of dark, locked-up storage place, packed away from life.

People tell me that I didn't even cry at the funeral — that I talked to everyone and thanked them for coming. Jason's dad organized a big celebration at their house.

"A celebration? Dad and Grams are dead and he wanted to celebrate???"

"No. No," Danni rushed to explain. Celebrate their lives — not their deaths. You know, remember all of the good stuff and the funny stuff — sort of a really, really, totally sweet goodbye party."

She said people from Dad's work brought tons of food. They all talked about what a great guy my dad was, and how he'd help anyone in trouble.

"You know how your dad used to always tell us to be part of the solution, never part of the problem?" Danni asked.

"Yeah."

"Well, I guess he did that with everyone at his work, too, because at least five people who worked for him mentioned how he'd helped them be part of the solution when all they could see were problems."

She said later in the afternoon someone told a funny story about Dad, which got other people started on funny stories, and pretty soon it seemed more like a comedy show than a funeral. She told me that I even talked about how Dad and Grams and I always reported our dreams, and about Dad's pancakes. I guess I led a bunch of people in the yellow submarine song. I don't remember any of that.

Casper and Grams' trainer, Wayne, drove all the way down from the guide dog center. He said what a great match Casper and Grams made, and he also talked about what great potential I showed when I did my internship there. I wish I could at least remember that part.

The night after I started remembering, and after Danni told me about the funeral, or celebration, or goodbye party, or whatever, Carole came into the kitchen where Danni and I were at the table, doing our homework. Well . . . we were sort of doing our homework. I'd been in such a fog, for such a long time, that nothing on my assignment page made sense. As for Danni, she always only sort of did her homework.

Carole pulled a chair up next to me.

"I don't know if now is the time to give this to you, but . . . it was such a nice . . . celebration, and you don't remember, and . . . I thought . . ."

She put a dark green photo album down on the table in front of me.

"I've been saving this for you, for when you'd start remembering. But you don't have to look at it right now. Just put it away for another time if you want."

I opened the album to the first picture — a group shot of a bunch of Dad's friends, and all of the Hopkins family, and Jason and his family, and Casper's trainer, and me. We're standing in front of a big banner that says "IN CELEBRATION OF THE LIVES OF TIMOTHY GRANT, AND MARTHA GRANT, AND CASPER."

The following pages are snapshots of people talking in small groups, or gathered around a table full of food. There are flowers everywhere.

In every picture I'm standing close to someone who has an arm around me. In the group picture it's Casper's trainer. Near the food, it's Carole and Donald. Outside at the door, it's Jason's mom and dad.

The next to last picture is of Grams and Casper at their graduation from the Guide Dogs for the Blind place. The last picture is of Dad, leaning against our yellow submarine mailbox, wearing a sea captain's cap.

When I finished looking through the pictures I started over again, this time remembering some of the things people said about Dad, and Grams, and Casper. When I started through for the third time, Carole eased the book from my hands.

"I'm sorry . . . I thought . . ."

"No. Thank you. Thank you," I said, wiping tears from my eyes. "I want to remember. It's just . . . I miss them so much . . ."

Carole sat close to me, rubbing my back, until my tears were all used up.

Since the funeral, I've gone to school every day. We just got preliminary progress reports, though, and my grades are in the pits. I guess I've just been sitting zombie-like in class, not doing any homework, or participating in discussions — just sitting.

I haven't played in any of the games or been to volleyball practice since the night of the accident. Carole says Nikki's left several messages for me, urging me to get back to it. She even stopped by after school one day and talked to me about starting easy, just with practices. I don't remember any of that, either.

It's strange, like maybe I've been abducted by space aliens or something, like those people in Nebraska. Maybe they left a zombie-like substitute in my earthly place, and they just now returned me to earth. Before they brought me back, they gave me an amnesia drug, so I can't remember anything about their world, or the time I've been with them. Back when we were laughing about space alien stories, I never actually believed any of it, but then I didn't believe I'd turn into a homeless orphan either.

Now that I'm back from wherever I've been, and I'm becoming more . . . conscious . . . the absence of my dad, and Grams, and Casper, the horrible accident — that's a constant ache with me all the time. But at least I'm noticing the details of everyday life again.

I met with each of my teachers to work out a plan for getting caught up. I've already checked off four assignments of missed homework in English and three in Government. It's not much in comparison to all that's missing, but it's a start.

I plan to tackle the Spanish catch-up plan next week. I'm in Spanish IV, but I got there partly because Jason was always around to help me. His grandparents on his dad's side of the family are from Mexico and they used to all live together, so Jason learned Spanish early on. Plus, being a year ahead of me, and smarter, he learns all the grammar stuff before I do. That's the hard part. The verb conjugations, pronominal declensions, and things that give me a headache just to think about. Of course, even if Jason was still here I wouldn't ask him to come over and help me. What if he noticed what I most want to keep hidden?

Anyway, all of my teachers are being amazingly nice — even Mr. Klaus, my math teacher. He's got to be the most rigid, demanding teacher in the whole school, but now he's like, "Take all the time you need." "Skip the test until you're ready to take it. No hurry." That's so not Mr. Klaus.

In a way, it bothers me how nice everyone's being. Like I'm the famous, sudden orphan and that's all people think about when they see me. Like they're being unnaturally nice. Whatever. At least I've got a "catch-up" plan now. I'm determined to stay focused, so I can graduate on time, with my friends, on the Hamilton High stage, like I've always dreamed of doing.

I haven't told anyone about this, but sometimes, when catching up seems completely and totally overwhelming, and all I want is to blow it all off, I talk to my dad about it. I mean, I don't exactly talk out loud. I don't want people thinking I'm crazy. I just talk to him in my head. And in my head, he talks back. He gives me one of his pep talks about how important school is, and how awesome I am. Even if it's in my head, it's his voice. I listen. Then I get back to work.

Here's something I don't talk about to Dad or to anyone else. Not out loud. Not in my head. After all of those weeks of not remembering, after my time with the aliens, or whatever, well . . . I guess the amnesia drug works as well for doctor's appointments as for everything else.

Yesterday, when Danni and her mom were at the market and Hannah was watching TV, I called Planned Parenthood to reschedule the termination procedure. The nurse told me it wasn't that simple. I have to wait a week to see a doctor again, and I may be past the cut-off date for termination. And all the time I'm getting bigger and bigger. Those little flutter kicks I was noticing just before my scheduled appointment?? Those are like elephant kicks now.

Yesterday, when Danni and I were walking to the bus stop, I was carrying my notebook in front of my belly, like I always do now. But I swear, one of those elephant kicks connected with my notebook and nearly sent it flying. I'm surprised Danni didn't notice. Lucky for me, it was one of those times when she was busy talking about Jason, and how he'll probably be home for Thanksgiving, and how she's been reading everything ever written by Luis Rodriguez, so she can impress him, and on and on and on. Danni's eyes still sort of glaze over whenever she talks about Jason, even if she doesn't talk about him as much as she used to.

"It's hard to maintain a relationship when you're a thousand miles apart," she'd told me yesterday. Like they had a relationship when she and Jason lived in the same town?

Grams used to have a whole bunch of old-fashioned favorite sayings, like "That's the way the cookie crumbles," or "The grass is always greener on the other side of the fence." I know what she would have said about Danni's relationship remark — "Wishful thinking doesn't make it true."

I know that. No matter how hard I wish my dad and Grams were still alive, or I hadn't done what I did with Jason, or I weren't pregnant, I can't make those wishes come true. Except maybe . . . just maybe . . . I can undo the pregnancy thing. At this stage, though, it will take a lot more than a wish.

7

I know I've got to get better organized if I'm serious about passing all of my classes. After dinner I go into Danni's room and dump everything out of my backpack onto "my" bed. It's horrible, going through stuff that hasn't been touched for so long. There's Dad's wallet, and a stack of his business cards he gave me to hand out at the Hamilton High job fair. And Gram's neatly organized purse.

I take a twenty from Dad's wallet. It's about time I quit mooching off of Danni for lunch money. I fold the twenty neatly into thirds and tuck it into the check-out pocket of *Ordinary People*. Ever since someone stole my picture money from a compartment in my backpack, back in the ninth grade, I've kept fives and over in book card pockets. No one ever thinks to look there.

The wallet and Gram's purse I tuck under my sweatshirts in the top drawer of Danni's chest of drawers, the one she has emptied out for me. Maybe this weekend I should use some of Gram's and Dad's money to buy some new, bigger tops. I'm running out of clothes that are baggy enough to hide things. I don't want to spend much money on that stuff, though, because I won't need baggy things much longer.

I go back to the pile of things on the bed — my cell phone, useless without the charger, which I suppose is in storage. And there's my pregnancy termination appointment from before, and my temporary Medi-Cal card. Crumpled homework papers, a half-eaten, now-rotten apple wrapped in a paper towel, and a maxi-pad. Talk about wishful thinking! Also, there's Gram's hairbrush and her small can of hairspray.

I pick up the brush, remembering. One of the few things Grams couldn't do very well was fix her hair. It was never matted, or tangled, or dirty, like with some blind people. But there was this one spot at the back of her head that would stick straight up if it wasn't brushed down and sprayed at just the right angle. She used to ask me to help her with that one, stubborn spot. She could feel it sticking up, but she couldn't always fix it. Even if Grams was old, like in her sixties, and she couldn't see how she looked, it was still important to her to look good.

A few days before the accident, Grams and I had gone shopping. She needed help finding the right colors and sizes of things, and she didn't like to depend on sales clerks. She'd tried on a turtleneck sweater and decided to buy it, but before she left the dressing room she asked me to fix her mussed up hair. She'd handed me the brush and the hairspray she always carried in her purse, and I'd flattened down that one spot.

"Done," I'd said, and Grams and Casper went to pay for the sweater. I tossed the brush and hairspray into my backpack and forgot about it.

Now, dropping the brush onto the pile of things to throw away, I notice a strand of grey hair shimmering in the light. I pick the brush up again and pull the hair from between the bristles. Other strands are buried in the brush, mostly grey with a few brown, the way Gram's hair was.

Carefully, I remove all of the hair and hold the strands to the light, examining them for color, and texture, wondering if they were from the unruly batch at the top of her head, or if they were from the hair that curled softly at the sides of her face. I roll the hair into a tight, tiny, almost invisible, ball. I clutch it in my fist, wanting it to grow to the length and weight of Rapunzel's braids, to become a heavy, substantial essence of Grams.

Tears gather in my eyes, then slide down my cheeks. More tears. A flood of tears. And I think that's all that's left of the substance of Grams. Or Dad. Or Casper. Tears and more tears.

I'm still crying, rocking back and forth, with my fist clutched tight over my chest, when Danni comes into the room.

"What's wrong?"

I can only shake my head and keep crying.

Danni leaves the room and comes back with a box of tissue. I wipe my eyes, my cheeks, and my nose, but the tears don't stop.

"You've been doing so much better," Danni says. "What is it?"

I open the palm of my hand to show her the hair but there's not enough for her to notice. I point at the tiny speck in the palm of my hand but she still doesn't get it.

Then as quickly and with as much force as the tears came, laughter takes over. I look at the speck in the palm of my hand — a hairball. I'm hoping to replace my grandmother with a hairball. She didn't even like cats. Now I can't stop laughing. Rocking and laughing. Gasping and giggling.

"I don't get it," Danni says. "What's so funny?"

"So funny . . . so funny . . . ." I manage to choke out, "So funny I didn't forget to laugh," which gets me going again.

Danni sits looking at me like I'm crazy. Maybe I am.

"Are you okay?"

All I can do is shake my head no and keep laughing.

Danni gives me another long look.

"Fine, then," she says. "Don't tell me."

She gets up from the bed and goes out of the room, leaving me to laugh-cry-laugh-cry, and to wonder if the aliens gave me a drug that's messed with more than my memory.

Finally, exhausted and embarrassed, I wrap Gram's tiny hairball in a tissue and carefully place it inside the plastic zip bag in the back of my notebook, next to my heart-rock. The zip bag in the front of my notebook is jammed with pens, pencils, Wite-Out®, erasers, loose change and a few sticks of gum. It's an opaque gray, cluttered with bits of lead and eraser dust and the grime of constant use. But the back zip bag, holding only the rock and tissue-wrapped hair, is still clean and transparent.

In bed, propped against two pillows, I turn to page one of *Ordinary People*, the book the rest of the class is nearly finished with.

When Mr. Mosier and I were working out a plan for me to catch up in English, he'd said, "You can choose a different novel if you'd like. This one's about a tragic death, and the effect it has on remaining family members. It might not be a good time for you to read it."

"It's okay," I'd told him.

"I can help you find something more cheerful," he'd offered.

"I'll read this."

No way was I eager to read a story of a tragic death. But I didn't like the idea of special treatment, either.

By the time Danni comes to bed I've read enough to know that the dad was an orphan. The kid, Conrad, is a mental case, but also kind of funny. The mom is so uptight she makes Carole look like some kind of Woodstock hippie.

I close the book and turn out the reading lamp.

"I'm sorry I was so weird."

"It's okay," Danni says, not very convincingly.

I try to explain about my crying-laughing fit, but nothing comes out in a way that makes sense.

Danni sighs. "I just wish things could be . . . remember how we used to laugh all the time?"

"I was laughing tonight."

"Not like that! You know what I mean."

"I guess things don't seem as funny as they used to," I say.

After a long silence, Danni says, "It must be so horrible to be you," which doesn't exactly make me feel any better.

"For more than a month I've been leading you from home to school and class to class and home again, like I was . . . I don't know . . . like I was Casper. And then that day when you smiled, and when we all prayed, I thought . . ."

Danni pauses and I wonder if she's going to cry.

" . . . I thought you were going to be my friend again. Like you used to be."

"I am your friend. I'll always be your friend," I tell her.

"I mean my funny friend. And my friend who wants to help me with Jason, and who plays volleyball like no one else in the world, and who gets me to play volleyball like a champion, too, because we know all of each other's moves and tricks and set-ups, and my friend who listens to me and talks to me and . . ."

"I'm your friend," I repeat. "I don't know if I'll ever be like I used to be or not, but I'm still your friend."

I try to explain about feeling like I'm in storage, but that doesn't come out right, either.

"I'm sorry," I say.

"I'm sorry, too," she says. "I feel so guilty now because you've been through so much! You've lost everything! And here I am wishing you'd get over it and start having fun. Really, I'm sorry for being such a selfish witch."

"Don't say that. You've totally stood by me," I say. "I wouldn't even have a place to live if it wasn't for you and your family."

"I feel so helpless, though. I don't know how to help, or what to say . . ."

Danni gets up and comes across to sit on the edge of my bed. I scoot over to make room, and turn on my side. The big illuminated clock on the table between the two beds casts a dim glow on Danni's face. Here in the almost dark, with her worried look, I'm reminded of how she looked back in the second grade, when she had to carry a disciplinary note home to her parents. I think about how we've been sister-friends for such a long time. I guess Danni may be thinking the same thing.

"Pinky sister-friends forever?" she says.

"Pinky sister-friends forever," I say, linking my pinky with hers.

"Danni . . ."

For a moment I think I can tell her, my for-always sister-friend, that I'm pregnant, and worse, that Jason's the guy.

"Danni . . ."

She watches me, waiting. The words are there, all backed up in my throat, but they won't come out. Then in the late-night stillness of the room, I get a powerful elephant kick. It seems like it's aimed right at Danni's leg but I don't think it actually reached her.

"I'm sleepy," Danni says, getting back in her own bed.

I drop off to sleep replaying the moment when I might have told Danni everything, imagining what would have come next. After I'd spit out the blocked up words, then what? I do remember how angry she was when I went out to dinner with Jason. Pregnant with him? She'd be angry to infinity and back.

We hardly talk at breakfast. It seems like Danni's watching me, but pretending not to. Maybe it's because of all we said to each other last night and she's just being thoughtful. Or . . . maybe . . . she noticed the elephant kick?

I'm just getting out of the shower when Carole gives a quick knock on the door and comes in.

"Sorry," she says, "I just need to . . ."

I pull the towel around my belly, fast.

"Autumn . . ."

I reposition the towel, wishing it were beach-towel size.

Carole looks me up and down.

"Are you pregnant?"

I nod, keeping my eyes focused on a spot on the floor.

She takes my face between her hands and raises it until we're eye to eye.

"Were you raped?" she whispers.

I shake my head no.

"What happened?"

I look away.

"Who's the father? Is he planning to marry you?"

I step away from her, again shaking my head.

"I don't want to get married."

I can feel her eyes on my face, my barely covered belly and boobs. I can't look at her.

"Blessed Jesus," she says, still in a whisper. "Lord help us."

I stand, still feeling her eyes on me. The room is so quiet I hear every breath, hers and mine.

"Well . . . get dressed. I'll take Danni and Hannah to school and then we can talk."

"But . . . I'm already way behind in first period . . ."

"This is more important than first period class. I'll tell Dannielle you're not feeling well, which I suppose is the truth."

When Carole returns she calls me into the kitchen. She fixes us both a cup of hot chocolate and we sit across from each other at the table.

"Do you want to tell me about it?" she asks.

I shake my head.

"Does Dannielle know you're pregnant?"

"No one knows."

"I want to know how this happened."

"I made a mistake," I say.

Carole looks away from me, toward the window. Moments later, when she looks back, I see tears. She shakes her head slowly, back and forth, then breathes a deep sigh.

"When your mother died way back when you and Dannielle were in kindergarten, I promised myself I'd do whatever I could for you. Remember how you ate dinner with us practically every night that first year after your mother died? And when I packed Dannielle's lunch for school I just automatically packed one for you, too?"

I nod.

"I've loved you as if you were my own daughter. You know that, don't you?"

Again I nod.

"If it were only me and Donald, you could stay with us, but we've got to consider Hannah and Dannielle, too."

I shift in the kitchen chair, trying to get comfortable, wondering what Carole's getting at. She reaches across the table and takes my hands in hers.

"Autumn, I'm sorry, but it just won't work out for you to stay with us any longer. Hannah's too impressionable. She looks up to you. You know that, don't you?"

"Sort of."

"Whatever you do, she wants to do. If you stay with us, Hannah will think it's just fine to have sex and get pregnant before you're married. We don't want that. And Dannielle — it wouldn't be good for her reputation for everyone to know that her best friend is pregnant and not even married. Do you understand?"

"I guess."

"Our church helps support a home for unwed mothers — Helping Home. It's a nice place where you can stay until you have the baby. I already called about it."

"I don't want to go to a home for unwed mothers."

"Just until you have the baby," Carole says.

"No! I'm not going to have a baby! I already decided!"

Carole looks at me puzzled, then gasps.

"An abortion?? You're planning an abortion??"

I look away, not wanting to answer.

"Oh, God! Oh my God!"

"I can't have a baby," I tell her.

"Yes you can!" she screams. "I won't have you murdering a baby!"

She takes both cups from the table and jams them into the dishwasher, then sponges off the table and counters in quick, jerky motions. She opens the refrigerator door, then slams it shut again. I sit watching, not knowing what to do or say. She leans against the sink counter with her back to me. After a while, she sits down again.

"Even if you didn't get any religious training at home, our family always offered you good Christian values. You know it's wrong to kill a baby. I want you to do the right thing. I'll take you to Helping Home this morning and help you get settled."

She reaches for her purse, takes an address book from it, and starts fumbling through the pages.

"No. I won't go there."

Carole stops looking through the address book. After a long while of silent, angry, staring, she tells me to pack my things and she'll take me to the County Home.

"We can't be your foster family any longer," she says.

"Fine," I say, walking past her to Danni's room.

I zip all of my school stuff into my backpack and cram everything else into three big grocery bags. By the time I get everything together, Carole's waiting in the car with the engine running and the passenger door open. I toss my things in the back and get in. She doesn't say anything. She just drives.

I gaze out the window as we go past Palm Avenue School, past Hamilton High, and onto the freeway, heading in the direction of downtown Los Angeles. Thirty minutes later we pull into a parking lot next to a large building with a sign that says "County Receiving

Home." Carole shuts off the engine and gets out of the car.

I gather up my bags and backpack and follow Carole through the big glass doors into the reception area. She takes my arm and walks me up to the reception desk. Reaching into her tote bag, she gets a large brown envelope labeled "Foster care papers." She flips through papers, slides them back in the envelope, and puts it on the desk in front of the receptionist.

"It isn't working out for Autumn to stay with us anymore," she says.

"Let me have you talk with a social worker," the receptionist says.

"No thank you," Carole says. "All of the papers are in order."

She turns and walks out the door without a backward glance.

"Sit down," the woman at the desk tells me, shuffling through Carole's papers. She picks up her cell phone and calls for an intake person.

After a few minutes, a short, plump black woman with a kind face comes out to the desk. Her badge says Felicia Fenton, M.S.W.

"Autumn? Come on back, Honey. We'll get you settled."

I get up to follow her.

"Bring your things," she says, picking up my largest shopping bag and leaving the rest to me.

"It's going to be just fine," she says.

I don't think so.

8

Ms. Fenton unlocks a heavy steel door leading into a broad corridor and clips her keys back on her belt.

"Our doors are locked from the outside, for the protection of our children. But they're not locked from the inside."

To prove her point, she opens the door we've just walked through, then closes it again.

"You can walk out these doors any time. We hope you won't, but this is not a locked facility. You're not a criminal. You're not in jail."

Ms. Fenton walks me back to the intake area, unlocks the door and leads me into a small windowless cubicle.

"Meet Ms. Smeal," she says. "Eleanor, this is Autumn Grant."

Ms. Smeal looks up from her paperwork.

"I'm happy to meet you, Autumn," she says, though I wouldn't say the look on her face is exactly one of happiness.

"If you'll bring Autumn back to my office when you're finished . . ."

"No problem," Ms. Smeal says.

Ms. Fenton closes the door behind her and Ms. Smeal motions

for me to sit in the chair beside her desk. She puts her paperwork on a side table.

"Let's go through your backpack first," she says.

I look at her, not understanding what she means.

"Put your backpack on the desk and we'll inventory it," she says.

I put my backpack on the desk, still not understanding what's going on. Ms. Smeal removes every item, one by one, then makes a list of everything. Cell phone (not in service), my dad's wallet and all of its contents, Gram's purse and contents, my notebook and everything in it, dividers, assignment sheet, zippered plastic packets, each book by title. When she finishes noting every single thing from my backpack, she puts it all back and places it in a large, mesh bag.

"You'll get everything back when you leave," she says. "We'll provide you with everything you need while you're here."

"But I need my backpack. It's got my books, and . . ." I think about my grandmother's hair and the heart shaped stone but decide not to mention them.

". . . and some things I care about."

"They'll all be locked away in a safe place. No personal items are allowed here."

She writes my name, date of birth, date and time of arrival on a label, and attaches it to the bag.

She takes a "Physical Description" form from a stack of papers on the side table and attaches it to a clipboard. She has me stand up straight, back against the wall, and takes a Polaroid picture of me.

While she's waiting for the picture to develop, she fills out the top of the form with the same information that's on the bag label.

"Now, Autumn, if you'll just take off your shoes and sweatshirt, we'll get you weighed and measured.

I'm surprised to see that I weigh 133 pounds. It doesn't seem like I've been eating much at all, but maybe I was and I just don't remember. Usually I weigh somewhere between 118 and 122.

"Turn facing the other wall, please."

Ms. Smeal measures my height with one of those long sliding ruler things.

"5'61/2" she says, filling in more blanks.

She attaches the now-developed Polaroid to the form. I'm glad this picture won't be appearing in any yearbook.

"Now, let's see. Eyes."

She looks into my eyes, cocking her head as if trying to find a better angle.

"Brown? Not exactly. More hazel, I'd say," more like she's talking to herself than to me. She cocks her head in the other direction for one more look.

"Definitely hazel," she says, filling in another blank.

"Hair? Blond? Light Brown? We'll just say blond."

"Skintone? Light."

"Distinguishing characteristics? Any scars, piercings, tattoos, birthmarks?"

"Just . . . two of my toes are sort of . . . webbed."

"Let's have a look," she says.

I take the sock off my left foot and point to the two toes next to my big toe.

"Ummm. Born that way?"

"Yes. My father has . . . had . . . had the same thing."

Ms. Smeal jots a note under distinguishing characteristics.

"Anything else?"

"No."

"Okay. Take everything off but your underwear."

"Why???"

"It's just part of the check-in routine."

"I don't want to!" I say, thinking how obvious my pregnancy is when it's not hidden beneath clothes.

"Nobody wants to, but we have to do it. It won't take long."

"What if I won't do it??"

Ms. Smeal shakes her head. "You don't want to be like that — like you've got something to hide."

I just sit there with my arms folded. No way am I taking my clothes off for this . . . this . . . jail warden.

"Well . . . I can call two more attendants in here, and they'll forcibly remove your clothes. Or you can do it yourself."

I still don't move.

"I promise you, you'd rather do it on your own. Give yourself a break."

Ms. Smeal has her hand on the phone, watching me. So, okay, I take off my other sock. Then my baggy pants. Then my loose tee shirt.

"Stand up, please."

I do, and she looks me over from every angle.

"No other distinguishing characteristics," she says. "Except it looks like you're pregnant. Right?"

"Wrong!"

I don't even know why I said that except I don't like this woman and it's none of her business whether I'm pregnant or not.

"Have it your way," she says.

She adds a note to the form. I reach for my T-shirt, but she takes it from me, along with my pants, shoes and socks, and puts them in the mesh bag next to my backpack.

"Time for a shower," she says, walking me through a side door to a shower stall. She hands me soap and shampoo and tells me to wash thoroughly.

"I just took a shower this morning!"

"All right. Now it's time for another one."

She pulls the shower curtain aside and I step in.

"Hand me your underwear please," she says. "I'll have clean things and a towel waiting on this bench," she says, pointing to a wooden bench along the wall. "I'll wait here for you."

I take my time in the shower, even though I don't need another shower. When I get out, Ms. Smeal hands me a towel and points to the stack of clothes — jeans, T-shirt, socks, underwear, sitting on the bench.

"These will do for now. You can choose something more to your liking tomorrow."

"I don't want these clothes! I have my own clothes!"

Ms. Smeal shakes her head.

"Your clothes will be laundered and kept safely stored for you," she says. "While you're here we'll provide you with clothes."

What can I do? I'm trapped here. After I'm dressed again, Ms. Smeal asks me to be sure all of the tangles are out of my hair. Then she has me sit in a chair under a bright light.

"We have to check for lice," she says.

"Lice! Shite! I don't have lice!"

She takes a very fine-toothed comb and starts to comb my hair. I jerk my head away.

"This won't take long, and it has to be done. Again, I can call other attendants to help if that seems necessary."

She takes the comb to my hair again. Starting at my scalp, she combs roughly through a few sections of hair at a time. She checks the comb carefully after each harsh stroke — strokes that leave my scalp stinging.

When she's finished with my hair, we go back to the other room where she takes all of the items from my shopping bags and lists them. Then she puts them back in the bags and puts the bags in with my other stuff in the labeled mesh bag. She locks the bag behind a door leading to a large storage room.

"Perfectly safe and waiting right here for you," she says, smiling.

Like that's supposed to make me feel good? I no longer can get to anything of my own. Absolutely nothing! Not even my little stone heart. Not even a single strand of my grandmother's hair!

"I'll have you see the nurse before you go back to Ms. Fenton's office," Ms. Smeal says, picking up the phone and dialing.

"Daisy? I've just done an intake on a new girl, Autumn Grant. She says she's not pregnant, but . . . Okay. We'll be right down."

She hangs up and tells me what I've already figured out. The nurse wants to see me.

"What size shoe do you take?" Ms. Smeal asks.

"A nine."

She goes back through the "clothes" door and comes out with a pair of new, cheapo running shoes.

"Nine and a half. The closest we have right now," she says, handing them to me.

"I have my own shoes that fit! Why can't I at least have my own shoes??"

"It's just how we do things here. Put these shoes on and we'll go see the nurse."

The nurse, Daisy Lee, her badge says, is dressed in those green pajama things like they wear on TV hospital shows. She motions me into a smaller room where there's a scale, a blood pressure thing, and all that other stuff nurses have in their offices.

"How are you, Autumn? Any physical complaints?

"No."

"Slip your shoes off and step on the scale."

"I already did that with Ms. Smeal!"

"I know. I'm sorry. We need to do it again"

I slip off the shoes, easy because they're too big for me, and step on the scale. Then I move over to a chair where the nurse does the blood pressure thing, looks in my ears, mouth, nose and throat. When she looks in my eyes she asks if I may be anemic.

"I don't know."

"Please take off your top and jeans and sit here on the examining table," she says, motioning to one of those high, narrow bed things. "You can leave your underwear on."

She listens to my heart and lungs, then has me lie down. She pokes gently around my belly. She listens with her stethoscope at several places, then goes back to a spot just right of my belly button, where she listens for what seems a long time.

"You can put your clothes on," she tells me. "We'll talk in my office."

I dress and go back to the area where Ms. Lee's desk and files are.

"Have a seat," she says, nodding toward a little couch against the wall opposite the door.

I sit down and Ms. Lee sits beside me.

"Everything looks good. Your lungs are clear, blood pressure is good, good heart rate . . . Are you aware that you're pregnant?"

I feel my face getting hot and I'm pretty sure I'm turning bright red.

"Pregnant?" I ask, as if I've never heard the word before.

"Yes. Pregnant. Do you know that you're pregnant?"

I sigh. "Yes."

"Have you been receiving prenatal care?"

I look at her blankly.

"You know, things to protect your baby's health, like getting monthly check-ups from a doctor? Taking prenatal vitamins? Eating a balanced diet?"

"I'm not going to have a baby," I say.

Ms. Lee looks puzzled.

"But you do know you're pregnant."

"Yes, but . . ."

Ms. Lee, who has been nothing but businesslike up to now, takes my hand in hers. She looks directly into my eyes, searchingly.

"Tell me," she says, holding my gaze.

I look away, focusing on a poster urging "Wash often, for your health and the health of others," and showing soaped up hands over a bathroom sink.

"We're here to help," Ms. Lee says.

With a soft smile and warm dark eyes, she again encourages me to talk about my pregnancy."

And so . . . finally . . . the words that were blocked in my throat with Danni, come rushing out, filling the room with so many secrets so long kept. Jason's birthday. The champagne. The waiting/hoping for my period. The positive results of several home pregnancy tests. The jumping jacks. The trip alone to Planned Parenthood to arrange for termination. The accident. The missed appointment. The weeks lost to amnesia. The new appointment at Planned Parenthood.

"Are you certain you want an abortion?" Ms. Lee asks.

"I have to," I say.

"No one has to if they don't want to. Are you aware that there are plenty of other options?"

I nod.

"What does your boyfriend say?"

"He's not my boyfriend."

"Well, then . . . the father. What does the father say?"

"Jason," I say, unable to think of him as the father.

"All right. Jason. What does Jason say?"

"He doesn't know."

"What would he say?"

"He'd want us to get married and be Mommy and Daddy. I can't do that. I know I can't. I'm going to college. I'm up for a volleyball scholarship. I'm not the teen mom type."

The phone rings and Ms. Lee answers.

"No . . . we're not quite finished . . ."

She hangs up and turns back to me.

"That was Ms. Fenton. She's ready to do your orientation and get you started on academic testing, but that can wait a while . . . Do you know when you had your last period?"

"May 9."

"You're sure?"

"Pretty sure. I had to figure it out when I got my first termination referral from Planned Parenthood."

Ms. Lee takes a calendar from her desk and starts counting weeks back to May 9.

"It's pretty late for an abortion," she says. "When is your doctor's appointment?"

"Next Wednesday."

"In a week?"

"Yes."

"And then it will probably take another week to get you in for the abortion," she says, still looking at the calendar, frowning.

"I'll call and see if we can move your appointment up. In the meantime, though, I'll take you back to see Ms. Fenton."

In her office, I sit across from Ms. Fenton at a desk that's cluttered with papers and sticky notes and what looks to be the remains of someone's McMuffin breakfast. She spends a few minutes glancing through the papers in the file Carole left, then looks up.

"You've been through a hard time," she says.

I nod.

"You're not alone. All of our young people have been through some kind of hard time. But we're all here to help. People care. I care. You'll see."

I'm wondering if the aliens are coming for me again. It's like I'm floating over the desk, looking down on a scene from a movie.

"Autumn . . . Autumn!"

Ms. Fenton looks at me strangely.

"I was asking if you'd eaten yet this morning."

"Oh. Yeah. I had fruit and cereal at Danni's."

"Danni?"

"My friend's house — where I was staying."

She glances again at my file.

"Oh, yes. The Hopkins family . . . Things didn't work out with them?"

"I guess not."

"Well . . . Come with me. I'll show you around and then we'll get on with the paperwork. Always more paperwork," she says, smiling.

I follow her into a large area lined with shelves. Clothes are stacked according to type and style.

"You can choose from any of these things in the morning. Everything gets laundered after each use."

She shows me to a small room with two beds. The bedspreads are colorful and everything is clean but . . . it doesn't feel right to me. It's not like home, or like a place I belong. And where would that be, I wonder? Where would I belong now?

Back in Ms. Fenton's office there's a message waiting for her from the nurse.

"Well . . . Ms. Lee managed to get an appointment for you at Planned Parenthood this afternoon. I guess the academic testing will have to wait until tomorrow."

"I've passed all my high school proficiencies."

"Right. We'll call for your records. In the meantime, though, we always do academic placement as part of our intake. It lets our teachers know what level of work to offer you while you're here with us."

"I'm a senior at Hamilton High," I say.

"Well . . . we like to get students back to their home schools if they've been doing well in that setting. Unfortunately, Hamilton High School is beyond our transportation boundaries so until we find a closer placement for you, you'll attend school here."

It's late afternoon when we arrive at Planned Parenthood. This is a different place than the one I went to near Hamilton Heights, bigger, with a crowded waiting room. Ms. Lee leads the way to the receptionist window.

"Hi, Shirley. Thanks for getting us in," she says to the woman sitting behind the window.

"We got lucky with a cancellation."

I sign in and show the temporary Medi-Cal card I got back in September, for the first termination appointment.

Shirley takes a copy and then hands the card back to me. "It'll be a few minutes. I'll call you."

Ms. Lee and I sit next to each other on blue plastic chairs. She takes some adoption pamphlets from the table next to her and hands them to me.

"I already saw these before," I tell her, trying to hand them back. She doesn't take them.

"That was a while ago, right?"

I nod.

"You may need to start thinking about what you'll do if you're too late for an abortion."

I gaze at the top pamphlet, not really looking at it. I can't be too late for an abortion!

A young black woman in the same kind of green pajama things Ms. Lee was wearing earlier in the day opens the door next to the reception window.

"Autumn Grant?"

"I'll wait here for you," Ms. Lee says.

I follow the woman down a long hall where again I'm weighed and measured. Then she leads me to a small examining room where she takes my temperature and blood pressure.

"Doctor will be with you shortly," she says, leaving me to wait on the examining table with nothing on except this paper thing that just barely reaches to the waist and is open in the back. I'm gazing at my belly when one of those forceful kicks jars me. This gets me thinking about Danni and last night. Did she feel that kick? Did she tell her mother about it? Did Carole plan to barge in on me just as I was getting out of the shower? Are we still pinky-finger sister-friends? What'd Danni tell people when I didn't show up at lunch today?

The doctor, Dr. Singh, taps lightly on the door and comes in. She checks my chart and asks the same questions Ms. Lee asked earlier today. Then she asks me to lie back and put my feet in the stirrups. I hate what's coming! I frown at the sign on the ceiling that says "SMILE."

Dr. Singh calls for the nurse to come in. As soon as she enters, the doctor puts on sterile gloves, applies a lubricant, tells me to relax, and pushes her finger way up into my vagina. At the same time, she puts pressure on my belly, feeling all around the outside as she pokes around inside. Again she encourages me to relax, and to take deep breaths. Relaxing's not that easy right now.

After that torture, I'm sent to the lab for blood tests.

When I come out into the waiting room, loaded down with prenatal vitamins and information on "Healthy Mom, Healthy Baby," and a handful of tissue, Ms. Lee takes one look at my tear-stained face and walks toward me.

"Too late?" she says in a whisper.

"Uh-huh," I say, wiping at my face with the tissue.

Ms. Lee takes the vitamins and puts them in her bag.

"I'll hand these out to you each morning, to be sure you're getting them. You should look over the reading material though."

On the way back to the home Ms. Lee says, "It'll be okay. Lots of girls get through this just fine."

I know she's just trying to help but I'm really tired of people telling me things will be okay when I know they won't.

Traffic is heavy. We're moving along between a big gravel truck on the right and a red Honda on the left. The Honda's just like ours except ours was white. With its right blinker flashing, the Honda zips in front of us, causing Ms. Lee to hit the brakes.

"Some people!" she says.

I watch as the Honda speeds forward, cuts in front of the gravel truck and catches the Avenue 62 off-ramp.

"Did you see that jerk?"

I saw it. The Honda. The gravel truck. I know what could have happened to the car and the people in it. But why is it that drivers like the one in the red Honda get to crowd in front of a gravel truck and escape untouched and my dad, who was always careful, gets crushed? And why is it my mother died when I was only five? If there's a good and loving God, like Carole and Danni say there is, why does He let such bad things happen to such good people?

And why is it that some girls have sex with anyone, anytime, with no protection, and get away with it, and I do it once and I'm caught? And why, why, why, wasn't I returned to earth in time to get an abortion?

9

It's dinnertime by the time we get back to the county home. Ms. Lee walks with me into the dining hall.

A girl yells out from clear across the room, "Hey, Lee!"

She comes racing over to us.

"Tell them I'm special. I need more than one dessert!"

Ms. Lee laughs.

"Madison, this is Autumn. Will you show her the dinner routine?"

"Happy to," she says, "for an extra rice pudding."

"Deal," Ms. Lee says, stopping to talk to one of the servers on her way out.

Madison's taller than I am, and sort of heavy, but not in a sloppy, obese way. She's wearing a badge with her name, Madison Peters, written at the top and LEVEL ONE in big bold letters spread across the middle.

"You're in good hands, now," Ms. Lee says.

She puts her arm around me and gives me sort of a half hug.

"I'll see you tomorrow."

"Bye. Thanks."

Ms. Lee stops to talk to someone at the counter on her way out. "She's nice," Madison says, watching Ms. Lee leave. "She helped me a lot when I first came here."

I wonder if Madison was pregnant when she first arrived, or if Ms. Lee helped her in some other way.

It looks as if everyone else is pretty much finished eating, but the food is still out and there's a woman in a white smock and one of those tight hairnets standing behind the serving table. Madison shows me where to get a tray and utensils and I check out the choices. I get a cheese enchilada with red sauce, refried beans and rice. My dad never liked cafeteria food — said it was institutionalized. But I didn't realize how hungry I was until just now and this tastes good.

The woman in the white smock hands Madison a bowl of rice pudding and we take our food to an otherwise empty table.

Madison flashes a big smile at me. "Thanks for helping me get an extra bowl of rice pudding!"

"No problem," I say, swallowing a bit of enchilada and smiling back.

"Why are you here?" she asks.

"My friend's mom said I couldn't stay there anymore," I tell her, not knowing what else to say.

"Did you piss her off, or is she just a bitch?"

"Both, I guess," feeling guilty about agreeing to the bitch description.

"Why are you here?" I ask.

"My mom's in jail. She's a druggie."

Madison says this like it's nothing. I've never known anyone whose mom was a druggie, or who was in jail. At least I don't think I have.

"What's 'Level One' mean?" I ask, pointing to her badge.

"It means I've earned enough points to get privileges. Like, I'm free to go anywhere in the facility I want to, and I get special snacks, and trips to the mall, that kind of stuff. It's easier if you're a Level One, so you should start working on your points right away."

I let Madison have my rice pudding, too, since I'm not wild about sweets. When we finish eating, we go back to the so-called living room, where there's a TV, a bunch of board games, some books, four upholstered chairs and a couple of couches.

"It's visiting hours now, so some of the girls are out in the common area," Madison says, glancing at the clock. "Do you know which bed is yours?"

I point in the direction of the room Ms. Fenton showed me earlier in the day. Madison makes a face.

"I hope you don't need much sleep."

"Why?"

"You're in with Dericia. Sometimes she gets kind of . . . loud . . . after she's had visitors. Like tonight. Her mom's here tonight."

It's only a little after seven, but I'm so tired all I want to do is take a shower and go to bed. This will be my third shower for the day, but I feel all sticky from the examination at Planned Parenthood. I search the shelves for pajamas, then go into the bathroom for a shower. Except it turns out the "bathroom" only has a toilet and sink in it.

"Madison?"

She glances up from the TV — some ancient Cosby show re-run.

"Where are the showers?"

"They're down at the end of the hall, past Ms. Lee's office," she says.

"Thanks. I know I'll sleep better if I take a shower," I say, walking toward the door.

"Whoa!" Madison yells. "You can't take a shower now."

"Why not?"

"The doors are locked. Everybody showers in the morning. No nighttime showers."

"That's so lame!"

"Tell me about it," Madison says. "When I get to be God people will shower whenever they feel like it."

I'm sooooo tired. According to the clock, it's been about twelve hours since Carole walked in on me in the bathroom and saw I was pregnant. It feels more like weeks ago, though. I browse the book-shelves, hoping to find a copy of *Ordinary People*. No such luck. Now that I'm finally getting into it, I don't get to read it anymore. None of these books looks very interesting. *Anne of Green Gables*, which I read in the fourth grade. *The Face on the Milk Carton*, fifth grade. There are two of the early Harry Potter books, which I've also read, a bunch of beat up paperback romance stories and a copy of *Gone with the Wind*. Maybe I'll try that. I heard it was pretty good.

I change into the loaner PJs and crawl under the covers of my assigned bed. It's not nearly as comfortable as the bed at Danni's.

I try to concentrate on reading, but I can't. What's going to happen to me? For the first time I think about the baby inside me. Dr. Singh assured me it is a baby at this stage, not just a blob of cells. I've got a baby inside me and I don't want a baby inside me. Why didn't I get it taken care of as soon as I knew I was pregnant? Now I've got to go the full nine yards, only with me it's the full nine months.

I finally give up on reading and close my eyes, drifting between scenes of gravel trucks and Hondas, babies and guide dogs. In my dream I'm back at my old house with Dad and Grams except it isn't exactly like my old house and Grams looks a lot like Carole. We're telling our dreams and it's like I'm two people, the one who's dreaming and another one who is thinking about how weird it is to be telling a dream in a dream. Then there's a sudden shift and the house starts shaking and we're sliding around in our chairs.

"Earthquake!" Dad yells. "Earthquake!"

Except it isn't a dream-earthquake. I struggle awake, caught for a moment between dream and reality, trying to make sense of the strange place I've awakened in. A short dark-haired girl stands at the foot of the bed across from mine, yelling and throwing things.

"That cocksucking, motherfucking prick!"

She hauls off and throws a shoe against the wall. I rub my eyes and sit up, still half asleep.

"That shit for brains maggot infested asshole!"

Another shoe, this time hurled against the wall by my bed. Now I'm awake.

"Fucking . . ."

A woman in a Raiders sweatshirt and black jeans rushes into the room and puts her arms around the girl.

"Shhhhh. Dericia. Shhhhh."

The girl struggles to get loose but the Raiders woman keeps a tight hold. Several girls are standing at the door, peering in.

"Get back to bed, girls," Raiders says.

"Told ya," Madison says to me before she turns and walks away. "She talks in her sleep, too."

"He's a PRICK!!!"

"Dericia! Enough! . . . And you girls get back to bed NOW!"

The remaining girls drift away.

"Go back to sleep," Raiders says, looking over her shoulder at me as she walks Dericia out of the room.

Back to sleep? After that?

It's not like any of those words are new to me, but . . . I've never been awakened by someone screaming them so up-close and personal, or witnessed within arms length such an earthquake force of anger.

After breakfast and hygiene we get fifteen minutes to put our rooms in order and gather things for school. Dericia's picking up her shoes and placing them neatly beside her bed when I get back to the room. I fold my pajamas and put them on the shelf beside my underwear and socks. When I reach for my sweatshirt — their sweatshirt — at the foot of my bed, Dericia stands up and makes eye contact.

"I'm Dericia," she says.

"I'm Autumn."

"Sorry 'bout last night," she says, smiling.

Dericia's dark hair is pulled back in a neat ponytail. Her features are delicate, like you might see on some old-fashioned pre-Barbie doll. She's wearing a "Level Three" name tag.

"I get pretty pissed off sometimes," she says, still smiling.

"I noticed," I say.

I don't mean to sound sarcastic but I guess maybe that's how it came out because Dericia stops smiling.

"You'd be pissed off too, if you had my asshole father."

"My father's dead," I say.

"Lucky you," she says, walking out into the corridor.

After I take the tests, Ms. Fenton looks over the evaluation print-out.

"Your test scores are excellent," she says, smiling.

Madison comes rushing around the corner, practically running into Ms. Fenton.

"Hey, Miss F. You better watch where you're going!" she says, laughing as she zips past us.

Ms. Fenton laughs, too.

"That was Madison. You'll get to know her soon."

"She showed me around last night."

"That figures. She probably got an extra dessert or two in the process."

"Rice pudding," I say.

Ms. Fenton laughs again. "That's a girl who knows how to work the system."

Ms. Lee joins us in Ms. Fenton's office to talk about my school options.

"One possibility would be for you to attend our on-site school for a month or so while we try to place you with a family in your old school district. That way you could return to your home school."

"Okay," I say.

But really, what's the use now? Pretty soon it'll be obvious to everyone that I'm pregnant, no matter how loose my clothes are. I don't want to be waddling down the halls of Hamilton High, pregnant. If I were back living in Hamilton Heights and going to Hamilton High School, someone would be sure to tell Jason I'm pregnant. And even though it seems like things can't get worse, it would be way worse if Jason knew I was pregnant. The baby's due in three months! I wish the aliens would come back for me and keep me until this is all over.

"I'd like to encourage you to enroll in our district's Teen Moms program," Ms. Lee says. "You'll learn how to take good care of yourself for the rest of the pregnancy, and what to expect during labor and delivery. Plus you can work at your own pace to complete your academic credits."

"A school van would pick you up in the morning and drop you off in the afternoon," Ms. Fenton says.

I think about Sarah, all dejected, standing on the corner waiting for the special van to pick her up. It's not how I want to see myself.

"Think about it," Ms. Fenton says. "We'll talk again later this afternoon."

I walk back to the nurse's office with Ms. Lee to take my morning vitamins. She unlocks a file cabinet and opens a drawer filled with all kinds of prescription medicines, vitamins, and over-the-counter pills and lotions. She pulls out a plastic baggie labeled "Autumn Grant," and places three different kinds of vitamin capsules into my outstretched palm. She hands me a paper cup filled with water and watches as I swallow what Grams would have referred to as "horse pills."

"Dr. Singh called this morning to say that your blood test shows that you're slightly anemic. It's not serious, but you'll need to start taking iron capsules, too."

"I hate taking pills! Can't I get everything in a multi-vitamin?"

Ms. Lee shakes her head.

"It's very important that you get the added iron. You want the baby to be healthy."

I stare at a spot on the floor. In my vocabulary, "want," and "baby" are two words that definitely do not go together.

"Autumn . . ."

Ms. Lee waits until I look up.

"You've got to face your situation. You're more than six months pregnant! You're going to have a baby!"

CHAPTER

10

I'm sitting by myself at lunchtime when Madison brings her tray to my table and plops down across from me.

"When's your baby due?"

I keep chewing my turkey sandwich as if I haven't heard.

"What?? You think you're in a home for the blind and retarded, and no one's noticed?"

I stop chewing and look up.

"It's that obvious?"

Madison hoots with laughter.

"Ms. Lee wants me to go to a school for pregnant girls," I say.

"Damn! I wish I was pregnant so I could go to that school!"

"Why?"

"So I could get out of this place every day — at least get a look at the outside world!"

"But Ms. Fenton says we can walk out anytime we want to."

This time Madison laughs so hard she has to clamp her hand over her mouth to keep from spewing food out.

"What?"

"The old 'We hope you won't leave, but you can walk right

through that door any time you want to? This is not a jail,'" she says, wiping her mouth.

"Yeah."

"Here's the deal. The minute you walk out that door, they call the cops.

"The cops find you and bring you back. We're all minors. We have to be under the care of our parents or guardians. We can leave, but we're not legal."

Madison looks longingly at the chocolate cake still sitting on my tray. I pass it across to her.

"If you go to Teen Moms you'll at least get out every day. And you'll see different people. Do you know how boring it's going to get, seeing the same old faces at school, at every meal, at recreation, in the dorm?"

Madison licks her finger and dabs up every last crumb on the plate.

"Everywhere you go, the same old faces, except in the shower room. Then you see the same old butts!"

After lunch, we go outside to sort of a combination soccer/ baseball field for "recreation." Someone named Edna leads the group in "calisthenics." If Nikki could see what they call calisthenics here, she'd laugh her head off. As easy as they are though, I'm excused from doing them because of my "condition." If not everyone knew before that I was pregnant, they do now.

After calisthenics we do five laps around the perimeter of the high-fenced field. Walking is supposed to be good for pregnant women, so I do the laps. Then we're excused back to our dorms for forty-five minutes of homework. Since I don't have any homework, I pick up the copy of *Gone with the Wind* again.

A woman, Ms. Solano, goes from one girl to the next, checking their homework and offering help. She's sitting next to me, telling me how *Gone with the Wind* was the first book she ever liked, when Dericia calls her.

"Hey, Solano! I don't get this stupid question!"

"Try reading it again, carefully," Ms. Solano says.

A few minutes later Dericia calls out, "I still don't get this fuckin' question!"

Ms. Solano goes over to Dericia's table and sits down beside her. I'm trying to concentrate on *Gone with the Wind*, but I keep hearing Dericia. She starts to read a question, stumbles, stops, then starts over again.

"Let's work on this word," Ms. Solano says.

I keep my eyes on my book, listening to Dericia try to figure out what some word says. After a lot of help — "Look at the first syllable, 're.' How might that sound? Now try the second syllable. Now put them together . . ." etc., etc., etc. Dericia finally figures out the word is "remained."

Another girl, Jessie, asks for help and Ms. Solano goes over to her desk. I glance at Dericia, her head bent over the book, frowning, moving her lips as she reads, or tries to read. How awful is that, to be seventeen and still be reading like a little second grader? I feel sorry for her — no wonder she's such a witch.

Later in the afternoon, we go to something called Group. There are five of us — the same five as are in our dorm section. Madison, Dericia, and I are all seventeen. The other two, Amanda and Jessie, are fifteen. We sit in a circle on metal folding chairs in a small "counseling" room. Ms. Fenton, who everyone calls "Miss F," leads the group. We go around the circle for a quick check-in, how are we feeling, anything bothering us, etc.

It's okay to listen to other people's problems, but I don't like to talk about my own. The only people I've ever talked over my problems with are either dead or unavailable but they're still the only ones I'd want to talk to. The trouble is, everybody's supposed to talk in group.

During the check in, Dericia complains that she's still on Level Three.

"Why do you think that is?" Miss F. asks.

"Because my asshole father makes me puke buffalo turds!"

"Is there another way to say that?" Miss F. asks.

"Yeah, but you won't like that either!"

"Can any of you help Dericia come up with another way to talk about what's bothering her?

No one says anything.

Miss F. sits quietly, looking from one to another of us. I guess the silence finally gets to Amanda because she says, "Well . . . Dericia . . . Can't you just say that you're really angry with your father, without all the bad words?"

"No! I fuckin' can't! Because that wouldn't say enough!"

Here's some of the stuff I learn in this group session.

Jessie doesn't like to talk in group, either.

Madison's worried about her two younger sisters who're in a foster home over near the airport. She's trying to figure out a way to see them, but even though she's a "Level One," she can't go off on her own on a bus.

Both of Amanda's parents are in jail and her twenty-five-year-old boyfriend is trying to adopt her.

Dericia hates her dad because he beats up on her and her mom and her little brother. She talks more than anyone else. Well . . . she more yells than talks.

The last time her dad beat up on Dericia, he hurt her so bad she had to go to the hospital. When she told the Emergency Room doctor she got her bruises and broken ribs from falling down the stairs at school, he said her injuries were more consistent with battery than with a fall.

"Why didn't you just tell the doctor what happened?" I ask.

"And why don't you just put your head back up your butthole?"

A flash of anger rises in me and I say, "Sure, I'll put my head up my butthole, if you can spell butthole for me!"

It's like Dericia doesn't get what I've just said. Then she does. She flashes a look of pure hatred at me — a look way worse than anything that ever came my way across the volleyball net, or anywhere else for that matter.

Miss F. threatens to take points away from both of us. Then she goes on to tell Dericia, "Autumn asked a reasonable question. Why didn't you tell the doctor what really happened?"

"Because if I tell them my mother-fucking dad beat me up, they'd put me in some hellhole like this for my own protection! Which is what happened anyway, but it wouldn't have if the doctor hadn't bugged my mom so much he got her to say that my dad kicked me in the ribs with his steel-toed work boots. If my mom'd stayed with my story, I'd still be home. But no! I'm here, and he's home! They take the kid away and leave the asshole wife-beater and kid-beater guy at home!"

Dericia's half-screaming, half-crying, now.

"And when I'm not there, he goes after my little brother worse than anything!"

She runs from the room, pushing out of her chair with such force that it falls backward.

Miss F. uses her cell phone to report that Dericia's left group, upset, then asks the rest of us how we feel about what just happened. When it's my turn all I can think to say is "Bad."

"Bad?" Miss F. says. "What is it you feel bad about?"

"I feel bad about what just happened," I say, not looking up.

"Can you say more about that?" Miss F. asks.

I shake my head. She keeps looking at me and waiting. Luckily, the timer on Miss F.'s watch beeps and the session's over.

I stop in at Miss F.'s office later in the day to tell her I've decided to sign up for the Teen Moms school.

"Have a seat," she says, motioning to the big, soft chair at the side of her desk.

"Want a kiss?" she asks, handing me a bowl of foil wrapped candies.

"No, thanks."

"I'm glad you've decided to take our advice," she says. "Teen Moms will offer you more academically than you would get here in our basic on-site program, plus, of course, the specialized pregnancy/parenting program and the advantage of being with girls who are going through some of the same things you are."

I nod. I don't have the heart to tell her my decision was based on Madison's advice, not hers.

"I'll call Brenda Miller, the Sterling School District's teen pregnancy/parenting director, and get things set up for you."

"Okay," I say.

Miss F. gives me her broad, friendly smile, and I force a smile back. I like her and I know she's trying to help, but it's hard to be enthused about going to a school that's only for pregnant girls, or teen moms, or whatever, when only a few months ago I went to a real school, and had real friends, and lived in a real home, with a real family, and had a real future.

It turns out that the Teen Moms program is in the middle of some kind of standardized testing, so I won't be starting there until next week. In the meantime, the on-site teacher, Ms. Guerra, sets me up with an American Government textbook and a senior English text, both classes I need to complete for graduation.

"Could I read my book from Hamilton High for English credit?" I ask.

"What's the book?"

"*Ordinary People.*"

"I don't have a copy of that," she says.

"There's one in my backpack, in the storage closet."

She shakes her head. "I'm sorry. . . I can pick one up from the library for you next week, though."

"I'll be at the other school next week," I tell her.

I hate all of the stupid rules they have here. Like, we can't have our own cell phones here and we can't use their phones unless we've got signed permission from our parents or guardians, which sure leaves me out. So last night I started a letter to Danni. I'm worried, because everything seems so weird with Carole right now. But I'd just started pouring my heart out in the first paragraph when Madison asked what I was doing.

"Writing to a friend," I said.

"Is your friend on the approved list?"

"What approved list?"

"You know. It's the same as the telephone. No communication unless with someone on the approved list."

"Shite!" I said, crumpling the paper.

"Someday you're going to have to learn to talk like a big girl," Madison told me.

I've been getting points for good behavior since I've been here, but I can't move up to Level One without Group points. Everybody's supposed to talk in Group. If you don't talk, you don't get any points. Friday, walking into the counseling room, I'm thinking I've got to come up with some pretend problem to talk about, so I can keep my private problems private. Maybe I'll talk about how unfair it is that I don't get to read *Ordinary People*. That'll be easy.

How lame is this? Two weeks ago I was working on getting caught up in my classes, so I'd keep my scholarship, and play volleyball on a top college team, and now I'm working on points so I can go to the bathroom when I want?

Today is another day of Dericia venting. I hate when she goes nuts at night, in our room, but I like when she carries on in Group because there's less time for the rest of us to be put on the hot seat. The only trouble is that today she gets so mad, so fast, she slams out of the room before the session is halfway over. Again, Miss F. calls security on her cell phone, and then continues the check-in.

When Miss F. gets to me with the "How are you feeling, anything bothering you" question, instead of my usual one word "okay" answer, I say how unfair it is that I can't even read the book from my old high school. I tell her how I was in the middle of it, and it had great meaning for me, and I'm totally bored in the classroom, and there's a perfectly good book locked away three doors down the hall and I hate these stupid rules!

The rest of the girls sit looking at me, surprised, I guess, since they've never heard me say more than a few words in any Group session. I don't care, I should at least get points for participation today. Maybe next time I'll tell how I was abducted by aliens. That should be good for a few points, too.

On the afternoons when we don't have group therapy, I meet with Dr. K., the psychologist. Next week I'm supposed to start a "grief group." Dr. K. says it's for people who have "lost" loved ones. And, since I've not been under a doctor's care for my whole pregnancy, they'll be taking me once a week to Planned Parenthood for prenatal care, too. It's like I've landed in this giant repair shop and everyone's trying to fix me and everyone else who's here. Except some things aren't fixable.

Madison sits with me at dinner again. I don't know if it's because we're getting to be friends, or because she likes my desserts. Either way, I'm glad not to eat alone.

Tonight, as soon as she sits down, she tells me Dericia ran.

"You know. She ran away. Right after group. I heard the housemother talking to Dr. K."

"Good. I can do without her screaming fits. She's such a bitch!"
Madison bursts out laughing.

"What?"

She points at me, still laughing.

"What?"

"It's just . . . you've finally . . . learned to say bitch with a B."

"Well, she is a bitch!"

"You know what Amanda said about you?"

"What?"

"She said, 'That Autumn chick wouldn't say shit if she had a mouthful.'"

"Shit," I say. "Shit! Shit! Shit!"

Madison laughs even harder.

"Seriously, I can stand a good night's sleep."

"You want your dessert?" Madison says, her fork poised over my applesauce cake.

"You can have it," I say, sliding the plate across to her. "I don't even like this stuff."

She takes a big bite of my cake and this look of pure pleasure comes over her face. She chews slowly, as if that's all in the world she's thinking about. Then she gets back to me.

"Dericia's pretty smart. Not like, smart in the way that she can spell 'butthole,' but smart in the way that she knows how to stay away from the law."

"Yeah, well I hope she can stay away for a long, long time."

"Sooner or later she'll show up at home and then they'll catch up with her."

"She hates home. Why would she ever go back there?"

"She's always worried about her little brother. Besides, after a while she'll want to get caught."

"Why??"

"Because it's so fucking hard on the streets! She'll get hungry, and she'll need a bath, and a bed," Madison says. "For a smart girl you sure don't know much."

I hate when Madison acts like such a know-it-all. I reach across the table and pull my dessert plate back. I take a bite of my cake.

"I thought you didn't like that kind of cake!"

"I'm developing a taste for it."

She watches as I force another bite of cake down.

"So, okay. I'm sorry about the smart girl remark."

I push the plate back across the table to her.

"The thing is, for a lot of us in here, this is the only place we've felt safe in our whole lives."

Madison sits quietly chewing the last bite of cake, then she tells me, "I was seven the first time I came here. A neighbor called a child abuse hot line about me and my sisters."

"Who was abusing you?"

"We weren't being abused. We just weren't being taken care of. My mom and her boyfriend would leave us alone for days, looking for drugs I guess. The house was filthy. There was no food. I was trying to take care of my little sisters, but I was only seven so I wasn't doing a great job."

"This was the first time I ever had a new pair of shoes. I slept in a warm, clean bed, I got clean clothes, and for the first time I could ever remember, I didn't go to sleep hungry."

I think about the cheap shoes they gave me the day I arrived here. They would have seemed pretty special if they were the first new shoes I'd ever had.

By the time Madison is finished with it, my dessert plate looks as clean as if it has just come out of the dishwasher. I guess maybe she's still trying to make up for all those years of going to bed hungry. I decide never again to take back a dessert, even if I'm mad at her.

By now everyone knows my family was killed in that accident and they know I'm pregnant. They know about my family because of the "grief group," and they all know I'm pregnant because it's obvious.

"It's good that you're pregnant," Madison says. "Now you'll have your own family again."

I like Madison, but she says some really stupid stuff sometimes.

"You think a baby's going to be a dad to me? Or a grandma?? I don't want a baby!"

"Sorry!" she says, sounding more angry than sorry.

"I wanted an abortion but I couldn't get one."

She rolls her eyes upward, like she can't believe how stupid I am.

"It's not that hard. My sister's only thirteen and she's already had two abortions."

"I missed the time."

"Oh . . . That's fucked," Madison says, then she laughs like it's the funniest thing she could ever possibly have said.

I miss Danni. I miss having a real friend who I've known forever and who knows me, and who can find wittier things to laugh about than just "bitch," and "shit," and "fucked."

I miss the emails with Jason, too. And I miss real school. All school is here is read and answer questions, read and answer questions. No discussion. No group work. No independent research. And it's so easy, you hardly even have to think about it. Now that my brain is finally awake, it's about to die of boredom.

I miss volleyball, too. And I'd be starting track about now. I know . . . I wouldn't be running track pregnant, but still . . . it feels like my muscles are getting soft. I don't like it.

I miss telling my dreams in the mornings. Yesterday I was sitting across from Jessie at breakfast and I said, "I dreamt this horse was . . ."

"Who gives a fuck about your fucking dreams!" she'd said, picking up her tray and moving to another table.

11

In the morning, on our way to class, Miss F. catches up with us.

"Here's your book," she says, handing me my copy of *Ordinary People.*

I take it, surprised.

"And your notebook, too. There's no reason to keep these things from you," she says, smiling.

"Thanks."

"You're welcome," she says, turning around and walking back toward her office.

"She's cool," Madison says. "You're lucky you got her for a social worker. I've got that Bronson bitch. She wouldn't bend a rule for a free trip to Hawaii. If Miss F. likes you she'll let some shit slide by."

The first thing I do when I get to the classroom is turn to the back compartment of my notebook. The little heart is still there, next to Gram's hairball. I know it's dumb, but I'm so happy to have these things back, I feel like crying.

Twenty minutes into the class period, I tuck my book under my loose sweatshirt and ask to be excused to the restroom. Because I'm pregnant, Ms. Guerra always excuses me.

In the stall, behind the closed door, I open the cover of *Ordinary People* and slide my finger inside the book pocket. I feel it. The twenty-dollar bill. I scoot it up to the edge of the pocket, just far enough so I can see that it's really the money, then I scoot it back down. It doesn't even make the slightest bulge in the pocket. Even though it's only twenty dollars, I feel rich.

The thing about this place is that no one is supposed to have personal money. The points we make for good behavior we can "spend" on treats and things from a little "store" that's open in the patio in the afternoons.

But real money is not allowed. Here's what I think. My dad's money is none of their business.

Back in the classroom, I lean close to the desk and slip the book out from under my sweatshirt.

In the afternoon Ms. Lee takes me back to Planned Parenthood for my weekly visit to the doctor. This time, besides the standard examination, I get a sonogram. It's weird, the technician smears this gel stuff on my abdomen and then uses something called a transducer to send sound waves into my uterus. The result is a picture of the fetus.

"Everything looks fine," the doctor says, showing me the picture. "You've got a girl in there."

At first, the picture looks kind of creepy to me — sort of like E.T., except not as cute. But then Dr. Singh points out the baby's eyes, and eyebrows, and that she's sucking her thumb, and I see that it is no longer just a mass of cells.

I take the sonogram and put it inside the cover of my *Ordinary People*.

When I tell my psychologist, Dr. K., that the sonogram looks like E.T., she asks if I think I'm dehumanizing my baby because I'm afraid of attachment. That's what she thinks, but she'd never say that straight out. Everything she says is a question, like it's some kind of rule for psychologists to only talk in questions.

I go into what is now my private room, even if only for a little while. I fold my pillow to make it thicker and lie down on my side, *Ordinary People* propped open beside me. I've got to have a bed-time story. Tonight's the night I'm going to tell my dad that I'm pregnant. I've waited too long as it is. So, tonight, first the bedtime story, then the serious talk.

The tragic death Mr. Mosier told me about when he gave me the book turns out to be a seventeen-year-old guy. He drowned, and his brother, Conrad, blames himself. I guess he was sixteen or so when his brother drowned.

The part I read tonight is about Conrad going to see a psychologist. It seems like Conrad's psychologist follows the same "only talk in questions" rule that Dr. K. lives by.

I slip the sonogram between pages forty-six and forty-seven to mark my place, then get the heart rock from its place at the back of my notebook.

I turn out the light, grip the rock tightly in my fist, and move over close to the wall, making room for my dad. I wait, very quietly, wanting to feel the weight of his body as he sits beside me at the edge of the bed.

"Dad? Daddy? I have something to tell you."

"I'm all ears, Kid."

"It's bad," I say.

"Tell me."

"I'm pregnant."

As soon as I tell him, I start crying, just like I know I would have if I'd told him back in . . . back in real life.

"Well . . . your timing's off on this one, isn't it?"

"It's already too late for an abortion," I tell him, crying even harder.

"Daddy? Do you think I'm an awful person?"

"I think you're Awesome Autumn. I think this changes a lot of things for you, but you'll figure it all out."

"It's a girl."

"You'll be part of the solution."

"I miss you so much, Daddy," I sob, wishing I could feel his arms around me, comforting me.

"I love you, Autumn. You're awesome . . ."

In the morning my eyes are nearly swollen shut from crying and there is a deep indentation in the palm of my hand from where I've clutched the heart stone all night long. I feel better, though — relieved that my Dad finally knows, and that he still loves me. I'm not crazy even if I do have to see a psychologist. I know he's dead. But he's not dead to me.

I'm on my way to wait for the Teen Moms' van when Madison flashes her Level One badge at the receptionist and we walk through the front door together. I lower my awkward body onto the bench out front and Madison flops down beside me.

"You're going back out into the big tough world," she says. "Remember, it's "bitch," not "witch." It's "shit," not "shite.""

I laugh.

"I mean it. You're in the real world now, you've got to talk like a grownup!" Madison says, looking as serious as if she's just given me her very own secret passwords to happiness.

"Say "fuck," she demands.

I laugh harder.

"Come on! Just once! Show me you can do it!"

"Fuck," I whisper, half covering my mouth with my hands.

"Oh, that is the weakest fuck I ever heard," Madison says. She sighs, "I guess it's a start, though."

A yellow van with Frank Sterling Unified School District painted on the side rounds the corner. I stand up and lift my just-released backpack over my shoulder.

"Laters!" Madison says, waving as she walks back toward the building. "Have fun with all the other big mamas!"

I get on the van and show my temporary bus pass. "Sit anywhere," the driver says. Like I expected assigned seats?

There's only one other girl in the van and she's looking out the side window like she didn't even notice me get on. I sit on the opposite side and stare out the opposite window. A few miles later the van picks up two girls, one with a baby and one who looks like her baby's due in about five minutes. The one with the baby carries it to the back seat and sits down with it. The other girl eases herself into the seat in front of me. She sits sideways, resting her back against the window, and turns to face me.

"When's yours due?"

"February 15th."

"Really? Mine's February 2nd."

She takes a long look at my belly.

"You're not very big for being February 15th, are you?"

"I don't know. I feel huge!" I say.

"But look at me!" she says, rubbing her hands over her belly, laughing. Huge doesn't begin to describe it. Giganticus?

"My name's Madonna, after the singer," she says.

"I'm Autumn, after the season."

"People just call me Donna."

"People just call me Autumn."

We both laugh. The girl on the other side turns to stare at us long enough to show she's not amused, then looks back out the window. The baby in the back starts whimpering, then escalates to a full cry.

We're passing rundown houses with wrought iron bars on the windows and doors. There's a strip mall with graffiti sprayed on the sidewalk and on some of the storefronts. It reminds me of where Jason used to live. I wonder what he's doing right now. It's 8:10. He's probably in class, maybe discussing like how to combat world hunger, or what to do about global warming. Jason loves to come up with big ideas for big problems.

Danni's in Peer Communications, maybe hearing an interesting discussion. That's where I would be, if I were still at Hamilton High. If I hadn't been so stupid. And if I hadn't lost time in outer space.

The van pulls into a wide driveway and stops in front of a cemented area with a tall flagpole. The American flag hangs from the top, and the California bear flag hangs below it. I walk with Donna through the gate that says Teen Age Pregnancy and Parenting Program into a small classroom with pregnancy/childbirth/baby care displays lining the walls. There's a large whiteboard on a wall at the front of the room, and there are six large tables like the kind they had in the study room of the library at Hamilton High.

A very tall, very large woman with bright red lipstick and jet black hair pulled back in a ponytail calls out to me from across the room.

"You must be Autumn! Right?"

"Right," I say.

She gives me a quick smile and walks across the room to meet me.

"I'm Brenda Miller. Just call me Brenda. We're all on a first name basis here.

"You've got enrollment papers for me?"

I dig the envelope out of my backpack and hand it to Brenda. A woman carrying a load of papers comes in through a side door.

"Hey, Lupe. Come meet our new student," Brenda booms out.

The woman stacks her papers neatly on a back shelf, next to a row of computers, and comes over to where we're standing.

"I'm Lupe Mendoza," she says, extending her hand to me.

"Autumn," I say, giving her the kind of firm handshake my dad taught me to do.

"Welcome to TAPP. I think you'll like it here," she says. Her voice is as soft as Brenda's is loud. She's about a foot shorter and probably a hundred pounds lighter. She's wearing beige pants and a beige blouse.

By now the room is buzzing with the chatter of fifteen or so girls. I'm guessing maybe twelve of the girls are in various stages of pregnancy and the other three already have babies.

"Lupe, would you get a journal for Autumn and help her get started with the morning's writing?" Brenda asks.

"Sure. Let's sit over there," Lupe says, pointing to an empty table near the back wall.

Lupe brings me a three-ringed notebook with dividers.

"This is the journal you'll keep for your baby," she says. "That's the first thing we do every morning."

Lupe tells me that only Brenda reads the journals and she keeps everything she reads confidential. The only exceptions to confidentiality are if we write that we're in any kind of danger, or that we're putting ourselves or someone else at risk. We're supposed to write at least a page every day, and we write directly to our babies. Pens, not pencils, are to be used, so the writing will last for a long time.

"Students usually like to decorate their journals," Lupe says. "Some of them are just beautiful! They'll be such a treasure to the babies when they're older."

I glance around the room.

The girls are seated three or four to a table, with their journals open in front of them. The only sound now is of pens on paper and an occasional sniff or sigh.

"I'll leave you to do your writing, then I'll come back and show you how to set up the notebook sections," Lupe says. "Do you have a pen?"

"Yes," I say, bringing out my old notebook and getting a pen from the front zipper bag.

"Don't worry about the dividers for now. Just put the day and the date at the top and start out with 'Dear Baby,'" Lupe says, placing the opened journal in front of me before she walks away.

I read what's on the whiteboard.

Write to your baby about one hope you have for him/her. Explain fully.

At the top of the paper I write "Tuesday, November 13." I drop down two lines and write "Dear Baby." Then I stare at the page and doodle in the margins, then finally write:

I'm supposed to tell you about one hope I have for you, but I didn't even think you were a baby until I saw your picture yesterday, so it's not like I've got hopes.

When the fifteen minutes of writing time is over, Lupe comes back with labels for the notebook dividers.

One says "Dear Baby, From Mom to You." One says, "Your Physical Development," and another is "My Plan for Baby and Me." There's a label for "Your Family History," and one for "Random Thoughts and Images."

Lupe's showing me which labels go where when Brenda comes over. "If you can help Brittany with her math, I'll go over Autumn's credit evaluation with her," she says.

"Sure," Lupe says. "We can finish setting up her journal later."

Brenda sits down next to me and puts my transcript and a chart that lists the requirements for high school graduation in front of me. Most of my requirements are checked off.

"You only need to complete English, American Government,

and Economics to get your diploma, a total of eighteen credits."

"What about Spanish IV?" I ask.

"I see that you were taking Spanish IV at your previous school, but it's not a graduation requirement. Neither is Peer Communications or Art or Physical Education."

"But don't I need those other classes to qualify for my scholarship?"

The phone rings and Lupe answers it.

"Superintendent's office," she says to Brenda.

Brenda groans.

"I'll be right back," she says, getting up. "You might want to check your requirement assessment to be sure I've included everything."

I sit staring at my transcript — the record of my whole high school life to now. Except for Spanish II, and Chemistry, I've got all A's and B's — mostly A's. There's the art class that I loved so much it made me want to be an artist, at least until I realized I had zero talent. And there's Peer Communications, which was an awesome class. If it hadn't been for PC, I probably would never even have heard of Planned Parenthood, or known about birth control, or how to arrange for an abortion. Not that knowing all that stuff did any good. But it could have.

There's English with Miss Oldham from last year. "Hard work and a laugh a minute," she'd promised. And chemistry with Dr. Frankel, also known as Dr. Frankelstein. If they gave out national awards for worst teacher of the year, he'd be a winner every year.

Brenda comes back to the table.

"Did I get everything listed?" she asks, pointing to the Graduation Requirement Evaluation sheet.

"I think so," I tell her.

The phone rings again, and again it is for Brenda.

"I'm sorry, " she says, handing me a red pencil. "Check everything off to be sure I've got it all, would you? I'll be right back."

I put little checks beside everything on my transcript that's listed on the evaluation sheet. The only thing missing is the drama class from last year. I add that in the electives column. I only signed up for the class because Danni wanted to take drama and she didn't want to be the only person in the class who couldn't act. Then, when Carole saw drama listed on Danni's preliminary program, she told her to choose an elective more in keeping with their Christian values. So then I was the only person in drama who couldn't act. But I ended up doing lights, which was fun, and was worth an A.

When we were sophomores, the drama department had chosen a play that dealt with AIDS for their spring production. Danni's parents and a whole lot of other people complained the subject was inappropriate for high school students. I guess that's why Carole didn't want Danni to be in drama.

Danni was hecka mad that Carole wouldn't let her take drama. She didn't speak to her mom for days. But then when they met with their weekly mother/daughter prayer group, everyone prayed that the hurt between mother and daughter could be healed, and that Danni would always be careful to use her talents in the service of God. Danni got all teary-eyed when she told me about it.

"My mom loves me so much, she wants me to be with her in Paradise for all eternity. She doesn't want me to take any chances."

I didn't quite get the connection between not being in drama and living in Paradise for all of eternity, but I guess it made sense to Danni because she wasn't mad at her mom anymore.

Even though I didn't understand the whole thing about the prayer group, I couldn't help wondering what it would be like to have a mother, and to be in a mother/daughter prayer group with her, and to have her want me with her for all of eternity. I wonder now if my dad and Grams and Casper are in heaven with my mom, or if it's only church people like Danni and her family who go to heaven.

Once, not long after my mom died, Carole took me on her lap and told me I didn't need to be sad about my mother, that she was with God in heaven and they were watching out for me from up above. I remember liking that idea, but I wasn't sure I could believe it.

Carole had always made a big deal about how Santa Claus went all over the world on Christmas Eve, delivering presents to good little boys and girls. She'd even had Danni and me help bake cookies to put out for Santa because he'd be so hungry from all of his travels. She'd been so convincing in the Santa stories she told us that I believed her version of Santa Claus more than I did my own

Dad's. According to Dad, the Santa story was kind of a nice fairy
tale to help people remember the joy of giving.

Anyway, whenever Carole talked to me about God, I thought He
sounded a lot like Santa Claus, and I'd already figured out that was
all make-believe.

I decided to check things out with my dad, because he'd been
right about Santa a few years back. I waited until after our bedtime
story, because that was when it seemed best to talk about important
things. So after Dad finished reading to me about a kid who lived in
the jungles of Africa, I asked him, "Is Mommy in heaven with God,
watching over me?"

He was quiet for a long time. Then he told me that if anyone
at all was in heaven Mom was. She was the best person that ever
lived, and if they had the right kind of telescopes in heaven, she'd
definitely be watching over me.

"What's heaven like?" I'd asked.

"I don't know, Kid. I think it's a lot like the yellow submarine.
Our friends are all aboard, and more of them live next door, and
everyone has all they need."

"Are there angels playing on harps?"

"Well . . . truth is, I really don't know about heaven, but here's
something I do know. Your mom will always be in my heart, and
in your heart, and her happy, loving spirit will see us through. Hold
her in your heart, Kid."

"Autumn? Wake up."

I look up at Brenda.

"I'm not sleeping," I tell her.

"Well . . . it looked like you were, with your head down on the
desk and your eyes closed . . . but who could blame you? I'm sorry
that took so long. Where were we again?"

In a yellow submarine I think, but have sense enough not to say.
Instead I just shrug, trying to leave the old times behind.

"Oh, yes. We were talking about how close you are to earn-
ing your high school diploma. It looks as if you've been a good
student," she says, running her index finger along the columns of
grades on my transcript.

"As I was saying, all you need to graduate is to complete those six credits each in English, Government, and Economics. You can manage that pretty quickly here, working independently."

"But for my scholarship . . . "

"Well . . . for now, let's work on the basic requirements. Then maybe you'll want to make up some classes at a more comprehensive program in summer school, or in the fall, at a community college."

Brenda sets me up with Senior English, American Government and Economics textbooks along with a book titled *Your Pregnancy and Newborn Journey*, and the worksheets that go with it.

"You can start Spanish IV on the Sterling High School campus next semester, if you'd like. The only trouble is, you'll probably have to miss at least two weeks when you have the baby. It might be hard to make that up."

"Can I complete Peer Communications?"

"I can set you up with some activities to meet those requirements."

So, okay. It is better here than back at the county home school because I can get more of the courses I need. But it's weird to be around so many pregnant girls.

"Would you mind taking your enrollment forms over to the office?" Brenda asks.

"Where is it?"

Brenda walks outside with me and points in the direction of a sign that says "OFFICE." But what really catches my attention is the pay phone on the wall near the office door. I give my papers to the secretary and walk back to class, thinking only of the phone call I want to make.

When the van drops me off at the county home in the afternoon, Madison rushes out to greet me, like she's been standing at the window waiting or something.

"Guess who's back?" she yells.

"Who?"

"I'll give you a hint. You'd better be caught up on your sleep!"

"Not . . . ?"

"Yep! Your old friend Dericia!"

"Shit," I say. Not shite, but shit, shit, shit!

12

After dinner I'm in the community room, writing a paragraph for Economics homework, minding my own business, when Dericia plops down beside me.

"I dumped your shit out of my side of the closet."

"Whatever," I say, not looking up.

I keep writing, feeling her eyes burning into me.

"Must be hard to act like such hot shit when everyone knows you're nothing but a knocked up slut."

I stop writing and turn to her.

"Why don't you just leave me alone and I'll do the same for you."

"Hey, yeah! Thanks, Rodney. Let's just all get along," she says, oozing sarcasm.

"Why don't you just forget the drama?" I say, picking up my books and walking to a table on the other side of the room.

"Fuck you, bitch!"

"No thank you," I say. "I'm not in the mood right now."

Dericia pauses long enough to show she doesn't get what I've just said, then throws another "fuck you" at me as she storms out the door.

Jessie looks up from her letter to her grandmother.

"You're going to have to fight her or she'll never leave you alone."

"Fight? That's soooo stupid!"

"I'm just saying . . ."

"Maybe she'll run away again pretty soon."

Jessie shrugs her shoulders and goes back to writing. I try to finish my homework but I'm having a hard time concentrating. I haven't been in a fight since I got mad at Danni for scribbling on my picture of a tree. I was six years old and even then I knew it was stupid.

I wait until Raiders comes through with a five-minute warning for lights out before I go into my room. I'm hoping for a miracle, like Dericia will already be asleep or something. She's not. She's sitting on my bed, in her pajamas, clipping her toenails. I scoop up the clothes, which are strewn all over the floor, and reach for hangars from the closet. I shove Dericia's things over to her side and hang mine back up where they belong.

"Lights out!" Raiders calls from down the hallway.

I stand looking down on Dericia.

"Do you mind?" I say in my most sarcastic tone.

"Do you mind?" she says, mimicking me.

She moves over to the other bed.

"I didn't want nasty toenail clippings on my bed," she says, crawling under the covers and turning out the light.

I yank the spread from my bed and shake it out over Dericia, then climb under my covers. Trembling with anger, I lie with my face to the wall and count to ten. Then I do it again, remembering the words of Coach Nicholson. "Count to ten, then again. Anger loses. Control will win."

After about the eighth time of counting to ten, my heartbeat is regular and my hands are steady.

"Goodnight, Bitch," Dericia says.

"Goodnight, Dericia," I say, keeping my calm, grateful for what Nikki taught us. Which gets me thinking again about my old life. I'm still awake, thinking about how much I miss my old friends, and thinking how maybe I'll call someone from the telephone near the TAPP office, when I hear Dericia snoring. The sound is light, and gentle, and reminds me of how Grams snored when she first fell asleep. It's such an innocent sound, not loud and grating like I'd expect from someone like Dericia. What isn't an innocent sound comes later — Dericia thrashing around in her bed, crying out "mother-fucker-cock-sucker."

In the morning, Dericia's apologetic, sort of. Like after the first time I met her when she was in such a rage.

"Sorry about the toenails," she says, smiling.

We walk to the dining room together.

"Know what I dreamt last night?" she asks.

"What?" I say, longing to hear somebody's dream, even if it's Dericia's.

"I was running from my asshole father. He had his belt out, buckle first, and was swinging at me and getting closer and closer. And then, I just lifted up and flew high into the sky. And I shit on him, like I was a bird! Dumped a big load right on his head."

She laughs so hard she has to lean against the wall to catch her breath.

"Cool, huh?"

"No wonder you're in such a good mood this morning," I say, joining in her laughter.

"How about you?" she says, wiping her eyes.

I look at her blankly.

"Dreams? Did you have any dreams last night?"

I think for a minute.

"Yeah. I was at my old school, at lunch with my friends and I took a bite of my hot dog and all of my front teeth came out."

"Weird!"

"Not as much fun as yours, I guess."

Once inside the dining room we go our separate ways. But for hours after our brief conversation, I am strangely reassured by having heard, and told, a dream.

After three days of thinking about the phone, I finally get up enough nerve to make a call. I break my carefully saved twenty at nutrition time, so I'll have change for the phone. At 11:37 I ask to use the restroom. Brenda never questions anyone about using the restroom because a major symptom of pregnancy is that you have to pee practically all the time. It's exactly 11:40, ten minutes into lunch-time at Hamilton High, when I dial Krystal's cell phone number. She picks up right away.

"Hey, Krystal. It's me, Autumn."

"Autumn!" she shrieks, practically rupturing my eardrum.

"Hey, it's Autumn!" she says, and I envision the lunch table — Danni with her peanut butter and jelly sandwich with the crusts cut off, Jasmine with her giant diet soda, and Krystal and Shantell with whatever the cafeteria's offering today.

"Autumn?" Krystal says. "Where are you?"

"School," I say, but I don't think Krystal hears me because there's a lot of noise in the background. Then I hear Danni's voice.

"Gimme the phone!"

More sounds of confusion and then it's Danni.

"Autumn?"

"Yeah. How are you?"

My stomach feels all fluttery and this time it has nothing to do with being pregnant.

"It's about time you called! Where are you? Where have you been?"

"I'm at school."

"How could you just disappear like that? You didn't even bother to say goodbye!"

"I couldn't . . . your mom . . . I'm sorry," I say, my voice tight with tears.

"Where are you? Krystal's got her car. We'll come get you."

Donna comes rushing over. "Can you hurry? I need the phone."

I nod at Donna, then tell Danni, "I'm over near Frank Sterling High School, but I've got to go back to the county home in twenty minutes."

"The county home?"

Donna gives me a pleading look.

I get a recorded one-minute warning and Danni asks for my number so she can call me back.

"I'm at a pay phone at the school, and somebody's waiting to use it."

"Okay, so what's the number where you're staying? I'll call you tonight. We've got to talk!"

"I can't get phone calls there."

"What? It's like a jail or something? What's happened anyway? Email me then. Something . . ."

The phone goes dead and I hand it to Donna.

Back in class, Brenda calls me to her desk for a private consultation. She has my journal open to the "Dear Baby" section.

"I see that Tuesday you don't have any hope for your baby," Brenda says, turning the page. "The topic for Wednesday was to tell your baby the names you're thinking about for it, and why. All you wrote that day was 'Dear Baby,' and the rest of the page you left blank. And today is a blank."

"I just . . . I couldn't think of anything to write."

She turns to the "My Plan for Baby and Me" section, which is also blank.

"Let's work on this one together," Brenda says.

"Due date?"

"February 15."

Brenda writes February 15 on the "Due Date" line.

"Where will you and the baby be living?"

I shrug.

"Who will you be living with?"

Another shrug.

"What hospital?"

"I'm not sure," I say.

"Is it safe to say you haven't thought much about life with a baby?"

"I didn't want a baby," I say.

Brenda glances at the clock.

"Oops. Just five more minutes. We'll have to work more on your plan tomorrow, but you might take a look at these."

She hands me some adoption pamphlets and a card for someone to call if I'm interested.

In the van on the way back to the county home I read the pamphlets. Donna, sitting in front of me as she did on my first trip to TAPP, notices.

"That sucks!" she says, pointing to "The Facts About Adoption."

"It sucks having a baby to take care of instead of going to college, too."

"I'd never give up my baby! Why would I want someone else raising my own baby?"

"Because you have other things to do before you get tied down to a baby?"

"That's the most spoiled, selfish, mean thing I have ever heard!" Donna says, turning around and facing forward.

When we get to her stop she gets off without looking at me, and without saying goodbye.

Madison is sitting at an outside table cluttered with blunt scissors, construction paper, glue, crayons, and everything else that would go with an elementary school art project. I ease down on the bench opposite her.

"What're you doing?"

"Thanksgiving," she says, carefully tracing the outline of her left hand onto a sheet of heavy white paper.

"What about Thanksgiving?"

She does the eye-roll thing.

"Well?"

"It's next week, and I've got to send something to my mom, and my little sisters."

She does another tracing of her hand, then hands me the pencil. She takes a fresh sheet of white paper and places her right hand down on it.

"Here, trace this hand for me. I don't want all of the turkeys to be facing the same direction."

"Turkeys?" I say, tracing her hand like she asked me to.

"You know. Hand turkeys. Didn't you ever make hand turkeys?"

Then I remember about hand turkeys from back in the third grade with Mr. Westley. Our whole class made turkeys like that. The thumb was the neck and head and the fingers were feathers. We drew in details, and colored them, and on the back we wrote "Happy Thanksgiving" to take to our families.

"Here, trace one more right hand for me," Madison says. "So I'll have two facing one direction and two facing the other — two for each of my sisters."

I put my pencil at the base of her thumb and start to trace, then I start laughing. I'm laughing so hard I can't even hold the pencil.

"What?" Madison says.

"I . . . You . . . You could trace four left hands and just turn two . . ." I'm gasping and Madison is looking at me like she still doesn't get it. " . . . you could just turn two of the left hands over and they'd be going the other direction."

Madison looks at one of the papers with a traced right hand, turns it over and peers at the barely visible outline on the backside of the paper, then turns it over again.

"You're always soooo fuckin' smart," she says, laughing.

I sit with her for awhile and make my own hand-turkey, carefully coloring the feathers and drawing a beak, and eyes, and that ugly thing that hangs from turkeys' necks. Wattles, I think. It's a pretty good turkey — definitely better than the one I made in the third grade.

Madison chooses the best of her turkeys and writes on the back, in pen, very carefully, "Dear Mom, Have a Very Happy Thanksgiving. I hope I get to see you soon. I love you." She signs her name and decorates the edge of the card with hearts.

"I've got homework," I say, standing up and taking my backpack from the table. "See you later."

"Hey, don't you want your turkey?" Madison calls after me.

"You can have it. I don't have anyone to send it to, anyway."

CHAPTER

13

In my dream a red-faced, howling Penny lies in the crib in the pink room, her arms and legs hanging out between the slats. Nikki stands over her, trying to give her a bottle. Penny throws her head from side to side, refusing to drink. The dream is so strong that when I first awaken from it I don't even know where I am. My old bedroom on Camellia? Danni's room? Then I hear Dericia's soft snore and it all comes back to me.

First thing in the morning, while we're gathering our clothes to take to the shower room, I tell Dericia my dream.

"It was so strange — that big, grown-up woman in a baby crib."

Dericia nods.

"How about you?"

She stops her search for a shoe, thinking. She smiles.

"Yeah. I dreamt my little brother could fly, too, like the way I flew in that dream about the asshole."

We both laugh at the memory of her "dumping" dream.

Dericia and I don't always get along great. She doesn't get along great with anyone. But we haven't come even close to a fight since we started telling each other our dreams. Maybe my mom had been right about her dream theory.

While everyone else is at breakfast, I scribble a quick note to Madison. I thank her for being my friend and tell her I've figured out what to do about the baby, so I've got to go somewhere else. I tell her I hope I'll see her again some day, and that's true. I ask her to say goodbye to Dericia for me, then fold the note, sneak into Madison's room and put the note under her pillow. I walk out the front door to wait for the TAPP van.

I'm sorry I couldn't say goodbye to Miss F., or Ms. Lee, because they both did everything they could to help me out. But you can't really run away if you're going to tell everyone you're leaving.

In class this morning, I finally have something to write in my baby journal:

Friday, November 16
Dear Baby,

I don't want to hurt your feelings, but I don't want to write a bunch of lies to you. The other girls are writing to their babies about how much they already love them, and how they can't wait to hold them in their arms. Now that I've seen your picture, and I feel you moving around all the time, I like you a little. I can't say I love you, though. I've known from the beginning I don't want a baby. But I think I know someone who will want you. My life has been so messed up lately that I haven't even been able to think right. And when I do think, all I can think about is me. I haven't always been like that. I used to care a lot about other people, just not lately. But I just now figured out how I can do something for someone else, and it'll work out better for you, and for me, too.

All of the other girls sign their letters to their babies with things like "Love you forever," or "Your loving mother," but even if I know it's true, I don't feel like anyone's mother.

Autumn

When the van drops me at the county home Friday afternoon, I walk quickly past the entrance, down the street and around the corner. It's four blocks to the bus stop and I hope the bus comes soon, before anyone at the home figures out I'm missing. I drop my backpack on the bench. All that's in it is my notebook and *Ordinary People*. I didn't take any of my textbooks from school because I don't expect to be going back. I hope someday I can get the stuff back that's still locked up at the home, especially Dad's wallet and Gram's purse. Not only for the money, but because it's something from them, something they touched every day.

I try to make sense of the posted bus routes. I'm pretty sure the red line will take me in the right direction, but San Remo isn't even shown on any of the routes.

Even though it's November, the afternoon sun is warm on my face and I soon feel tired and sleepy in that relaxed way the warm sun can bring. I lean my head against the back of the bench and wonder if Madison's found the note I left for her yet, and how long it will take me to get to San Remo. I don't even know if I can find their house or not. And what if they already have another adoption started? I hadn't thought about that possibility until this minute.

I feel the swoosh of the approaching bus and open my eyes.

"Can I get to San Remo from here?" I ask the bus driver.

She laughs. "Yeah. If you've got all day and half the night."

I heave my backpack up the steps and dig money from my book.

"$1.85," she says. "That'll take you to the end of the blue line, then you'll have to transfer to the red line."

"Thanks," I say, walking to the back of the crowded bus, to the first vacant seat.

I sit by the window, watching the neighborhood change from trash-littered, graffiti-ridden sidewalks, and buildings with junk cars lining the streets, to freshly painted buildings with flower boxes and clean sidewalks, and back to graffiti and trash.

There are now only two passengers on the bus, me and an ancient lady who keeps muttering to herself, sometimes laughing and sometimes seeming very angry.

In another mile or so the driver calls out, "End of the line. Everybody off."

I pick up my backpack and make my way to the front of the bus.

"You'll get the next red line bus, probably in ten minutes or so, and then you'll be halfway there."

"Thanks."

"Hey, Irma! End of the line, Honey!"

The old woman keeps talking to herself and the bus driver walks back to where she's sitting. I get off and plop down on the bench. The digital clock in front of a bank across the street says 2:47 p.m., but it also says it's forty-four degrees, which must be at least twenty degrees off. Not that it matters much to me what the accurate time is. It's not like I've got an appointment or anything.

It's dark by the time I get to San Remo. I'm tired, and my back aches from sitting for hours on buses, and from hauling my backpack on the bus, off the bus, on the bus, off the bus, from the blue line, to the red line, to the green line. The baby keeps kicking me in the gut and I've got to pee so bad I'm about to burst.

I get off at the San Remo shopping center and rush into the Safeway in search of a restroom. Luckily, it's near the front of the store and I make it into a stall just in time. I wash my hands and splash cold water on my face. I don't even look like the same person I used to be. My hair is dull and lifeless, nothing "glowing" about it now. Pale face, dark circles under my eyes, fat as a cow — will Nikki even recognize me when she sees me? I smear on some lip gloss, run the brush through my hair and pull it back tight in a scrunchy, then pat my cheeks hoping to bring some color to them.

Standing in front of the Safeway, I try to get my bearings. This is where we got paper plates for last summer's team party at Nikki's place. I'm sure we drove out the far end of the parking lot, by the Starbucks, and turned right to get to her house. But then what? I've only been to her house twice. Once for the party, when Danni drove, and then the night Dad and Grams were killed. I wasn't noticing much about how we got anywhere that night.

There's a pay phone outside the gas station across the street and I waddle over there to see if I can call Nikki, or find her address, or something. There are about thirty Nicholsons in the phone book. I remember from grade reports and notices home that her first name is Jean, but there is no Jean Nicholson listed. There are seven J. Nicholsons. I guess it's worth a try.

A man picks up at the first J. Nicholson.

"I'm trying to reach Jean Nicholson," I say.

"Not here," he says, and hangs up.

No answer at either the second or third numbers.

On the fourth try I get a familiar voice.

"You have reached the home of Jean and Penny. Leave a message and we'll get back to you soon."

"I . . . Nikki? This is Autumn Grant. I . . . I need some . . ."

"Autumn! Don't hang up!"

"Nikki?"

"How are you? Where are you?"

"I'm across the street from the San Remo Shopping Center."

"San Remo? You're just around the corner from us! What're you doing there?"

"I came to talk to you."

"Jesus! I'll come get you. What're you close to?"

"I'm at the Arco station across from Safeway."

"Okay. I'll be right there."

"Thanks."

"Wait! Autumn! Are you okay?"

"Sort of."

"I won't be more than five minutes."

I've barely hung up and walked out to the sidewalk when I see Nikki's silver Subaru turn the corner. She honks when she sees me, then pulls to a stop at the curb and rushes to greet me. Gad it's good to see a familiar face from my old life!

"Autumn! Where've you been?" she says, throwing her arms around me and giving me a tight hug.

She pulls back, her eyes on my belly.

"Oh, my God!"

I look away, trying to hold back the tears.

"Come on," Nikki says. "We'll go back to my place and you can tell me all about it."

She opens the door for me and I heft my tired, clumsy body up into the passenger seat. Nikki tosses my backpack on the floor behind me and comes around to the driver's side.

"Thanks for coming to get me," I say.

She starts the car and pulls away from the curb.

"Thanks for calling," she says. "Danni said she talked to you on the phone yesterday but you got cut off before she could find out how to reach you."

"Yeah. I ran out of time on the pay phone."

"Where've you been? Your friends, teachers, we've all been so worried about you."

"But didn't Danni know where I was?"

"She knew her mom had taken you to another foster home, but she didn't know where. She kept expecting to hear from you."

"I was in the county home. I couldn't call out."

"County home? Clear out there by the old fairgrounds?"

"I guess," I say, thinking about the big fenced off place of vacant land we passed every day on the way to TAPP.

Nikki pulls into her driveway and shuts off the engine, then comes around to meet me as I get out of the car. I reach for my backpack but she gets to it first.

"I'll take that. You look like you're dead tired."

"Yeah. I've been on buses since early this afternoon."

"So . . . Did you run away?"

"I just left."

Nikki unlocks the front door and we go inside.

"Does anybody know you're here?"

"No. I left a note for my friend, but I didn't tell her where I was going."

"Hmm," Nikki says. "Sounds a lot like running away to me."

Nikki goes straight to the kitchen and I follow close behind her. "I'm starved. I bet you are, too," she says. "Want a quesadilla?"

"Okay."

"Here. Have a seat."

She pulls a chair away from the table. I sit down, tired and achy. Nikki sets my backpack on the floor beside me, then opens the refrigerator and peers inside.

"Penny usually does the cooking but she told me she stocked up on a few things that would be within the range of my culinary skills — all microwaveable." Nikki says, laughing.

She pulls a package of grated cheese, tortillas and salsa from the refrigerator, sticks a spoon into the salsa jar and sets it on the table.

"You want onions?" she asks.

"No, thanks."

"Penny always visits her parents at Thanksgiving. They live clear across the country in New Hampshire. I'd just walked in from taking her to the airport when you called. Lucky timing."

Putting a big, flour tortilla on a plate, she loads it with cheese and puts it in the microwave. She slices an avocado onto a plate, puts it on the table next to the salsa, then readies another quesadilla for the microwave.

"Milk? Soda? Water?"

"Just water is fine," I say.

Nikki gets two bottles of water from the refrigerator and puts them on the table, then takes the first quesadilla from the microwave and puts it in front of me.

"Dig in," she says.

"Thanks."

It tastes soooo good — made especially for me, not like something cooked in huge pots to feed fifty people.

Nikki brings her finished quesadilla to the table and sits across from me. She adds avocado and salsa to it and takes a big bite.

"Mmm. That's tasty! I don't care what Penny says about my culinary skills. I make a mean quesadilla!"

Nikki waits until I've swallowed my last bite of quesadilla and then she says, "Talk to me. Why did you run away? What's with the pregnancy? How can I help?"

I take a deep breath, hardly knowing where to start.

"Was it awful at the county home?"

"Well . . . the teacher and counselors were nice. Some of the girls were pretty crazy, but . . . they were okay, I guess, considering what they'd been through."

"Do you have any friends there?"

"Yeah, a girl named Madison. She's there because her mom is in jail and there's no one else to take care of her. She's been there lots of times."

"And you're pregnant," she says — a statement, not a question.

"Yeah."

"How far along are you?"

"About six and a half months."

I can see Nikki doing the math in her head.

"So you were already pregnant when volleyball season began?"

I nod.

"Probably four months or more in the play-offs with Wilson?"

"About."

"You played a pretty good game for a pregnant chick," she says, laughing.

She gets up and goes to the counter where the quesadilla fixings still sit.

"Want another one?"

"No thanks."

She stacks cheese on another tortilla and stands waiting for the microwave to beep. When it's finished, she sits back down at the table.

"You know, I've had a lot of surprises in my teaching career, but if someone had asked me to rank our team in order of who was most likely to get pregnant, I'd have put you at about the bottom of the list."

"Yeah. Me, too."

"So? What happened?"

"I just . . . I was really stupid and . . ."

"And?" Nikki prompts.

I tell her the whole story, except I don't name Jason.

"It wasn't Nathan, was it?"

"No!"

Nathan was a guy I was in love with for about five days last spring. He was such a total jerk, even Nikki knew about him.

"It was just a guy I went out with, this guy who was really only a friend and . . ."

"What does this guy think about being a dad?"

"He doesn't know. I don't want him to know. I wanted an abortion. I'd gone through the counseling at Planned Parenthood. I had an appointment and everything. But then, I guess I sort of lost it after the accident. I don't know how to explain it. It was like I was in a fog, like my brain stopped thinking."

"Understandable," Nikki says. "That was a horrible shock."

"By the time I came out of the fog, it was too late to get an abortion."

"Did your dad and grandmother know you were pregnant?"

"No. I didn't want them to know. I didn't want anyone to know."

"Danni?"

"Not even Danni."

The big grey cat ambles into the kitchen, jumps up in Nikki's lap, then walks onto the table.

"Off the table, Elvis," Nikki says.

Elvis lays down on the table, twitching his tail. Nikki picks him up and puts him back on the floor. He jumps up again. I sit watching, trying to get up the nerve to say what I want to say. Nikki holds Elvis on her lap, scratching behind his ears. I take a deep breath, then just blurt it out.

"I want to give you the baby!"

Nikki freezes. Her hand sits unmoving on the cat's head. She looks up, wide-eyed, not seeming to notice when Elvis gets back on the table. She blinks.

"What?"

"I want to give you the baby — you and Penny. I want something good to come from this."

CHAPTER

14

The luxury of a long, hot, private shower — no one yelling to hurry up, no one casting sideways looks at my naked belly — I've missed privacy! I sit on the edge of the tub rubbing cocoa butter across my midsection, thinking about Nikki's reaction to my offer of a baby. I expected her to be really happy about it, but all she'd said was "We're both tired. Let's talk in the morning."

In the pink room, the crib is folded flat against the wall. The bare mattress leaning next to it. No teddy bears. No baby monitor. No framed Disney characters looking down on me from the walls. It is quiet here, no sweet snoring sounds or outbursts of motherfucker-cocksucker. I take the heart-shaped stone from the back pocket of my notebook for a bedtime talk with my dad.

"Hey, Dad. I'm at Nikki's. I figured out how I can be part of the solution."

"You're awesome. I know you'll . . ."

His voice is getting harder and harder to hear. I hold the stone against my chest, hoping the beat of my heart brings new life.

"Dad? . . . Daddy?"

In the morning on the patio, while we're eating cereal and toast and watching Elvis stalk a sparrow, Nikki tells me she's got to call the county home and let them know where I am.

"By law, I should have called them last night. But I just couldn't bring myself to do it. You were so tired, and there was so much to talk about."

"But . . . I've been reading about adoptions and . . . can't I just stay here with you and Penny until the baby is born? And then you can have the baby?"

"Maybe we'll work something out further down the road, but for right now . . . I don't want to lose my job over this."

"But lots of people who adopt let birthmoms stay with them while they're pregnant," I say.

"It's not about that. You're a minor, someone who's been in my program at Hamilton for four years, you're here illegally and I'm harboring you. That's definitely grounds for dismissal. And even though I'm a popular coach with winning teams, there are some people who're just waiting for a chance to get rid of me."

"That's ridiculous! You're the best coach in the whole league. Who'd want to get rid of you?"

"Well . . . some of the people from Danni's church. And some others from that big church just off the freeway . . . You know, they think people like Penny and me are trying to corrupt the youth. Like we're trying to influence you all to become lesbians."

"That's crazy!"

"I know that, but they don't. Things can get pretty nasty sometimes."

Nikki picks up the cereal bowls and carries them inside. I pick up the butter dish and jar of jam and follow. Watching Nikki put the bowls in the dishwasher, wipe down the counter top — take care of the everyday things that people everywhere take care of, I don't understand the whole "bad influence" idea.

I remember in the ninth grade, when Danni and I first started playing volleyball. Carole and Donald had warned my dad that Coach Nicholson was homosexual. They wondered if we should be exposed to someone like that. Dad said he wasn't going to worry about what any of our teachers did in their private lives. He said Nikki was an excellent coach, and that's what mattered. I guess they ended up thinking the same thing, because Danni's played volleyball every single season without complaints from her parents.

"We should get going pretty soon," Nikki says.

"Maybe . . . couldn't I stay just one more day?"

"I wish," Nikki says, "but both of us being teachers, Penny and I have to keep a low profile. We've got to be careful not to do anything that looks bad. And letting you stay here as a runaway wouldn't only look bad, we'd actually be breaking the law."

I think of the long, leisurely shower I had last night, and the one-of-a-kind quesadilla, and the pink room that I had all to myself, and I'll have to go through that whole "intake" ordeal again and I can't hold back the tears.

Between sobs I manage to gasp out, "I . . . I thought . . . I thought you'd help . . . I thought . . . I'd give you a baby."

"Don't . . . Please don't cry," Nikki says, putting her arms around me. "I'd absolutely love to have you stay here. My God! You've been through so much, and we've got that empty room just sitting there, but . . . I can't jeopardize my whole career . . . You know?"

"Yeah, I guess," I say, reaching for a napkin to wipe my nose.

"I'll do my best to get you released to me, but for now . . ."

"What about that temporary guardian paper, like you used before when the sheriffs wanted to take me with them?"

"You weren't a runaway then."

Nikki looks at her watch.

"Let's go sit where it's comfortable. We can talk a little longer before I call."

We go into the den, with the matching recliners facing the TV screen. I sit in one and Nikki sits sideways in the other, facing me.

"Tell me more about your baby. Are you sure you want to give it up for adoption?"

"I can't keep a baby. I want you and Penny to have it," I say.

Elvis comes sauntering in and jumps up on the empty couch.

"We're thinking maybe we should give up on the idea of getting a baby," Nikki says.

"But I thought you really wanted one."

"Right. But we've had so many disappointments. We . . . ." Nikki shakes her head. " . . . this is all absolutely confidential. Okay?"

"Okay," I say.

"It's not something I want spread around the team."

'I don't even see anyone anymore."

"No, but you will. And even if you don't see anyone until your ten-year high school reunion, it's still strictly confidential."

"Okay."

"Before we decided to adopt, we tried to have a baby of our own with artificial insemination."

I stand up and tap my foot against the floor, heel-toe, heel-toe.

"Foot cramp. It's a pregnancy thing," I explain. "But what's artificial . . . what?"

"Insemination."

Nikki gives me a long look.

"I'm telling you this because it has to do with . . . your offer."

I sit back down, slip off my shoe, and rub my cramped foot.

"Artificial insemination is a way for women to get pregnant when they don't want sperm to be delivered in the usual way."

"Oh, yeah. We talked about that in biology. I just didn't remember what it was called."

"But it's complicated. You go through all of this stuff of trying to figure out your fertile period. The sperm arrives in a metal canister that looks like an old-fashioned milk can. When you open it, on that supposedly fertile day, cold steam rises out, like maybe a genie is about to appear. It's eerie. Packed inside the big can is a little vial of precious sperm. You squirt the sperm into the vagina of the wanna-be-pregnant woman, and then wait, and hope."

I lean the recliner back, trying to get comfortable. It's hard to imagine why anyone would want to be pregnant. Foot cramps, leg cramps, back aches, constant peeing . . .

"It's more complicated than I just said," Nikki continues, "but that's the general idea. It works great for some people, but it didn't for us. First we tried with Penny, because she was the one who was craziest about having a kid. We tried three times, and on the third time she got pregnant. I was pretty happy, but Penny was insanely happy. The day after her positive pregnancy test she bought that crib and a stroller and about twenty teddy bears. We called all of our friends with the good news and started making lists of names we liked. Then at about three months she lost it — miscarried."

"That sucks," I say.

"It was horrible. The doctor said she might have some problem with her uterus or something, so then we decided to try it with me. We'd do the deed, following instructions to the letter, and we'd get our hopes up. Then we'd wait, hoping against hope that I wouldn't get my period. Once I was five days late and we were sure I was pregnant. But I wasn't. Eight tries in seventeen months. Each time a horrible disappointment."

Elvis jumps up on my lap, what there is left of it. He stretches full out across my legs, purring. He's got the loudest purr of any cat I've ever heard. Nikki laughs.

"You must be special. Usually someone has to be coming around here for years before Elvis gives them the honor of jumping onto their lap."

I scratch behind Elvis's ears and he purrs even louder.

"After five tries, five failures, we felt like we just didn't want to keep putting ourselves through that kind of emotional trauma. So that's when we decided to go the adoption route. You know what happened from there."

"But now you can really get a baby."

"Yeah . . . well . . ."

The phone rings and Nikki goes inside. I get up and walk around, trying to get rid of the lingering cramp. Back out on the patio, I sit with my legs stretched out straight, turning my face to the sun and closing my eyes. It doesn't seem fair that Penny had a miscarriage when she wanted a baby so much, and I'm getting a baby when I wanted a miscarriage so much. But that's just one little thing that doesn't seem fair. How about Dad and Grams and Casper. Talk about unfair!

Nikki comes back outside.

"That was Penny," she says, scooting the cat off her chair and sitting down. "It's snowing there. I said I'd call her back in an hour. I didn't want to talk to her about any of this just yet."

Another phone call. This time Nikki comes back laughing.

"That was Penny again. She said, 'I know something's up. What's going on?' It's like she can read my mind!"

"What did you tell her?"

"I told her, 'Yeah, something's up.' Why lie about it when she knows she's right? But I told her she had to wait another fifty-five minutes to hear the details."

She laughs again, then shakes her head, sadly.

"All of this has been so hard on her. She's probably gained about twenty pounds since the baby deal fell through. 'Feeding the emptiness' is what her therapist says . . ."

I think the therapist probably doesn't exactly say that. If she's anything like Dr. K., or the psychologist in *Ordinary People*, she probably does that question thing. Like "Do you think you might be feeding the emptiness?"

I flash on Dr. K.'s question, "Do you think you might be in total denial about this baby?" Not now, I'm not, but . . . I turn my attention back to Nikki.

" . . . on antidepressants but I'm not sure that's helping her. I'm sad, too, and sometimes it's easier for me to stay late at school than to come home to Penny all gloomy and depressed. I don't think we could stand another disappointment."

"But I'm really pregnant, not like that other person who just faked you out."

"I know, but things happen. You could still miscarry. Or sometimes women go full term and the baby's born dead. Or you could change your mind . . ."

"No way! All I've ever wanted since the strip turned pink on my first home pregnancy test was not to be pregnant and not to have a baby. I definitely don't want a baby. And . . . I know it sounds kind of lame, but . . . I keep thinking about how my dad always told me to be part of the solution, not part of the problem. And all I've been seeing for months are problems. And now I see part of a solution."

Nikki stands up and does a series of calf and hamstring stretches, like she's getting ready for a game or something. Then she sits back down.

"It would be complicated," she says. "I've never heard of a teacher adopting a student's baby."

"I'm not really your student right now."

"Well . . . we'd have to be sure to have all of the legal issues in order. Last time we were so eager to get that baby, and it seemed like such a good situation, we let some details slide by. If we'd visited the doctor with Sherry, like the adoption guidelines suggest, we could have saved ourselves a lot of heartbreak, not to mention money."

"You can go to the doctor with me whenever you want," I say.

Nikki nods.

"Well . . . If we can clear everything officially, you can stay here for a while. But I'm not sure about the baby thing."

She looks at her watch again.

"I've got to make that phone call to the county home. Is there anyone in particular I should ask to speak to?"

"My social worker is Ms. Fenton, but she won't be there today."

Nikki goes inside to make the phone call and I wander over to the side of the yard, where rose bushes border the white picket fence. I think they bloom in the springtime, so there are only a few flowers left on a couple of bushes. I lean down to smell a white rose, but it has no scent. I move a few bushes up and take a whiff of a deep red rose. Wow! This is one Grams would definitely have liked. I'm caught by a sudden, sharp sadness for all they've missed. Dad never to plant the roses he was so excited about. Grams never to experience the fragrance of a "Wow!" rose in our own backyard. More tears. I'm so sick of crying, but I don't know how to stop.

I'm still wiping my endless supply of tears when Nikki comes back outside.

"You okay?"

I nod.

"It doesn't look like it."

"It's just . . . sometimes I miss them so much," I say.

Nikki puts her arms around me.

"I know. I miss them, too. Sometimes during a game, I get a glimpse of something in the Grant section and for an instant I think I see Casper, sitting so tall next to your grandmother, like he's analyzing the game."

We laugh at that vision of Casper. That's exactly how it seemed. Like he was watching every move and second-guessing every play.

"I've missed you, too," Nikki says. "We all have."

"I've really missed everyone, too."

"I talked with your social worker. She wasn't there, but they gave me her cell phone number."

"What'd she say?"

"She wants you to call her. She sounds like a nice person, though."

I nod.

"I told her I'd like for you to stay with us for a while."

"Can I?"

"You've got to go back there for now. But we may be able to get things worked out."

"When do I have to go back?"

"The first person I talked to over there said to get you back there right now. But Ms. Fenton said if you're back by three o'clock, before the shift changes, it will be okay."

"What time is it now?"

"It's almost ten . . . Ms. Fenton will call the police and let them know you've been found and that you'll be returning on your own. They'll file another report, though, if you don't show up on time."

"Can I check my email before I have to go back?"

"Sure. My computer's set up and ready to go in the den."

I have hundreds of email messages dating clear back to September 20. There are a bunch from friends saying how sorry they are about Dad and Grams and Casper, and a bunch from the people Dad worked with. There are a few of the usual sicko spam things. I sort the messages by name and start on Jason's.

For weeks after the accident he emailed every day, always asking for a response. He said he'd heard from Danni that I wasn't doing much, or saying much, but he hoped I would email back, just a word or two, to let him know I was getting his messages. Then he emailed less often, mostly short stuff, like "Are you there?" His latest message said he was tired of emailing into a void. He hoped I was doing okay. If I ever needed help, let him know, otherwise I wouldn't be hearing from him again.

I click on "reply" and write:

Hey Jason, :=(about not answering your emails. I haven't been able to use a computer for weeks. And before *that I was in outer space or something, like those people in Nebraska. Remember them? From that **Weird World** paper? It's kind of like I was in some weird zone for a while. Anyway, I had this quick chance to use a friend's computer, but this is probably it for a while.*

How's college? Do you like Iowa? I'll email again next chance I get — L8RS — Autumn

Next I look at Danni's messages. Hers start on October 26, two days after her mother took me to the county home.

Where are you? My mom says she took you to a safe place, and to keep you in my prayers. That's all she'll tell me! What happened? I'm hoping you get this. Remember, if you want to call me, Tuesday night before ten is a good time because that's one of Mom's meeting nights. XOXOXO

Just this past Wednesday, she wrote:

This is so weird. I'm wondering if you could possibly have been right about the whole space alien thing, and you've been abducted again. How else could you have just disappeared without a trace? XOXOXO

Then, from Thursday night:

Finally, I know you're still on earth. At least I think your phone call was from earth. Where are you? Call again! :=)

I click on reply, then sit staring at the computer screen. What can I say? Where can I start? I go into the kitchen and get a banana. I'm supposed to be eating a lot of fruit whether I'm hungry for it or not. I gaze out at the back yard. It's so peaceful here. And it smells good. And I really, really don't want to go back to that place. I go outside for another whiff of the Wow! rose, then settle back in to my email task.

Hi Danni, Finally, I've got use of a computer. Where I was staying before I couldn't use a computer, or telephone, or anything. I couldn't even write letters. So, I've had a little break, but I've got to go back to the other place again. If I can sneak a phone call out, I'll do that. How are things with you? I miss you, and everybody else, and I really hope I can see you soon. Say hi to everyone at the lunch table, and to Hannah, too. XOXOXO

I close my email and go back to the pink room. I've got $6.27 in my jeans pocket. I fold the five into tight thirds and slip it into the card pocket in *Ordinary People*. The rest of the money I leave on the dresser. Better here than locked in the mesh bag.

I dread going through that whole routine with Smeal again, but I know from Dericia that whenever you're gone without permission it's like starting all over again when you get back. I think about the lice check, and how Smeal seemed to like seeing me wince with each tug of my hair. I go into the bathroom and start brushing furiously, trying to get my hair absolutely tangle free. It's still going to hurt, though.

I search through the bathroom drawers and finally, in the bottom one, I find a pair of scissors. I stand in front of the mirror and take one last look at my long hair. It's not that pretty anymore, anyway, sort of dull like my skin. Ms. Lee says it's because I wasn't eating very well or taking vitamins until just recently, but institutional shampoo may also have something to do with it.

I take the first cut, close to my head, then another and another. There's a light knock on the bathroom door.

"Autumn?"

"Just a minute," I say.

"We should go pretty soon."

"Okay."

I chop off the last long section and then try to even it up. It looks horrible! But it won't hurt much when Smeal puts her fine-toothed comb to it.

"Autumn?"

"Yeah. Coming."

I gather up as much of the hair as I can and dump it in the waste-basket, then open the door.

"Do you have a dustbuster?" I ask, walking into the den where Nikki is sitting at the computer.

"Above the washing machine . . . Oh my God!"

The look of shock on Nikki's face confirms my suspicion that I didn't give myself a good haircut. I get the dustbuster and go back to the bathroom to finish cleaning up. Nikki stands watching at the bathroom door.

"Why?"

I tell her about the lice check I'll have to have when we get back.

Her eyes fill with tears.

When we back out the driveway we turn in the opposite direction of the county home.

"We'll take time for one quick stop," Nikki says.

A few miles south of the shopping center, we pull up in front of a Super Cuts. After a short wait, a stylist leads me to a chair and asks what I want done.

"Whatever you can," I tell her.

She has to cut it very short just to get it even. She rubs a little gel in her hands and runs them through what's left of my hair, giving it a kind of spiky look.

"Not bad," Nikki says.

Not good, I think, but all I say is "Thanks."

On the way back to the county home, Nikki tells me about her phone conversation with Penny.

"I told her if we could work things out, you might be staying with us for a while. And I told her about your offer."

"What did she say?"

"She wanted to know all about your pregnancy — have you been eating right, taking your vitamins, are you sure it's a girl, do you ever have any cramping or spotting, is the baby active, etc., etc. I've told her we're not making any quick decisions."

"But Penny wants my baby, doesn't she?"

Nikki sighs.

"Yes."

"I knew it," I say, smiling.

"But it isn't just Penny's decision. You know?"

CHAPTER

15

Back at the home I have to go through the whole search thing again — stripped down, checked for cuts, bruises, needle marks, new tattoos or piercings, any changes at all, and, of course, the lice check. But no matter how quickly Ms. Smeal jerks the lice comb through my hair, she can't catch a snag. Right now, I don't care how awful my hair looks. Her disappointment makes it all worthwhile.

The things I wore out of here are sent off to laundry and I get another batch of plain label clothes, including shoes. Smeal takes my backpack, with my notebook and *Ordinary People*, and puts it back in the mesh bag.

"Miss F. let me keep those," I say.

"Running away changes things."

I get a new badge — Level Three.

Everybody from my section crowds around me at dinner. When they've all run out of things to say about my hair, they start pounding me with questions, getting all buzzed about how they would have done things differently.

Where'd you go? . . . How'd they catch you so soon? . . . Did

you get high? . . . Shit — that's the first thing I'd do . . . Anytime I
run I'm gone for at least a week . . . One day's not even worth the
fuckin' trouble . . . You must have gone the first place anybody'd
know to look for you . . . Did you see your boyfriend? . . . Get a
good hot lay? . . . blah, blah, blahdie-blah.

I take a bite of rubbery, institutional spaghetti and think about
last night's quesadilla, made just for me. I think about the long,
hot, private shower, a yard with roses, a purring cat lying across
my legs, a computer hooked up to the Internet, a telephone, a nice
room, a comfortable bed, waking up when I want to, going to bed
when I want to, all of those things I never thought twice about before, things my outside friends take for granted, things that might
be mine again at Nikki and Penny's.

Dericia starts in on me after lights out.

"How stupid was that to run someplace where they'd deliver
you right back here?"

I turn my face to the wall and hold the pillow over my head, trying to block out her voice.

"And a teacher??? You went to a teacher!"

I count to ten.

"That's about the biggest pussy thing I ever heard!"

I shove the pillow off my head and turn to face Dericia.

"Shut the fuck up!!!" I scream. "Just shut your dirty fuckin'
mouth!!!"

Raiders stomps into our room and leads me out. At least I get to
sleep by myself, even if there is an attendant sitting right outside the
door of the tiny, windowless room.

Miss F. tells me I've lost the privilege of going to the TAPP
school. Boo-hoo.

"Can you get my backpack for me?"

"I only do favors for people I trust," she says.

On Monday two new girls, one fifteen and one sixteen, show
up in Ms. Guerra's classroom, making a group of seven. On Tuesday we're back to six. This time it's Amanda who's run.

"It's the holidays," Madison says.

"What's that mean?"

"You know. Things get crazier around the holidays. Haven't you ever noticed that?"

I shake my head.

"More people run away. More kids get beat up. More people go homeless. You know."

I'm still trying to figure out what Madison is getting at when she heaves a sigh of frustration.

"Oh, yeah. I forgot who you are," Madison says, all sarcastic. "Probably nothing like that ever went wrong in your goody-goody little world."

"You don't know shit about my world," I tell her.

In the living room I pretend to read *Gone with the Wind*, but really I'm just staring at the page, trying to figure out what's next. Somehow I've got to get out of this place. I'm turning into someone I don't want to be — losing my temper, losing my vocabulary, forgetting how to be the person my dad and Grams taught me to be. If I lose that, what will I have left of them? What will I have left of me?

Raiders stands over me, waiting for me to look up.

"Autumn?"

I pretend to be engrossed in the book.

"You have a visitor, Autumn."

I look up now, and so does everyone else in the room. Having a visitor is a first for me.

"Who is it?" I ask, closing the book and getting up from my chair.

Raiders hands me a slip of paper. "Jean Nicholson " is printed on the line next to "Name of Visitor." I follow Raiders down the hall to the common room. As a Level Three I can't go anywhere unescorted.

Nikki is sitting on the couch closest to the door. She stands and greets me with a big hug.

"Just ring the buzzer when you're ready to leave, and I'll come back for her," Raiders says.

"Okay," Nikki says, going back to the couch.

I sit down beside her. I can't believe she's here! I can't believe I've actually got a visitor.

"I've got good news for you," Nikki says, all smiles.

"What?" I say, afraid to even think about the possibilities, afraid to get my hopes up.

"I've been talking with your social worker, and filling out papers, and getting references for her. She's agreed to let you spend tomorrow and Thanksgiving with me, then I'll have to bring you back Friday morning."

"Cool," I say, happy I'll be getting out of this place even if it's only for two days.

Honestly though, as much as I tried not to hope for it, I wanted the good news to be that I was going to live with Nikki, not just visit.

"I'll pick you up in the morning and we can do some shopping," Nikki says, tugging on my sweatshirt. "Maybe do a little clothing upgrade for you."

"I can't have any clothes of my own," I tell her.

"You can keep them at my place, to have whenever you visit."

So . . . more good news — Nikki expects other visits.

"Thanksgiving we'll go to my friend's house for spectacular food."

"I'd be happy with another one of your mean quesadillas," I say, laughing.

"Oh, no. Once you've tasted Ella's corn and walnut dressing, you'll be throwing rocks at my quesadillas."

We both laugh at that one, then Nikki turns serious.

"How are you feeling?"

"Okay."

"And the baby?"

"Okay, I guess. I could show you the sonogram, if they'd let me get my stuff back."

"You mean you can't even keep your sonogram with you?"

"It got locked up with all of my other stuff. It's in my book."

"You can't have a book here?"

"Well, I could for a while, but then when I got back from your place they took it away again."

"Your book? Why?"

"I don't know. I guess they're afraid . . . like anything from the outside might have something hidden . . . or to show they're boss, or something."

"Well, maybe I can get it back for you. I'd like to see the sonogram."

That's more good news, I think, that Nikki wants to see the sonogram. Maybe things are looking up.

Wednesday morning Miss F. walks me up to the reception room where Nikki's waiting. Before she signs me out, Nikki asks if Miss F. will release my backpack to her custody.

"I'd like to see Autumn's sonogram, and it would be good if she could have her book to read, too, in case she gets bored with my company."

I'm surprised when Miss F. calls and asks that my backpack be brought out. She's still hecka mad at me for running away.

"We'll have to take it back when Autumn returns," she says, handing the backpack to Nikki.

"Thanks," Nikki says.

We walk through the doors out into the bright, sunny day. I think about Madison, and Dericia, and the rest of them back inside. Even when they get to be in the outdoor courtyard, the wall is so high it's like the sun never quite shines in there. I breathe deeply, breathing in freedom.

Our first stop is at a dress-for-less place where Nikki buys me a long, light blue top, and a short, but full enough to fit over my belly, denim vest. Nobody but Dad and Grams ever bought clothes for me before, and it's strange watching Nikki put down $62.73 for stuff for me.

"I can pay you back when I get my dad's wallet and Gram's purse back," I tell her.

"Don't worry about it! You still had your deposit money left in the team bank account, remember?"

"For new uniforms?"

"Yeah. I didn't order one for you, because I didn't know where you were."

She looks at my shoes.

"Those can't offer much support. Let's swing by the shoe department."

Even though I hate the shoes from the home, I tell Nikki they're fine. I'm pretty sure the leftover deposit money wouldn't cover shoes, too. What I really need is a better bra, but I'm embarrassed to say so.

Our next stop is at a place called "Polly's Pies." It's down a long driveway, tucked behind a dry-cleaning plant, in a converted garage. It's hard to believe anybody'd ever find this place, but there are people lined up clear outside the door and halfway down the driveway. We take our place in line.

"I may not be a great cook, but I know where to buy the best pies in the whole San Gabriel Valley. That's my Thanksgiving specialty."

"Grams used to make pumpkin pies every Thanksgiving."

"Before she went blind?"

"No. I never knew her before she was blind."

"She baked pies? Blind?"

"Yeah. And cookies, too."

Nikki laughs. "I can't even do that stuff with 20-20 vision!"

We take a few steps forward.

"What were your other Thanksgiving traditions?" Nikki asks.

"Well . . . we always had turkey with cornbread and sausage dressing. My dad made that. And we always invited some people from my dad's work. And we had a rule that at least one of the people we invited wouldn't have had anywhere else to go on that day."

"Nice," Nikki says, smiling. "When I was growing up we had all the aunts and uncles and cousins over to our house. Everyone would bring stuff and we'd have volleyball and croquet set up in the back yard . . . it was great. There were so many of us, the kids would eat outside on ping-pong tables. My parents still do that."

"Do they live a long way away?"

Nikki looks along the line of people in front of us.

"You can go sit in the car if you're tired," Nikki says. "We don't both have to stand in line."

"I'm okay," I say. "I like being out in the open like this, not all fenced in like at the home."

"Yeah, and it's great weather, isn't it? Penny says she practically freezes to death every time they leave her parents' house, and here we are in short sleeves, basking in the sunshine."

We move along in silence, a few short steps at a time. Then Nikki says, "To answer your question, my parents only live about eight miles from me. They're still in the house I grew up in."

We're almost to the front of the store now, and I hear a squawking "Polly wanna pie? Polly wanna pie?"

"That's the famous Polly. Wait 'til you see her," Nikki says, laughing.

She turns her face to the sun, eyes closed, breathing deeply, almost as if she were somewhere else, like maybe on a beautiful beach instead of standing in line in front of an old garage. Then she opens her eyes and turns to me.

"It's funny, all of those Thanksgivings at my parents' house, with tables and games set up outside — I don't think it ever rained. Like New Year's Day. It almost never rains on the Rose Parade, you know?"

I nod.

"Anyway, I don't think they have to set tables up outside anymore, unless they just want to. Some of the cousins have moved away, and some of the older generation are gone . . . It's still a pretty big group though, I think."

"Why don't you go there on Thanksgiving?"

"I lost my invitation."

Another silence. More attention to the line.

Then, in a voice so soft I can barely hear her, she tells me, "When Penny and I got together, my father . . . he's . . . he can't accept the fact that I'm a lesbian. My mother would still welcome me, but he won't. My mother and I went out for a pre-Thanksgiving lunch on Sunday. That's my family tradition now — my blood family."

Nikki turns her face back to the sun, but not before I see her tears. I finger the little heart in my pocket, wishing Nikki, too, had had a father with lasting love.

Finally we get inside and up to the counter.

"Polly wanna pie? Polly wanna pie?" the parrot squawks again.

People laugh every time the parrot squawks, but I think it could get irritating fast.

Nikki gives her name to a woman wearing a black apron with a parrot embroidered on the front. The woman goes to the back room and comes out with two large pie boxes and two small ones.

"Two apple and two chicken pot," she says, smiling.

"Right," Nikki says.

She pays for the pies and we walk out past the line, which now reaches nearly to the street.

"It's a good thing we got here early. By seven this line will be longer than the one at Disneyland's Splash Mountain."

Back at Nikki's I get the sonogram-bookmark out of my backpack and show it to her.

"God! It's not exactly the Gerber baby," she says, laughing. "Do you mind if I scan it and email it to Penny?"

"You can have it if you want," I tell her.

"No. I'll just scan it. I don't want you to lose your place in the book."

We're eating the chicken pot pies and watching women's soccer playoffs when the phone rings. Nikki answers in the kitchen, then comes back to the den. She points to the mute button on the remote and mouths "Do you mind?"

I shake my head and mute the sound.

"Not beautiful!" she says, laughing, watching the silent game. "No! It's absolutely porcine!"

She listens for a bit, then says, "There are vegetables in the pot pie . . . Hmmm . . . Yeah. Okay . . . So how're Thelma and Rod?"

Nikki takes the phone back to the kitchen and finishes her conversation beyond my hearing. I pick up the remote and turn the sound on again.

Thanksgiving morning I put on my new clothes. I like wearing something that belongs just to me, instead of getting some faded, pre-worn sweatshirt from a pile of rejects.

Nikki knocks at the door of the pink bedroom.

"Mind if I come in?"

"No. I'm just putting on my shoes."

"I got my morning run in," Nikki says, going to the chest of drawers and pulling out a stack of neatly folded shirts.

"I do four miles usually, but I did six today to balance the ton of mashed potatoes and gravy I plan to put away."

She takes the T-shirts to the bed and lays them out, one by one.

"I miss running . . . and sports," I tell her. "I feel like my muscles are turning to mush."

"You'll get it all back, after the baby."

Nikki looks up from the T-shirts.

"Hey, you look nice," she says, kind of like she's surprised.

"That blue's a good color for you." She looks directly into my eyes, long enough that I have to look away.

"No more dark circles under your eyes, either. You've lost that 'death warmed over' look you had when you got here last Saturday."

"It helps to be able to sleep in a quiet place," I say.

Nikki nods and turns her attention back to the shirts on the bed.

"I'm choosing my costume," she says, looking from one shirt to another. "Part of our Thanksgiving tradition is that we all wear something to dinner that shows what we're thankful for. Or something we hope for."

She picks up a pink shirt that says "Race for the cure," then folds it up again. There's a shirt with a picture of the earth that says "Save our planet," one that says "Hate is not a family value," and one with a big picture of a smiling baby.

"Penny wore this last year, when we were still trying the turkey baster trick." Nikki sighs. "She'd probably wear it this year, too, if she were here."

"But this year it would be a real thing."

"Well . . . she's very excited about the . . . your . . . offer."

Nikki refolds the earth shirt, and puts it on top of the smiling baby shirt.

"I guess all of those bad experiences got me out of the baby mood . . . Do you see anything here you'd like to express yourself with, for Thanksgiving? Not that you have to do that, but if you want to . . ."

I shake my head no. I would like a clean planet, and a cure for cancer, and I agree that hate is not a family value. But nothing jumps out at me as the thing I'd like for my own personal Thanksgiving statement. Besides, I'm really, really, tired of wearing other people's clothes.

Nikki puts the shirts away.

"I think I'll just wear one of our team shirts," Nikki says. "That's something I'm thankful for, and also have a lot of hope for."

If I could magically come up with the perfect T-shirt, I think it would have a picture of Penny on it, wearing a gold medal around her neck, because what I most hope for is for Penny to win Nikki over, and for them to get my baby. Letting me stay with them could be part of the adoption agreement, and then . . . well, I don't have it all figured out yet, but if Penny gets her way . . .

16

Going south on the 605 freeway, we take the Carson off-ramp, toward Long Beach.

"Okay," Nikki says. "I've only been here once before, but it's starting to look familiar . . . What's next?"

I check the Mapquest directions.

"Right on Oleander, two miles."

"Oh, yeah. I think I remember . . ."

"I thought you always came to their house on Thanksgiving."

"Yeah, for about six years now. But they've moved since last Thanksgiving. I've only been to this new place once, and Penny was driving."

"This should be Oleander coming up," I tell her.

"You're about to meet my true family," Nikki says, making the right turn. "Sometimes, for whatever reason, we have to find new families — love families rather than blood families. That's what Penny and I have done. Not that we don't still care about our first families . . . "

Nikki drives slowly, concentrating on the house numbers.

"I know nothing can ever truly replace your family, but somewhere along the way I bet you'll find a love family, too," Nikki says. "Lots of people do."

I can't imagine ever finding another family, but Nikki sounds convinced, and I don't want to argue with her. Especially since I'm hoping that she and Penny'll treat me like family for a while.

We park in front of a beige house with a big lawn and carry the pies, a six-pack of sodas, and a big jug of orange juice up the walkway to the front door. The orange juice is for me. Sodas are not on my list of "Approved Foods for the Mommy-to-Be."

"Ella's got this thing about the Virgin Mary," Nikki says, gesturing towards two large statues that look like the religious pictures you see in museums.

A woman in jeans and a bright green "PRO MARRIAGE" T-shirt walks out to meet us.

"Hey, Jean," she says, giving Nikki a quick hug before turning to me.

It sounds strange hearing Nikki called "Jean," but I guess that is her name.

"Here, let me take your precious treasure," she says, reaching for the pies. "You must be Autumn. I'm Sandy."

We follow Sandy into the kitchen where she puts the pies down on the counter and then waves both arms in the air.

"Hey, everybody! This is Autumn! She's one of Jean's top volleyball players."

"Not right now, she's not," the guy standing next to me says, looking straight at my middle.

"Autumn, this is Gavin," Sandy says. "You don't have to listen to one word he says. Not one!"

Gavin smiles and shakes my hand.

"And Barry," Sandy says, gesturing toward the man next to Gavin.

"Welcome to turkey day," he says. He's wearing a purple T-shirt with a rainbow-bordered sign across the front that says "Mom Knows."

Sandy goes around the room, introducing me to seven others.

"The goddess at the stove is Ella, but she probably can't look up from the sauce just yet."

Without a pause in her rhythmic stirring, Ella turns, flashes me a quick smile, and turns back to the stove.

A guy in a "Save the Los Angeles River" shirt gets up from his chair and turns it in my direction.

"Here, have a seat," he says.

"It's okay."

"No, sit down! I can't stay seated while an expectant mother stands!"

I sit down, just because I don't know what else to do.

"When's your baby due?" he asks.

"February 15."

He counts on his fingers. "Not quite three months? It'll fly by."

"Isn't that just like a man," a woman on the other side of the room says. "I'd like to see you hosting a fetus for the last three and a half months of pregnancy!"

Several others join in on how things might be if men had wombs, and what medical advances it would take, and on and on, with a lot of laughter in between.

The woman sitting next to me, Kim, leans closer and tells me how she and Penny have been friends since middle school.

"I hope this all works out for her, and for you, too," Kim says. "You couldn't find two nicer people to raise your baby."

I must look surprised because she leans in even closer and lowers her voice to a whisper.

"Oh, I know Jean is being very cautious. But Penny called me on Saturday, just after she heard you wanted them to adopt your baby. She was thrilled."

"But Nikki . . ."

"Penny told me that underneath it all, she's sure Jean still really wants a baby, too. Besides, if Penny really wants something . . . "

Nikki notices us talking and comes over. Kim makes a zip your lip sign and gives me a wink.

"Hey, Jean, Autumn was just telling me what a great coach you are," Kim says.

Nikki gives her a look that's not exactly friendly. I've seen that look when a player tries to make a phony excuse for showing up late for practice.

"How about a little air hockey?" Nikki says to me.

We go through the kitchen to a screened-in porch that has an air hockey game, a dart board on the wall with a bunch of darts stuck in it, and boxes of board games stacked in the corner.

"Heads or tails?" Nikki asks, taking a quarter from her pocket.

"Tails."

She wins the toss and bank-shots the puck straight into the goal.

The "Save the Los Angeles River" guy comes in. "Play the winner?"

"Sure," Nikki says, then turns to me.

"Glenn here is the unofficial Thanksgiving air hockey second placer."

He laughs.

"I've been practicing. This is the year I move up to champ."

I send the puck straight across to Nikki's goal — another bank shot back at me, another point for her.

"She's tough," Glenn says, "but this is her day of defeat."

Others come in to watch. I only score one point against Nikki. Then Glenn beats her, and I play against him. I get the feel of the mallet, the angle of bank shots, and beat him seven to five.

I like this lighthearted competition, thinking only about the little plastic hockey puck and how to get it where you want it to go, laughing at your opponent's mistakes, and your own, too.

"I've been beaten by the new kid," Glenn says, pretending despair as he hands the mallet to Nikki. I win that one, too, to great cheers from the rest of the group.

"This girl is a natural," Sandy says.

"It can be your winter sport," Nikki tells me.

"Hey, don't laugh," Glenn says. "There's a whole official air hockey association. They have leagues and tournaments and everything."

"Scholarships?" I ask, slamming the puck off the left side and straight into Glen's goal.

There's a noise from another room and Barry and Gavin both hurry out.

"My turn!" Barry says. "You got him last time!"

"Did not!" Gavin says.

Everyone laughs, except me. I just stand there smiling a stupid, I-don't-get-it smile.

"That's just how we were, isn't it, Honey?" a woman, Peggy I think her name is, says to her husband.

He laughs. "Oh, yeah. We were like, maybe if we let the little rug rat cry for another hour or so, he'll go back to sleep."

Gavin comes back in, carrying a baby in his arms. Barry's following along behind, carrying a tote bag of what I guess is baby supplies.

"Oh, look how he's grown," Nikki says. "Hi, Little Dalton."

She gives the baby a light kiss on the cheek.

"How old is he now?"

"Eight months tomorrow," Barry says. "Can you believe it?"

Ella comes into the room, stops to admire the baby, then says, "Okay everybody, the fun's over. It's time for some serious eating!"

People wander into the dining room, where a big round table is filled with so many heaping platters of food you can barely see the tablecloth. In the very middle of the table stand two carved wooden pilgrims and two Indians in headdress. Once the jostling's over and everyone's seated, Ella opens a beat-up book of poetry by e.e. cummings and reads:

"i thank You God for most this amazing day: for the leaping spirits of trees and a blue true dream of a sky; and for everything which is natural which is infinite which is yes."

Then we go around the table and people say what it is they're thankful for, or what special meaning their T-shirts have. When it's Gavin's turn he just points to the baby, who is sitting in a high chair gumming a teething biscuit and picking at slobbery crumbs. When it's Ella's turn she and Sandy stand up together and clasp hands. With their free hands they point to their T-shirts. Sandy's is green and Ella's is bright blue. Both of them have colorful abstract figures of people across the front, with "Pro Marriage" in black block letters below.

"Eighteen years together, and I'm still hoping I can sometime make an honest woman of Sandy," Ella says.

When it's my turn I say I'm happy for air hockey. Everyone laughs, and I do, too, but really, I'm serious. For the first time since that horrible accident, I had twenty minutes or so of being in the zone, my mind and body working together, with no thought of anything else.

For a while, when we first start eating, there's not much conversation. Then, once everything's been tasted, I guess, the talk and laughter gets back to a pre-dinner level.

I know they'll be having turkey at the home, and the tables will be decorated. It won't be like this, though, with people who've been friends for years, and who have lives in the world. I'm lucky to be here.

Besides Ella's specialty dressing, Glenn has brought his special, non-gourmet dressing, which turns out to be cornbread and sausage. One taste and I'm in a different Thanksgiving scene, at our big kitchen table in the old house on Camellia Street. Casper's relaxed, without his harness, lying at Gram's feet. Our neighbor, old Mr. Franklin, is next to Grams. He was the one who didn't have anywhere to go, since his wife died and his kids all lived far away. There's Lori and Jamie, from Dad's work, and Pete and Louise, who used to live next door. In the middle of the table is the big plastic yellow submarine which is what Dad puts on display each year . . . put on display . . . and he always starts dinner with . . . started . . . with the same toast — "our friends are all aboard and everyone of us has all we need . . ."

"Autumn?"

Nikki's voice comes through the fog to that other time.

"Autumn? Are you okay?"

The conversation is stopped and everyone at the table is looking at me.

I shake my head. "Sorry," I say, "I was just thinking about . . ."

"Are you sure you're okay?"

I nod and the others turn their attention back to their conversations. Nikki watches me a moment longer, then asks if I'll help her serve the apple pie. I take one more taste of the cornbread dressing, savoring remnants from that other time, then join Nikki in the kitchen. She slices pie onto dessert plates, and I carry the plates into the dining room.

Kim motions for me to sit next to her, where Barry'd been sitting before he took the baby back to a bedroom to change him.

"Did you see how Jean kissed Dalton? She'll love your baby,"

Kim says, talking in that low, confidential voice she uses.

"Now, tell me about the father. Is he smart, and good-looking, like you?"

I look around for Nikki, but she must still be in the kitchen.

"Do you see him very often, or did he skip out when . . ."

"Nikki may still need more help," I say, practically running out of the dining room and into the kitchen.

Friday morning, before I have to go back, I call Danni. Carole answers.

"May I please talk to Danni?" I say.

She hangs up without a word.

CHAPTER

17

J ust before dinner on the Saturday after Thanksgiving, I'm led to the visitors' area where Nikki and Penny are waiting.

"We came straight from the airport," Penny says, hugging me quickly, then backing away for a better look.

She reaches her hand toward my mid-section, pausing just inches from actual contact, hesitant.

"May I?"

I nod okay, even though I'm embarrassed.

Penny rubs her hand lightly over my abdomen.

"Where do you usually feel movement?"

I point to a place just above my belly button and to the right. Penny rests her hand over that spot.

"Is she pretty active?" Penny asks.

"Mostly late at night, when I'm in bed. Or sometimes just after I eat."

Penny keeps her hand on my belly a little longer, then, after nothing happens, we move to one of the "conversation groupings" and sit down.

"We've decided we'd like you to stay with us until you have the baby," Nikki says. "If you want to."

"I want to," I say, wondering if I really heard right — if it's really possible that I might again live in a real home.

"We're not sure about the baby . . ." Nikki starts.

"But we think . . . ."

"We'll take things one step at a time," Nikki says, more to Penny than to me. "We'll get the temporary foster home license completed and then, if it seems like a good idea, we'll think about the baby."

I can't stop smiling.

Penny puts her arms around me in a soft, warm hug.

"You've been through so much, Autumn. But you'll like it at our place. I know you will."

Before they leave, Penny puts her hand on my stomach again, just in time to feel a kick.

"Oh . . . Oh, that's the sweetest thing . . . that little baby in there . . ."

She takes Nikki's hand and holds it over the same spot, but everything's quiet again.

W ednesday, less than a week after Thanksgiving, I get a progress report from Ms. Guerra. Madison walks out into the hall with me, to tell me goodbye.

"You're so lucky! I wish they'd take me, too. I don't even care if they're muff divers."

"Madison! That's so disrespectful!"

"No, it's not! How can it be disrespectful when I don't even know them?"

"That's just the point."

"Well, anyway, I wish I could go with you." She shakes her head, sadly, then smiles.

"I bet you won't be gone for a week before you'll have forgotten everything I taught you! Say 'bitch'!

"Bitch."

"Say 'shit.'"

"Shit."

"Say 'fuck.'"

"Madison . . ."

"Come on! Don't be such a pussy!"

I laugh.

"Madison . . ."

"I knew it," she says, also laughing. "As soon as you get out of here you're going to revert to your old goody-goody self."

"I hope so," I say.

"Come on, then. Just once more — for old time's sake."

"No! There's got to be more interesting things to say than bitch, shit, fuck!"

"I wouldn't know," Madison says, suddenly sad again. She throws her arms around me. "Good luck!"

"You, too," I say, surprised that I feel like crying.

We promise to write each other, even though our letters will have to first go through Miss F.

I go down to the nurse's office to say goodbye to Ms. Lee.

"Thank you for all of your help," I say.

"Are you going to be okay out there in the big world?"

"I'm going to be soooo okay — more than okay."

Miss Lee smiles.

"I believe you will be. Just don't go near the river."

"Huh? What river?"

"You know! That most dangerous river of all. Da Nile."

It takes a moment, and then I get it. Da Nile. Denial.

"Ha, ha," I say, stone-faced.

"Really," Miss Lee says, still smiling. "Take good care of yourself. Drop in now and then if you can."

Miss F. isn't in her office when I stop to tell her goodbye. I think about leaving a note. Then I realize, hey, I can just call her! I'm going to be in the real world, where I can use the phone, and email and the U. S. Postal Service! Like real people do.

I take my paperwork down to the windowless room and give it to Ms. Smeal. She reads it over, slowly, then goes into the storage room and gets my stuff. She hands things to me, one at a time, as she checks them off her list. My shoes, my Hamilton High sweatshirt — each time she hands something to me, I have to write my initials beside the description. And each time it feels like I'm getting back a piece of my self.

Once I've got all of my belongings in front of me, I take the basics behind the folding screen and change clothes. My jeans, already too tight when I came in here, won't even zip halfway up, now. I put the "shared" clothes on an empty chair near the door.

"You can keep the shoes," Ms. Smeal says.

"No thanks." I say, lacing my Nikes. "I like my own shoes."

My dad's wallet and Gram's purse I put at the very bottom of my backpack, then my cell phone. Next goes my Hamilton High books and then my notebook. The red plastic purse with pictures and driver's license I put in a small zippered compartment. Then I stuff the rest of my clothes into the three shopping bags I came in with and go out to the waiting room. Nikki's already there, talking with Miss F.

"You weren't going to leave without telling me goodbye, were you?" she asks, flashing the smile that was so reassuring to me when I first arrived here.

"I stopped by your office but you weren't in," I say.

"Well, then, here I am now!" She opens her arms to me and I step into her soft embrace.

"The best of luck to you," she says.

"Thanks."

She fishes around in her pocket, pulling out candy kisses, pencils, notes on torn pieces of paper, until she finds her cards.

"Here. Call me if you need anything. Or just to say hi."

I take the card from her and put it in my jeans pocket.

In the evening, we're sitting in the den, watching the UCLA Stanford women's basketball game, on mute. I'm in the big recliner, with my legs and feet slightly elevated, a position Penny says is good to use during pregnancy. Elvis is stretched out on my lap.

"Let's talk about what you'll be doing for school," Nikki says. "We're thinking you can take the next few days to settle in here, then get started somewhere Monday morning."

"Where?"

"That's what we were wondering. Any thoughts?"

"Well . . . maybe . . ."

Both Nikki and Penny sit waiting for me to answer the "any thoughts about school" question, but apparently I don't have any thoughts.

"Penny and I have been talking about what might work for you. There are plenty of possibilities. Hamilton High, of course. We could get a district waiver and you could ride with me every day. Or you could go to the teen pregnancy program in the Hamilton Heights district."

"Or," Penny says, "You could go to the teen pregnancy program here in San Remo."

"Or San Remo High School," Nikki adds.

"I sort of want to go to Hamilton High. I mean, it is my school . . ."

"Oh, no!" Nikki yells. "Did you see that?"

She turns the TV sound on.

"Schmidt totally fouled Jeffers and the ref . . . listen . . ."

The announcer repeats the referee's decision. Nikki mutters something.

"Uh, Nikki?" Penny says. "We were talking about possible schools for Autumn?"

"Oh. Sorry," Nikki says, turning the sound off again.

"So, you were saying Hamilton High?"

"Maybe. I don't know. It would be weird, but at least I could get the classes I need, and maybe keep my scholarship . . ."

"What scholarship?" Penny asks.

"Autumn was in line for a volleyball scholarship to Cal Poly before all this happened."

"But now?"

Nikki shrugs. "I guess there may still be a chance," she says, giving me a long look. "I don't know, though. You sort of fell off the radar before the season was over."

I run my hand across Elvis' back, from head to toe, watching the hair rise slightly from static electricity.

"What are you thinking about for September?" Penny asks.

"I want to go to Cal Poly — like I planned."

Penny nods. "Could you go even if you don't get the scholarship?"

"I'm not sure."

Nikki turns off the TV and pulls a footstool over so she's sitting directly in front of me.

"I know you're going to have to get into the long-term planning for college thing eventually. But for now, let's just think about where you'll show up for school on Monday morning."

We talk about the pros and cons of a regular high school versus a teen pregnancy school, of Hamilton High versus San Remo High, of the Hamilton Heights teen pregnancy program versus the San Remo teen pregnancy program, until my head is spinning with pros and cons. Maybe Nikki's head is spinning, too, because she calls a time out.

"5:00 rolls around pretty early," she says. "It's past my bed-time."

She stands, does a few stretches, and sits down on the footstool again.

"That's another thing to think about for Hamilton High. You'd be riding with me. I leave at six on the dot and usually don't get home until at least five o'clock — that's a pretty long day for a growing girl, specially one who's growing a baby."

"Let's call it a night," Penny says, looking at her watch and yawning. "Do you want a glass of milk, or anything, Autumn?"

"No, thanks," I say.

"Well, help yourself if you change your mind. I'm off to bed now, too."

Nikki sits watching me, thoughtful.

"I'm glad you're here with us," she says.

"Me, too! It's . . . the home was . . . hard."

"Listen, it really is past my bedtime. But you can sleep late to-morrow morning, if you'd like, so feel free to stay up later if you want. Watch TV, use the computer, whatever . . . just make yourself at home."

"Thank you," I say, wishing I could come up with better words to tell Nikki how much it means to me to be here, in a real home, with real people.

"Just one thing, for now. When you contact your Hamilton High friends it might be better . . . it's . . . well . . . that low profile thing," Nikki says.

I have no idea what Nikki's talking about now, except she seems embarrassed.

"You know . . . we try to avoid gossip so . . . just for a little while . . . it might be better if your old friends don't know you're staying with us."

"Okay."

"I hate to ask that. It has nothing to do with you, or wanting to keep you hidden away."

"It's okay," I say. "None of my friends have known where I am for months, anyway."

Nikki's quiet for a while, then stands up. She looks down at the cat who's still sleeping on my lap.

"Bedtime, Elvis. Coming?"

He gives a barely noticeable twitch of his tail, opens one eye a tiny slit, then closes it again. Nikki laughs.

"Okay, traitor, but remember who feeds you."

There's a short email from Jason: November 28

Glad to finally hear from you. Keep in touch. Jason.

And another from Danni: November 23

Wow! GR8 2 hear from u! Where are u? Why can't u call? There's so much to tell u! Finally I'm in love, I mean RE-ALLY in love, not that puppy love stuff I felt for Jason. Can u believe how stupid I was? (Don't answer that.) A whole year of unrequited love? But I can only tell u this F2F. WHERE ARE U????

I write back to her that I'm staying in a different place now, and I want to hear all about her new love, and I've got a lot of news for her, too. I say maybe there would be a way to get together sometime Saturday, and then as soon as I press send, I get scared about seeing Danni in person. I don't think Carole told Danni I was pregnant or she'd have been asking about it in her emails. How will she react? And I know she'll want to know who the father is. I don't want to go there.

Whenever I think about school possibilities, I think Hamilton High. It is my school. But then when I picture myself pregnant — pregnant! — squeezing into a school desk, feeling curious eyes watching, knowing I'll be the subject of a lot of talk, some of it not so nice . . . I get scared.

CHAPTER

18

Nikki and Penny are both gone by the time I wake up. There's a note on the kitchen table for me from Penny: *Give me a call on my lunch break, between 11:00 and 11:35. My cell number is 286-3714.*

I put my clothes in the washer, get a bowl of cereal, take it into the den, and turn on the TV. I flip past the Home Shopping Network, news, some house make-over thing, a kiddie cartoon, and end up watching a Jerry Springer show where DNA testing results are about to be revealed. I have enough drama in my life without this.

I go out to the laundry room and put my washed clothes into the dryer. When I return, Elvis is licking the last of the milk from my bowl and Jerry Springer is lecturing the mother and the guy who was most certain he wasn't the dad about the responsibilities of parenthood. Here's what I don't ever, ever want to do — be on Jerry Springer's show.

By the time my clothes are dry and put away in the pink room it's time to call Penny.

She asks if I slept well, and how I'm feeling, and if I've eaten, and if the baby's moving around, and what I need from the market.

I ask for orange juice, the kind with light pulp.

"You got it. I'll see you around 3:00," she says. "If you think of anything more you need, just call and leave a message. I'll check my phone before I come home."

I start a to-do list, but so far all I can come up with is: get a new bra, get a charger and buy minutes for my cell phone. Like I need a list for that?

It's weird. It's been so long since I've had any control over my own life, I can't figure out what needs to be done. In the county home, every decision was already made for me — when to get up and when to go to bed, when to take a shower and when to brush my teeth, and on and on. Practically the only decision I ever made there was whether or not to let Madison have my dessert. I hope I haven't forgotten how to make decisions for myself.

Although the walk to the shopping center is only a few blocks, I'm short of breath by the time I get there. I'm so out of shape! I buy a charger for my cell phone and sixty minutes calling time and mark those two things off my list. There's no place in this center where I can buy a bra, though, so that will have to wait.

Back at Nikki and Penny's I plug in my phone and check email. There's a message from Danni saying she really, really, really, wants to see me, but she's in a pageant at her church and she's rehearsing all day. Their dress rehearsal is Saturday night.

I email her back, telling her my cell phone is working again and if I don't hear from her before, I'll call her Tuesday night.

Penny comes in loaded down with groceries and a heavy-looking tote bag.

"Why I ever chose to teach English . . . " she says, stacking a batch of papers on the table. "I should have had my head examined!"

She takes a large container of orange juice from one of the bags.

"This what you want?"

"Perfect," I say.

"How was your first day of residence at 6047 E. Ancourt, San Remo, California?" she says, opening a bag of chips and putting them in a bowl on the table.

"Quiet. Nice. I walked to the phone store and bought minutes and a charger."

"So you're connected again?"

"Yeah. As soon as my battery's charged up."

"Who's the first person you'll call?"

"Well . . . I'd like to call my friend, Danni, but she's hard to reach sometimes. Maybe Krystal."

"From volleyball?"

"Yeah. Most of my friends are from volleyball."

Penny empties the last grocery bag, putting lettuce and milk in the refrigerator, and cans of soup and tomatoes in the pantry.

"How about your boyfriend?" Penny asks.

"I don't really have a boyfriend," I say.

She looks at me as if she's not sure whether or not to believe me.

"I don't. Really."

Penny sits at the table and picks the top paper off her stack.

"Do you want to help a poor, overworked English teacher?" she asks.

"Sure."

She shows me how to enter the grades in her roll book and I sit across from her, reading *Ordinary People* and entering a grade each time she finishes a paper. At the fourth paper, Penny erupts in laughter.

"What?" I ask.

She shakes her head, still laughing.

I glance over at the paper, but don't see anything funny.

"Well . . . I tell my students that it's worth ten bonus points if they can make me laugh when I'm grading papers, and a student in my first period class, Nathan Taylor, is always amusing me with Tom Swifties."

"Tom Swifties?"

"An adverb that is also a pun, like . . . 'I can't hear anything!' Tom said deftly."

"Oh, yeah! My grams used to like those things. Like . . . 'I need a pencil sharpener,' Tom said bluntly?"

"Right! Not exactly sophisticated humor, but Nathan works them into his papers very cleverly. This is a personal essay about

the negative influence of online poker, and he managed to slip it in
. . ."

She runs her finger under a sentence that says, "I only have dia-
monds, clubs and spades," Tom said heartlessly.

We both laugh, and I'm about to enter ten bonus points beside
Nathan's name when Elvis jumps up on the table and stretches out
across the open book.

"Scoot, you big blob," Penny says, lifting him off the table.

He jumps up again, making us both laugh.

"He's got food in the laundry room. Do you want to open a can
and put half of it in his dish?"

I get up from the table and go get the food. Elvis rubs against
my legs, back to front, making it nearly impossible to walk without
tripping over him.

"Can opener's in the top drawer next to the washing machine,"
Penny says. "And lids for the cans should be right next to it."

After I feed Elvis and put his leftover food in the refrigerator, I
get back to the task of entering grades. Nikki calls to say she's on
her way home and Penny clears the papers and books off the table.

"This can wait until after dinner," she says, wiping the table off
and putting three placemats on it.

"Do you want to help?" she asks.

"Sure."

She hands me a big wooden salad bowl with tongs and gets lettuce, tomatoes, cucumbers and carrots from the refrigerator.

"How about doing the salad?"

I wash my hands, then the vegetables, and start cutting things
up. Penny cuts up two chicken breasts, an onion, some peppers and
garlic and heats olive oil in a skillet.

"I do the cooking and shopping and Nikki does the dishes and
laundry," Penny says. "Except on Sundays, when Nikki makes
breakfast."

Penny puts a pot of water on to boil and gets a package of pasta
noodles from the pantry.

"Do you like to cook?" she asks.

"I used to help Grams in the kitchen sometimes, but I don't really know how to cook. I'm pretty good at hot dogs and microwaved
macaroni and cheese."

Penny laughs. "It sounds like you and Nikki are about on the same level when it comes to cooking."

When Penny hears Nikki's car in the driveway, she puts the pasta into the boiling water and walks to the back door to greet her.

"Hi, Sweetheart," she says, giving Nikki a quick peck on the cheek.

"Hey, Babe, smells good in here! Hi, Autumn, how're you doing?"

"Fine," I say, mixing the salad with the tongs.

It all feels so . . . homey. At dinner we talk about the details of our days, though I don't have a lot of details to talk about except my walk to the phone store. I guess I could say I wrote a three-item list, but I don't.

Late at night, in the privacy of the pink room, I listen to the one saved message still on my cell phone.

"Hey, Kid. I'm bringing home pizza. What kind do you want? Call me. Otherwise, I'll assume you want pineapple." There's his wild laugh, then, "Only kidding."

I take the stone heart from my notebook and put it under my pillow.

"I still miss you so much," I say, letting the tears come.

There's this part in *Ordinary People* that says grief is ugly and isolating, not something to share with others. I guess maybe that's true for me.

Friday night is pizza and movie night at Nikki and Penny's. It's Penny's turn to choose, so we watch "Freedom Writers," about some high school kids down in Long Beach who were total gangbangers until this English teacher helped them figure out that their lives mattered.

The only one not crying by the end is Elvis, who is sleeping on my lap, which is his new favorite place to be. Penny says cats have super sensitive hearing and she thinks maybe he likes listening to the baby's heartbeat.

Nikki wipes her eyes and blows her nose.

"Next week we're watching a comedy!"

"You've got to admit it's a pretty impressive story, though," Penny says.

Talking about "Freedom Writers" gets us talking about high

school in general, which gets us talking about where I'll be enrolling Monday morning.

"I sort of want to go to Hamilton, but . . ."

Just then the baby gives such a strong kick that Elvis is pushed off onto the floor. He looks up at my belly with such a puzzled, irritated expression that Nikki and Penny and I totally crack up. I'm laughing so hard I can barely get to the bathroom in time. When I come back out, Nikki has Elvis on her lap.

"See, now you know who to trust," she says.

I sit back down, half expecting Elvis to come over to me and take his usual position, but he stays on Nikki's lap, sending bad looks in my direction.

"You were saying about Hamilton . . . " Penny prompts.

"Yeah, that's where I want to go, but I don't really want to go like . . . this," I say, putting my hand over my belly.

"Penny and I have been talking about it, and we'd like to make a proposal," Nikki says, looking very serious.

I hope the proposal doesn't have anything to do with going back to the county home.

"We want you to know we'll go along with whatever you decide, but we think the best thing for everyone right now is for you to go to the San Remo teen pregnancy/parenting program."

"You do?" I say, surprised that Nikki thinks that's better for me than Hamilton High.

"For one thing, it's a shorter day," Nikki says. "I'm afraid you'd be exhausted having to leave so early in the morning and be gone for ten or twelve hours. And the closer your time comes, the more easily you'll tire."

"And you'll be learning more about what to expect for the rest of your pregnancy, and the birthing process, and how to take good care of yourself," Penny says. "You wouldn't get any of that in classes at Hamilton."

"The other thing is . . ." Penny pauses and looks toward Nikki, as if for support.

"The other thing is, it's just best for people not to know you're living with us right now. And it would be hard to keep that from getting out if you're coming to school with me every morning and leaving with me every evening," Nikki says.

"But I'm here legally and everything. What's wrong with that?"

"Nothing," Nikki says. "It's just, like I said before, certain people would like to see me fired. They've backed off for now, because their demands are ridiculous and everybody, almost everybody, knows that. And it's not that I'd be fired for having you stay here, it's just that it's one more thing for them to get all fired up about, and that wouldn't be fun."

I'm trying to make sense of it — that my being here would get people "fired up" to get rid of Coach Nicholson.

"I don't get it," I say.

"I don't either," Nikki says. "I just know how certain people would react if they knew you were living with us."

We're all quiet for a while, then Nikki says, "If you feel like you've got to go to Hamilton High, we'll make it work. But we'd like you to at least try the San Remo TAPP school for now. Then we'll reevaluate before second semester, and if Hamilton High is still your choice, you can transfer."

"But what about those people? Will they be gone by then?"

Nikki shakes her head sadly.

"They're never really gone. A few leave and new ones come along. As for next semester, we'll cross that bridge when we come to it."

"At least think about it," Penny says. "I know the San Remo TAPP teacher over there, and I think you'd like her."

Between my worry about gossip, and squeezing into desk chairs, and being embarrassed about being pregnant, along with Nikki and Penny's push for TAPP, I decide to do as they suggest. Once decided, it's kind of a relief to me not to have to face all of my old classmates just yet.

CHAPTER

19

On our way to the TAPP school Monday morning, Penny says she's talked with the teacher, Karen Metcalf, about our situation.

"Karen suggested it might be better not to mention your adoption plans with the other students until you get to know them better."

"I won't."

"She said a lot of her students are totally against the idea of adoption, and they might not be very nice to you if they think you're giving up your baby."

"If they're anything like the girls at the other TAPP place, they'd hate me for it."

Penny sighs. "It's such a wonderful thing you're doing for us, and for your baby. It's utterly selfish of little fifteen/sixteen-year-old girls to think they can be good parents when they're still children themselves."

"I'm just coming here to get my credits," I say. "I don't have to be friends with everybody."

"Well . . . I thought I'd give you a heads up on this one . . . "

We get to the new school before any of the other students

have arrived. Penny walks with me into the classroom where a short woman with long, blond, curly hair is arranging pictures on a large bulletin board.

"Karen?"

"Oh. Hey, Penny," she says, turning toward us with a broad smile.

"And you must be Autumn. Welcome to TAPP."

She shoves scissors and thumb tacks into the big pocket in the middle of her apron and extends her hand.

"I'm Karen Metcalf. Everybody calls me Karen — unless they're mad at me, and I won't tell you what they call me then," she laughs.

"Don't believe her," Penny says. "I hear her students love her."

The three of us sit at one of the big tables while Karen explains the system here. It sounds pretty much like how things were at Sterling. Class work centers on issues related to pregnancy and parenting, and students work individually for academic credit.

"Did you and Penny talk about waiting a while before you tell other students about the adoption?"

I nod.

"But don't you think a lot of their babies would be better off if they were adopted?" Penny asks.

"I'm sure some of them would. But these girls are making difficult, life-changing commitments. Maybe they're afraid to think about adoption possibilities, even for someone else — afraid it would weaken their resolve."

"That makes no sense," Penny says, shaking her head sadly.

"I know. That's how it is, though."

"I'm glad Autumn's smart enough to know what's best for her and her baby," Penny says.

"I don't think it's a matter of smarts — it's emotions."

"Whatever it is, I'm glad for it," Penny says, smiling at me.

I smile back. I feel like things are finally getting better for me, and it's mostly because of Penny, and how much she wants a baby.

"I'd better be off to impart knowledge to the unkempt masses," Penny says.

Karen laughs. "You know you love it."

"Sometimes yes, sometimes no . . . I will pick you up at 1:00,

Autumn. You can start riding the school van tomorrow."

"Okay. Thanks," I say, waving goodbye.

Karen gives me a folder to keep my work in, and a multiple choice pre-test with fifty questions about pregnancy. Usually I do well on tests, but I think this one is going to be different.

I'm trying to decide if the definition of kegels is: (A) Protective layers of fat that form around the amniotic sac. (B) Exercises to strengthen muscles in the pelvic area. (C) Containers for pregnancy-safe, non-alcoholic beer. I've eliminated C and am wavering between A and B when three girls come into the room, one of them with a baby.

Karen introduces us all around and the girl with the baby, Heather, goes through the door that says NURSERY.

"When's your baby due?" one of the girls asks.

"February 15. How about you?"

"April sixteenth."

"Mine's due the end of January," the other girl says.

"Tiffany, I haven't had a chance to give Autumn the tour yet. Would you mind?"

"No problem," Tiffany, the one whose baby is due in January, says.

"You can finish the test when you get back," Karen says.

Tiffany drops her backpack on the chair next to mine. I get up and follow her into the nursery. There are five cribs, a refrigerator, a long counter with a sink, storage cabinets, and pictures of babies on every wall.

"That's Miss Goldfarb — Goldy," Tiffany says, nodding toward a woman sitting in one of the rockers, talking on a cell phone. She smiles and goes on talking.

"Goldy supervises the nursery. She's pretty nice unless you do something stupid with one of the babies. Last month this girl left a dirty diaper on the floor and one of the two-year-olds got into it."

Tiffany makes a face like she's about to get sick.

"Goldy really went off on that girl — Deena, I think her name was. She was only here for a few days and then she moved away or something."

On the other side of the room, Heather is standing at a changing table cleaning her baby's butt.

"That's Ryan," Tiffany says. "He's ten months old. Isn't he a cutie?"

I've never been one of those girls that gets all crazy over babies, but I guess he's cute enough.

Heather fastens the baby's diaper, pulls his pants up, and brings him over to where we're standing. "He didn't sleep at all last night," she says. "I think he's getting another tooth."

Goldy comes over and introduces herself to me, then turns her attention to the baby.

"Did he have any fever last night?" she asks, feeling his forehead.

"I don't think so," Heather says, yawning.

Two more girls with babies come through the door. Tiffany introduces us, then takes me out to the play yard. Next she takes me past the restrooms and vending machines, shows me the lunchroom, and then we go back to the classroom.

"No worry about getting lost on this campus, is there?" Karen says.

I shake my head, smiling, remembering how totally lost I was the whole first week of my freshman year at Hamilton High.

By now there are six more girls in the classroom, all at tables with books and papers out in front of them, but only two of them are working. The others are talking. Karen pulls a chair up next to the talkers and goes through some papers. Soon things are quiet in the classroom.

I finish the pretest and then check it with the answer key. Out of fifty questions, I missed eighteen! Even though I scored next highest in the "Vocabulary for the College Bound" tests we took at Hamilton High in September, I don't know half of the words on this pre-test. Episiotomy. Postpartum. Linea Negra. Fundus. Amniocentesis. God! It's not like I'm trying to be a gynecologist. I just want to have the baby and get a life back. Why do I need to know all this gross stuff?

Karen brings a stack of books to my table. One deals with pregnancy, one with being a good parent, and the others are for subjects I need to finish, like Government, Economics, and English. I can turn in a review of *Ordinary People* for English credit, plus do the poetry unit and a daily journal. Like at Sterling, everyone does a daily journal in this class.

Besides the pregnancy/childbirth/parenting classwork, most of the girls spend thirty minutes a day, three times a week, helping out in the nursery. Karen says it's up to me whether I include the nursery component in my work. She says since I'll probably raise a child someday later on, the parenting stuff is good to know. But I decide to skip it and use the time for my other requirements.

Penny's already waiting for me in the parking lot when school's out. She hands me a Baggie with slices of apple.

"Here. This is good for you . . . How'd things go?"

"Okay," I say, leaning the seat back and closing my eyes.

She wants to know a lot more than "okay." Like what's the title of my English textbook, what exactly will I be doing for Economics, and will we do anything experiential for American Government.

I bite into a slice of apple. It's cold, and crunchy.

"What do you mean, experiential?" I ask.

"You know. Beyond the books. There's an election coming up. You could work for a precinct, or participate in a debate, that sort of thing."

"Hmmm. The only experiential stuff I've heard about is for parenting credit if we help with the babies and toddlers in the nursery, but I'm not going to take that elective."

Penny glances over at me. "Why not?"

"Well . . . it's not like I'm going to be taking care of a kid. And I could use that time to work on my real credits."

She laughs. "Maybe I should come take the parenting class, and you could teach my third period hooligans."

The adoption consultant's office is in Hamilton Heights, close to Barb and Edie's. It's weird, driving past all these familiar places. I haven't been gone that long, but it seems like another lifetime — a time lived by someone else.

Penny and I take the elevator to the seventh floor of the tallest steel and glass office building in town, and I follow her down the hall to the Adoption Help Network. From the window in the waiting room I can look down to my left and see the intersection where the gravel truck demolished my dad's Honda, and all the life that was in it.

To the north the San Gabriel mountains rise above foothill suburbs, outlined against the sky. Giant TV antennas sparkle from the peaks of Mt. Wilson. It's a clear, crisp day and the view of the mountains is beautiful. But as hard as I try to focus on the mountains, my eyes are drawn back to the site of the deadly accident, my attention drawn back to the "what ifs." What if we'd talked longer in the parking lot? What if Danni hadn't shown up and delayed their leaving? What if Dad hadn't forgotten the escrow papers?

"Autumn?"

I turn away from the window to see Penny's look of concern.

"Are you okay? You're not worried about doing this are you?"

It takes a moment to understand what Penny is saying. I push the "what ifs" out of my thoughts.

"I'm not worried," I say, "just . . . my head was somewhere else."

A woman in a dark business suit and high heels opens the door to an inner office and invites us in.

"This is Audrey Hollenbeck," Penny says. "Audrey, this is Autumn."

Audrey smiles and shakes my hand.

"Nikki should be here any minute," Penny says.

"That's okay. We can start on some of the routine paper work for now. We'll save the gritty details for later."

Penny and I sit on a big leather couch and Audrey sits across from us in a matching chair. She sets a folder and a stack of forms on the long, glass coffee table that sits between the couch and the two matching chairs.

"Any changes here? Address? Phone numbers?" Audrey asks, taking papers from the folder and sliding them across to Penny.

Penny glances through the information.

"Everything's the same," Penny says.

"Okay. That's the easy part."

There's a light knock at the door and Nikki comes in.

"Sorry," she says, taking a seat next to Penny. "I had to help the substitute get set up for practice."

"No problem," Audrey says. "We're just now getting to the good stuff."

Ms. Hollenbeck pulls more papers from the folder and glances through them.

"You two already have most of what you need. Your home study is still valid. Your expectations for ongoing contact . . . have you discussed these items?"

"Only that Autumn definitely doesn't want to be a mom," Penny says.

"Autumn, will you want to visit the baby sometimes? Will you want to remain a part of his? — her? life?"

"Her," I say. "I plan to go away to college in September. I won't be around much."

"Where will you be living until you go away to college?"

"Ummm. I'm not sure."

" She can stay with us until September . . . longer if she wants," Nikki says, looking at Penny for confirmation.

Penny frowns.

Audrey looks from one to the other.

"Well . . . it's generally recommended that the birthmother not live with the adoptive family after relinquishing the baby."

"Why is that?" Nikki asks.

"It's hard on everyone if birthmother bonds with the baby."

"We'll make arrangements for a place for Autumn to stay after the baby's born," Penny says. "We're not just going to forget about her once we have the baby."

Audrey takes one set of forms and hands it to me. She hands a set of forms to Penny.

"This is just an update of what we already have on file for you and Jean," she says.

She hands me a packet.

"I'd like you to fill these out carefully. Of course, you should consider how you really want things to go during these next few months, and during labor and delivery. But it's very important that you have a realistic plan for your life after the baby is born."

She turns back to Penny and Nikki.

"Let's all get together again sometime next week . . . Autumn, you'll be signing the forms to show your intent, they're not binding. The only forms that mean anything legally will be the ones you sign after the baby is born."

On the way out, I sneak one last look down at the fatal intersection.

When we get to the parking lot, Nikki says, "Ride with me. Penny got you all to herself on the way over."

We decide to meet at "La Fiesta," a Mexican food restaurant in San Remo. On the way there, Nikki asks, "Are you sure you want to do this?"

"Positive," I say.

"Well, okay. The wheels are in motion."

At the restaurant Nikki and Penny order margaritas, virgin because they're driving. They offer a toast to me, the new baby, and their new lives as mommies.

"What shall we name her?" Nikki says.

"How about Virginia, after Virginia Woolfe?

"Oh, that's awful!" Nikki says. "How about Florence, after Florence Chadwick?"

"Who's Florence Chadwick?" Penny says.

"You know . . . the first woman to swim the English Channel."

"No! Not after a swimmer! At least not one named Florence."

"Better than after a writer who drowned herself," Nikki says, laughing.

"Well, then, how about Emily, after Emily Dickinson?"

"The one who spent her whole life hiding in her house?"

"Nooooo," Penny says, also laughing. "During her lifetime, she took several short trips to visit relatives."

"Don't ever get tied up with an English major," Nikki says, laughing even harder. "Especially if you want help naming a baby."

"What do you think about a name, Autumn?" Penny asks.

"I don't know. It's your baby," I say.

"Not bad," Nikki says. "We could name her "Our Baby," and call her O.B. for short."

"Beats Florence," Penny says.

"I've got it!" Nikki says. "A name that has literary resonance, for the English teacher, and is also a tough chick, for the sports fan!"

"What?" Penny and I ask at the same time.

"Nancy! As in Nancy Drew! A great role model for a girl!"

We laugh, but Nikki says she's serious. Penny seems to be thinking it over, then she gets a big smile.

"I like it. Nancy it is!"

"To Nancy," Nikki says.

We click glasses, laughing.

Leaving the restaurant, as I am walking between the two still-laughing mommies, I shove my hand deep into the pocket of my jacket and rub the stone heart between my thumb and index finger. Things are getting better, I think. And I'm part of the solution.

CHAPTER

20

The forms the adoption consultant gave me include a "health history" with questions like have I ever tested HIV positive, or had tuberculosis, or been committed to a mental institution, or had a whole list of surgeries and on and on. It's tedious, but easy. Then I get to the "Your adoption plan" packet.

The first question asks if I want the adoptive parents involved during pregnancy. That's a no-brainer, because they already are.

"Do you want the adoptive parents to be birth coaches?" I skip that for now.

"Do you want the adoptive parents to be in the labor/delivery room?" Skip.

"Do you want to spend time alone with the baby in the hospital?" No.

"Do you want letters and pictures over time? How often? When?" Skip.

"Do you want phone contact with the adoptive family?" Yes.

"Do you want to see the child occasionally over the years? How often?" Skip.

"Will anyone else want these privileges? Is there anyone you would specifically want to exclude?" Skip.

I read back over the items I've skipped, still not sure how to answer. I set that section aside and go on to the next one. Penny comes into the kitchen and glances at the "birth plan" forms.

"We can go over these things together after your next doctor's visit," she says.

"Good idea!" I say, relieved to set the whole thing aside.

"I'd like to go with you to the doctor, if you don't mind," Penny says.

"Sure."

I get my appointment card from my backpack and hand it to her.

"So, Friday at 2:00?"

I nod.

"I'll get someone to cover sixth period for me."

On Tuesday evening, when I'm sure Carole will be out, I dial Danni's number. I'm not sure what I'll say after hello. I just know I've got to talk to her.

"Hello?"

"Danni?"

"Autumn???"

"Yeah. How are you?"

"How am I? How are you???"

"I'm fine. Better."

"Better than what?"

"Better than I was," I say. "How about you?"

"I'm better than I was, too," she says, laughing. "Oh, Autumn, I can't wait for you to meet Evan! He's sooooo cool! And I can't wait to see you. Where are you? When can we get together? Where are you going to school?"

After a ton of questions, and more talk about Evan, and news of Krystal, and Stacy and Shantell, and the rest of the volleyball-lunch group, Danni tells me she has the car tomorrow because she takes Hannah to soccer practice every Wednesday.

"I could come get you after I drop her off," Danni says.

I tell her I'm staying with a foster family, but it's better to meet somewhere than for me to have visitors. I don't really lie to her, I just don't say anything about who I'm staying with.

"Well, where can I meet you, then? What's some place close to where you live?"

"Do you know where that big shopping center is in San Remo?"

"Near where Coach Nicholson lives?"

"Yeah, I guess."

"Where we got stuff for the party last summer?"

After more talk about the details, we decide to meet tomorrow afternoon at Jamba Juice in the San Remo shopping center.

"I can't wait," Danni says.

"Me either."

"I'll bring pictures of Evan."

"Cool."

"How about you? Is there a guy in your life?"

"Not exactly."

"What's that mean?"

"I'll tell you tomorrow."

I stand in front of the mirror in the pink bedroom, trying to see myself through Danni's eyes. My big belly. My chopped hair. My pale skin. If I were seeing me for the first time in months, I'd be totally shocked.

At Hamilton High, between volleyball and my jogging routine, I was outside a lot. And even though I always wore sunscreen, I had a year-round light tan. Not anymore.

Oh, well. I can't hide from my very best friend forever. At least I don't want to. I've missed Danni soooo much. I hope we can still find something to laugh about.

It's pouring down rain when the school van drops me off at the corner, about half a block from Nikki and Penny's. I hurry to the house and let myself inside with the key they had made for me. This is so different, so much better than being in the county home. I'm free to come and go as I please, as long as I let someone know where to reach me and when to expect me home. Now that I have minutes on my cell phone, I can talk on the phone whenever I want, and use the computer, and shower whenever I want. Stay up late, or go to bed early — it's up to me. More than that, though, I'm with people who care — not because they're paid to care, but just because they care.

I change into dry clothes and stretch out on the couch in the den, spinning past channel after channel, finding nothing I want to settle on. Elvis jumps onto the back of the couch, then eases himself down gently onto my belly, as if he doesn't want to disturb the baby. Maybe that swift kick he got the other night taught him some respect.

I go through the channels again, then press the off button on the remote. I'm so nervous about seeing Danni, I can't think about anything else. If she had a cell phone I'd call and say I was sick or something, but there's no way I can reach her right now. I think about just not showing up, but that'd be so cold, to let her drive all the way over here, in the rain, and me not be there.

I open my Economics book and try to read the assignment, but I can't stay focused. I lift Elvis off my belly and go into the bathroom, closing the door behind me. I hate when he jumps up on my lap when I'm on the toilet! With a light dab of gel, I scrunch my hair up. Some blush and lip gloss adds a little color. Taking an umbrella from the stand near the back door, I step outside into a light drizzle and make my way toward the shopping center.

At Jamba Juice I order a Strawberry Swirl and take a table in the corner, facing the door. It feels as if hundreds of butterflies are fluttering around in my stomach, and the baby isn't even kicking.

I'm halfway finished with my drink when I see Danni's blue Nissan turn into the parking lot. Now it's thousands of butterflies. I watch her pull into a parking place a few spaces down from the Jamba Juice entrance. When I see her, that curly red hair and round, smiling face, I forget the butterflies and rush to the door.

"Autumn!" she squeals, loud enough that everyone in the shop turns to look.

We throw our arms around each other, laughing, then push away. Danni's smile fades quickly.

"What'd you do to your hair?"

"I had to . . ."

"Oh, my God!" she says, her eyes now on my belly.

I feel my face grow hot while everyone in the shop seems to be watching us.

"I've got my drink over here," I say, walking toward the corner table.

I sit down, but Danni is still standing at the door, staring. At first I wonder if she's going to stay or go, but then she comes to the table and sits down.

"You're pregnant?" she whispers, her eyes wide with astonishment.

I nod.

"I didn't even think you had a boyfriend!"

"I don't."

"Oh, my God! Were you raped? God! That's awful!" she says, tears gathering in her eyes.

I shake my head.

"No. No . . . it's nothing like that."

"But . . . when are you due?"

"February 15," I say, watching as she counts backwards to May.

"You were pregnant all summer??"

I nod.

"And you didn't even tell me?"

"I . . . I couldn't."

"Why not?" she asks, anger creeping into her voice.

"I just . . . I don't know . . . At first I couldn't believe it, and then . . . it was so embarrassing, and I kept hoping it would go away, you know, like one of those early miscarriages . . . and . . ."

"Did your Dad know? Or your grandmother?"

"No one," I say, shaking my head. "I made a stupid, stupid mistake, and I knew I had to work through it on my own."

"Who's the father?"

I stare into my drink, not answering.

Danni goes to the counter, taking heavy steps, the way she does when she's angry. She orders a Mega Mango, loudly, as if she's angry at the counter person, too. I take a sip of what's left of my now warm strawberry drink, wondering if Danni and I are still friends, or if she's going to be like her mother and turn me away because I'm pregnant.

Danni waits for her drink at the counter, her back to me. I'm remembering when I was twelve, when I first got my period. I didn't tell Danni right away. I guess I was embarrassed or something. Then one afternoon, months later, Danni and I were hanging out at my house. She went into the bathroom and came out red-faced.

"You got your period???"

"Yeah."

"When?"

"Around Christmas."

"Three months ago? And you didn't even tell me?? Your best friend-almost sister???"

She'd stomped out the door and wouldn't even speak to me for over a week. Now, seeing her straight, stiff back as she waits at the counter, I'm thinking maybe my long-secret pregnancy will be too much for our friendship to bear.

When her drink is ready she still waits at the counter, as if trying to decide whether to turn back to me or walk out the door. Finally, she turns to face me. Tears are running down her cheeks.

"Let's go," she says.

I follow her to the car.

For what feels like a long time, Danni sits with her head against her folded arms, her arms resting on the steering wheel of her mother's car. The sound of the rain beating hard against the car adds an eerie rhythm to our long silence.

I'd like to say something, but I don't know what. Besides, it's hard to talk to a buried face. I sit watching giant raindrops reflecting light from the Jamba Juice sign, wishing my hair were still as long and pretty as Jesus's hair is in the laminated picture that hangs from the rear view mirror.

A crack of thunder startles Danni to attention.

"How long is this storm supposed to last, anyway?" she asks, looking at me for the first time since she ordered her drink inside.

"All week, I think."

A distant flash of lightning. A faint roll of thunder.

"I hate this weather!" Danni says.

She goes on about how she hates the rain, even if everyone says how much we need it, and how she really hates the lightning.

"More people are killed by lightning every year than they are by . . ."

"Stop talking about the weather!"

She gives me a surprised look, like maybe she'd forgotten I was here.

"Listen, Danni, I'm sorry I didn't tell you earlier, but it's not like there've been a lot of chances to talk lately with me locked away in the home."

"Oh! But you were already four months pregnant even before . . . before . . . And I tell you everything! I've always told you everything! And you were going to have a baby and you didn't even tell me!"

"It was just . . . I was pregnant, but I wasn't going to have a baby. . . . At least, I didn't think I was going to have a baby back then. I was going to get an abortion."

"You were going to murder your baby!" she shrieks.

"It wasn't a baby then!"

"Who are you anyway?? I don't even know you! I've missed you so much, and been so worried, and . . ."

"Oh, poor you! Poor Little Miss Dannielle! So betrayed by her best friend! Shit! This isn't all about you! How do you think I feel? I lost my whole family," I yell, choking back tears. "And then I lost my second family because your mother, my second mother, sent me away when she found out I'd been a bad girl! And now I am going to have a baby, and I feel like shit, and I've lost my scholarship, and so excuse me if I'm not joining in on your pity-party!" I scream, giving way to tears, sobbing, gasping for air, my chest heaving so hard it starts the baby kicking.

Danni puts her head back down on the steering wheel and I can tell from the shaky movements of her back that she, too, is crying. And it's pouring down rain. And there's lightning. And thunder. And I want the storm to let up. I want it all to let up.

"My mother sent you away?" Danni asks softly.

"You didn't know that?"

"She just told me we couldn't be your foster family anymore. I thought it was some state regulation or something. I kept wanting to get in touch with you, but she said that was against the rules . . . That's what you said, too, on the phone that day."

"You could have called, or come to see me, or written, you just would have needed an okay. She knew that. She just didn't want you to be exposed. Like pregnancy's catching or something."

We sit watching the rain. The parking lot is nearly empty now. There's no one in the Jamba Juice place except the two people who work there. I rub my belly, wanting to quiet the still active baby. Danni gives me a long, searching look.

"I'm sorry," she whispers. "I'm really sorry."

"Me, too," I say.

Slowly, we start talking, catching up on the details of our lives. I tell her about the home, being stripped down, and searched, and checked for lice.

Her eyes widen.

"That's horrible," she says.

I tell her about Madison, and Dericia, and their vocabulary lessons.

Danni tells me about Hannah, and everybody at the lunch table, and what she's wearing to the Winter Ball. She shows me pictures of Evan — one wallet sized graduation picture with him in cap and gown, and two snapshots taken on their front porch, one of him with Hannah, and the other with Danni. He's handsome, with a nice smile.

"He's so sweet," Danni says. "He calls every morning before school, and every night before phone shut-off time at the Hopkins house."

"Your mom lets you get that many phone calls? From a guy?"

"That's what's so cool. My mom loves him. He's a junior pastor at our church . . . "

"How old is he?"

"He's nineteen. He goes to City College now, but next year he'll be going away, to Bible College."

I pick up the picture of them together and look at it again. I know you can't always tell by pictures, but they both look pretty happy. I glance again at the picture with Hannah.

"Hannah's totally in love with Evan, too," Danni says, laughing.

"What about Jason?"

"Oh, you know Hannah. Short attention span. She loves whoever's around."

I hand the pictures back to Danni, wondering if Hannah ever thinks about me, her almost-sister, anymore. As if reading my mind, Danni reaches past the console and puts her hand on mine.

"Hannah still carries that picture of you in her Sleeping Beauty purse. Just a few nights ago she had it out looking at it when I went in to tell her goodnight. We talked about how much we both still missed you."

"Tell her hi for me. Tell her I miss her too, a lot."

Danni nods. The rain has let up now, and Jamba Juice is getting busy again. Five girls wearing San Remo High School hoodies are sitting at the corner table where Danni and I had been just an hour ago. They're laughing and goofing around. I try to remember what it was like to feel so lighthearted. I can't.

"Listen. I . . ."

I turn my attention away from the laughing girls, to a serious Danni.

" . . . I want to be there for you. I want to be your baby's god-mother. I want it . . . it ? . . ."

"Her," I say.

Danni smiles.

"I want her to call me Aunt Danni, let me fix her hair, and . . ."

"I don't think that's how it will be," I say.

Danni looks away.

"Please," she whispers. "Don't hold it against me, that I was mad at you. You know how I get. Don't not be friends with me anymore."

"It's not that! I always want us to be friends . . . you know that! It's just that . . . well . . . I've still got a lot to figure out."

"But you can't get an abortion now!"

"No. It's a baby now. I'm definitely having a baby in Febru-ary."

"You haven't promised someone else they could be the god-mother, have you? That Madison girl's not going to be the god-mother, is she?"

"No . . . Oh, Danni, there's still so much to talk about," I say, suddenly exhausted by the contrast between the laughing girls in the juice place and Danni and me, all out of laughs, in the car.

Danni looks at the clock on the dashboard.

"Uh-oh. I'm going to be late!"

She starts the engine. "I'll take you home," she says. "Just tell me how to get there."

"I'm not supposed to be hanging out with old friends yet, so it'd be better if they didn't see you drop me off. Can you just take me to the library? It's real close."

Danni backs out of the parking space and I direct her to the library, just two blocks away.

"We're close to Coach Nicholson's, aren't we?" Danni says. "If we had more time we should stop by and see her. I know she'd love to see you. She was totally worried about you until you called that day at lunch and said you were okay."

Danni pulls up in front of the library.

"Email me," I say, opening the car door.

"Who's the father?" she asks, wanting the other huge truth that remains hidden.

I shake my head.

"You're not going to tell me, are you?" she says, her face going closed again.

"I am going to tell you. But it's going to take more than three minutes," I say, pointing to the clock. "And please, please, please! Don't tell anyone I'm pregnant. Promise?"

"Promise," she says.

I get out of the car.

"I've missed you a lot," Danni says.

"I've missed you, too," I say, closing the door and walking up the library steps.

I wait inside, watching through a side window as Danni turns the corner. I give it a few more minutes, then step outside into the now gentle rain. I open the umbrella and walk back down the steps. The air feels fresh and clean, sort of like how I feel having finally let Danni know that I'm pregnant. It's been awful, keeping secrets from my best friend. I vow never to do that again. Except . . . how will I ever tell her the Jason part of the pregnancy picture?

21

I shake out the dripping umbrella and put it back in the umbrella stand near the door, then slip off my wet shoes.

"Sit right down and I'll get you some dry things," Penny says,
alarmed.

She's back in an instant with a towel, dry socks and fuzzy slippers.

"These should fit," she says, squatting down and pulling off my
barely damp socks, then briskly rubbing my feet and ankles with
the towel. It feels so good sitting here in the warm kitchen, being
taken care of.

"You shouldn't let yourself get wet like that," she says, starting
to put one of the dry socks on my right foot. She stops suddenly,
staring at my two unseparated toes.

"That's why I'm a good swimmer," I laugh. "Webbed toes."

She looks at the other foot.

"A matched pair," I tell her, stating the obvious.

"Do they hurt?"

"No. And look, I can even wear flip-flops," I say, showing her
the normal space between my big toe and second toe. "My dad had

the same kinds of toes, and Grams did, too. 'A rich heritage' my dad used to say."

Penny laughs, then slips the socks and fuzzy slippers on for me. She stands up with a groan, using the edge of the table for support. Penny is definitely not a physical fitness nut like Nikki is. I guess it's the difference between being an English teacher and being a coach.

"Where were you?" Penny asks, taking salad fixings from the refrigerator.

"I met a friend down at Jamba Juice. I told Nikki . . ."

"Next time tell me. Okay?" she says, smiling a sort of stiff smile. "I could easily have picked you up on my way home from school."

"Sometimes I like to walk."

"Well . . . not in the rain. You've got to be more careful. There's more than just one of you to think about."

I really appreciate Penny. Who wouldn't after being stuck in a place like the home. She fixes my breakfast every morning and she packs tasty lunches for me. This Saturday we're going shopping for more clothes that will fit. It's like she can't do enough for me. Nikki's nice, too, but she's not quite so attentive. The thing is, though, sometimes I'm not sure if Penny likes me because I'm me, or because I'm growing a baby in me. I know Nikki likes me for me, because she liked me a long time before I was pregnant.

In the morning before school I check my email. The only new message is from Danni.

It's strange. All of the time I wasn't able to use email, Jason sent messages every day. Now that I've been answering, he's stopped sending. I know I can't see him while I'm pregnant, but I would at least like to keep in touch. Things have changed so much, but I don't want all of our years of friendship to just be wiped out.

I search the Internet for the kind of math puzzle Jason loves and then forward one to him. Just so he doesn't forget me. Then I open Danni's message.

Let's get together again next week, same time, same place?
And don't forget, I'll be there for you! Promise! YBF

P.S. You could name the baby after me — maybe my mid-

*dle name? That'd be cool. Little Genevieve Grant. We could
call her Genny — She wouldn't be just any old Jenny, she'd
be Genny with a "G."*

Shite! There's still so much I have to confess to Danni! Maybe
it would be easier just to write it all out in an email. Or maybe I
should just drop a few hints in emails and then tell her the rest in
person. Gad! There's so much I wish I could undo!

Saturday morning, after breakfast, and household chores, we
spread the adoption packets out on the table. Really, it's mostly
Penny and Nikki who do the chores. Penny says the movement it
takes to vacuum strains the abdomen in a way that can be risky for
pregnant women. She doesn't want me to clean the cat box, either,
because of germs. I can rinse dishes and put them in the dishwasher,
but when it's time to put them away I can't put the plates on the
second shelf because reaching might also be a strain. Today I dust-
ed the furniture and wiped down the counter tops with an organic
cleanser that's guaranteed not to give off toxic fumes while Nikki
and Penny did everything else.

Nikki picks up my "adoption plan" packet and reads the first
unanswered question.

"Do you want the adoptive parents to be birth coaches?" she
asks, pen poised over the blank space.

"We talked with the doctor about that yesterday," Penny says.
"I'm planning to be Autumn's coach, unless you want to do it."

"I love being Autumn's coach for volleyball, and track, but I'll
leave this one to you."

"That's good," Penny says, laughing. "I already filled out the
forms with my name on them."

"Do you want the adoptive parents to be in the labor/delivery
room?"

"Definitely," Penny says, smiling across the table at me.

"You said here you don't want to spend time alone with the baby
in the hospital," Nikki says. "Are you sure?"

"I'm sure."

Nikki scans down to the next unanswered question.

"Do you think you'll want letters and pictures over time?"

I try not to go for that trip on "da Nile" that Ms. Lee warned me about. I try to think about how there really is going to be a baby, and how she's going to be here, in this house, growing up with Nikki and Penny.

"Yeah. I guess I might like to see some pictures."

"How often and when?" Nikki asks, her pen set to fill in the next blanks.

I shrug.

"Let's just say once or twice a year — maybe a birthday picture and a Christmas picture?"

"Sure," I say, unable to even think about how that might be. Like, will I be in a dorm room somewhere in San Luis Obispo, opening mail, and I'll get a picture of a little girl blowing out birthday candles? I can't even project my mind into that dorm room, much less to the pictures falling out of an envelope.

"Autumn?"

I look up at Nikki.

"Let's try to focus here. We want to drop these papers by Audrey's office on Monday."

"Okay," I say, standing up and stretching out my aching lower back.

"Are you all right?" Penny asks.

I nod and sit back down.

Nikki reads the next question.

"Do you want to see the child occasionally over the years? If so, how often?"

I sit looking at the form in front of Nikki, reading it upside down. It seems like a fantasy game, like that old game of "Life" where you have to make guesses about a pretend job, and pretend family — all pretend.

Nikki taps her pen against the unanswered question, getting impatient. I've watched her at practice, tap-tap-tapping her pen against her clipboard while she waits for a slow-moving player to get with the program.

"It might be better if Autumn doesn't see the baby, at least for the first couple of years or so," Penny says.

Nikki looks surprised.

"Why?"

"Well, you know . . . We'll want Nancy to know for sure that we're the moms. It could be confusing for her if Autumn was around."

"I don't need to see her," I say. "I'm not going to be her mom."

"Right. That's what I'm thinking," Penny says.

Nikki still doesn't fill in the blank.

"It wouldn't have to be confusing," Nikki says. "Not if we handle it right."

"I'm just saying it might be easier," Penny says.

"Well, think about it, Autumn. You can fill in this part tomorrow."

Penny goes to the freezer and gets a chocolate covered ice cream bar.

"Anyone else want one?"

"No thanks," I say.

"Too early for ice cream for me," Nikki says, tapping her pen against the next question.

Nikki taps when she gets nervous, and Penny eats. Me? I guess that's when I take a cruise on da Nile.

"Last question, Autumn — will anyone else want visiting privileges? Is there anyone you would specifically want to exclude?"

"No."

"You're sure?" Nikki says. "What about the father?"

"He won't even know," I say.

"That could be a problem," Nikki says.

"Why?"

"In California, the father has to sign a release for a baby to be adopted. It's not just the mother's decision."

Elvis jumps up on the table and licks at a dab of ice cream that's melted off Penny's Dove bar. I sit staring at Nikki, not believing what I've just heard.

"But it's *my* body — my decision!"

Nikki shakes her head. "That's true for abortions, but once there's a baby, the father has rights."

"According to Audrey, it's mostly just a formality," Penny says. "In her ten years of adoption consultation, she's never once had a father fight an adoption plan."

"She'd never had anyone pretend to be pregnant and cheat people out of thousands of dollars before, either," Nikki says, all sarcastic.

"But he doesn't even *know!*"

"Maybe it's better just to leave it that way," Penny says.

"And have him find out three years later and take the baby from us? That's not a chance we want to take. Besides, it wouldn't be right."

Elvis, having licked every last remaining molecule of ice cream from the table, slinks down onto my lap, purring. I scratch behind his ears.

Penny gets the disinfectant spray from below the sink, sprays the table, then wipes it down with a sponge.

"What about women who get raped by some stranger?" She asks. "Or who get so drunk they don't even know who they've had sex with? Or they've had sex with fifty guys in one month?"

"Every reasonable effort has to be made to find the father and inform him of the situation," Nikki says. "That's the law."

I'm thinking as hard and fast as I can. What if I say I don't know who the guy is? Like just somebody I met at a party, who maybe slipped some X in my drink, and I don't even know his name. That would be so much easier than trying to get Jason to sign a release. But . . . I'm tired of secrets, and half-truths. I want to get back to the old way, where I was honest with everyone and never had to worry about getting caught in a lie.

"Autumn? Is this going to be a problem?"

"I don't know," I say.

Penny looks shocked. "You mean he might not want to release the baby? Our baby?"

She closes her eyes, shaking her head slowly, back and forth, back and forth. Nikki reaches across the table and takes both Penny's hands in hers.

"Oh, Babe," she says, "Please. Don't cry."

She slides her chair close to Penny, who leans her head into Nikki's shoulder and lets the tears come.

I am suddenly tired — more than tired, exhausted. I push myself up from the table, barely aware of the surprised cat half-sliding, half-jumping to the floor. In the pink room I lie on the bed staring at the ceiling. The crib is put back together now, filled with teddy bears. Framed Disney pictures are back on the wall. What if it all has to be taken down again? I wanted to do something good, to be part of the solution, not part of the problem. I reach for the stone heart on the bedside table and hold it tight, trying to sense my father's love, trying to believe I'm still awesome.

By Sunday morning the storm has passed and the sky is bright and clear. Nikki asks if I'd like to go for a walk with her. I can tell by the way she asks that she's wanting more than just light exercise.

"Sure," I say, getting my sweatshirt from the pink room.

Nikki leaves a note for Penny, who still isn't up yet even though it's after ten o'clock.

We walk together, not talking, until we come to a little park I didn't even know was here. I can tell Nikki's making an effort to walk slowly so I can keep up. How sad! I used to be able to run way faster than Nikki and now I can't even keep up with her walking. I wonder if I'll ever get my old speed and strength back.

At the park, I follow Nikki over to the swings. We take the two middle ones and sit, barely moving, while Nikki drags her foot in the sand, drawing a line and covering it over. She finally looks over at me.

"We absolutely can't run the risk of losing another baby," she says. "We've got to get a release from the father."

I nod.

"If you want to go to another placement for teen moms, and release the baby to an agency, and let them worry about the father, then we'll help you get that set up."

I think about the place Miss F. told me about, where six pregnant teens, or teen moms, live together. A group home.

"I want to stay with you and Penny," I say, turning my swing to face Nikki. "I want you to have my baby."

Nikki takes a deep breath.

"Well, then, we've got to get a release from the father. You've got to let him know you're pregnant, and work it out. And you've got to do it soon because Penny and I aren't doing so well on the old baby adoption roller coaster."

Now it's my turn to drag my feet in the sand and cover the lines over.

I picture Jason in my mind — try to guess what he might say, how he might react. I'm not sure, but I don't think it's going to be easy.

"Do you know the guy's address?"

"Yeah. I've got it in my organizer."

"Write it down for me when we get back and I'll take it to Audrey when I drop the other papers off . . . I want her to get started on that paternal consent right away."

"How does that work?"

"I don't know for sure. I'll find out more about it on Monday. I think she'll send a letter informing him of paternity, and something for him to sign saying he gives his permission for the baby to be adopted."

"I'd like to tell him first," I say, "before he gets the letter."

"Okay. You just need to make it soon."

"He's in Iowa, in college. But he'll be home for Christmas."

"We need to get going on this before Christmas."

"But I'd like to tell him face to face."

"All I know is, we'll be moving along on the legal end of things. How you decide to deal with it personally is up to you . . . What's this guy's name, anyway?" Nikki asks.

"Jason. Jason Garcia."

"That guy that used to come to our games, and root for you and Danni?"

"Yeah."

"The guy that Danni had the hots for?"

I nod.

"Does Danni know who the father is?"

"No."

"Does she even know you're pregnant?"

"Yeah. I saw her just the other day. But I didn't say it was Jason and I didn't say I was giving the baby to you and Penny."

Nikki shakes her head. "It's like we're living a damned soap opera right now. I hope whoever's writing the script likes happy endings."

Back home I find Jason's address and write it out for Nikki.

"Thanks. I'll call Audrey first thing Monday morning and have her overnight the forms."

Gad! It's possible Jason could be getting information in the mail from Audrey as early as Tuesday! I go into the pink room and get my cell phone, wondering how I'm going to say what I have to say. I press the symbol beside Jason's name and wait, my heart pounding fast. An out-of-service recording comes on.

In the den, I log on to my email account. After a lot of starting and deleting and starting over again I end up with:

Hey Jason — I just tried your cell phone and got an out-of-service message. Do you have a new number? Or could you call my cell? It's working again. I really need to talk to you. I wish it could be face to face, but I don't think it can wait until Christmas. — Autumn

22

"If you'll please put your books away for now, we'll do a timed writing," Karen says.

Every day we do a timed writing as practice for the writing proficiency exam. I passed all of my proficiencies in my freshman year at Hamilton High, but I guess not everyone else has. I do the timed writings anyway, for English credits. I close my American Government textbook, happy to take a break from "The National Judiciary and a Dual Court System."

I take two sheets of lined paper from my notebook.

"Can I borrow a sheet of paper?" Tiffany says, holding her hand out as if she already knows the answer.

I hand the paper to her and look at the timed-writing topic Karen has just written on the board. She reads out loud:

"Write about life from your baby's point of view. What is he/she experiencing and noticing? What's she afraid of? What's he happy about? What might he/she be expecting from life?"

Tiffany groans. "How would I know?"

"You don't know," Karen says. "I'm just asking you to make

some guesses."

Heather asks, "Can I just write a whole page of 'My gums hurt and I don't want my mom to sleep?"

Karen laughs and shakes her head. "Get creative."

Another girl, Olivia, says "I haven't even met my baby yet, how can I write anything from his perspective?"

"Make it up," Karen says, sitting down at her desk and looking through a school furniture catalog, marking pages along the way.

There's more grumbling about how stupid the assignment is, but Karen seems not to notice. I feel a flutter kick on the lower left side and try to imagine what that's like from the baby's perspective. I think about the sonogram picture. I wonder if the baby can hear anything from inside me? I decide to pretend she can. I start writing from her imaginary point of view:

> It's dark in here, and comfortable, but it can also be kind of boring. It feels crowded sometimes, too. When I heard one of the girls in this class was carrying two babies I was shocked! I wouldn't want to be sharing this tiny space with another baby.
>
> Sometimes when I start feeling closed in, I turn a kind of somersault to get in a better position. And sometimes I kick my mom just to make her notice me. Sometimes she even groans when I do that. Oh, and there's a way I can turn that puts a lot of pressure on her bladder and makes her run to the bathroom. That's the best! But she's already told me she's not really my mom. She doesn't love me so she's going to give me to someone who will. When I hear some of the other girls in here talking about how much they already love their babies, and they can't wait to hold them in their arms, I wish I'd ended up inside one of them. But then, when I hear that those same girls drink sodas all day long, and never eat vegetables or drink milk, I'm glad to be growing strong and healthy inside Autumn. And then I think, maybe she does love me just a little bit, if she's being careful about what she feeds me. Or sometimes I hear another woman on the outside telling my not-mom to drink some milk, or keep her feet dry, and I think maybe that's the one who will love me. I hope someone will.

I put my name and date in the upper right hand corner and turn the paper face down. This is the first time I've ever even thought about how things might be for the baby inside me. The minute class is over I check my phone messages. There's one from Krystal, which I'll return later. Nothing from Jason. The first thing I do when I get home is check my email. There's nothing from Jason there, either. I try again.

Hey Jason — Not that I want to bug you or anything, but I really, really need to talk to you. — Autumn

Next I email Danni and ask if she has a new number for Jason. I call Krystal, but her phone, as always, is busy.

Finally, Tuesday afternoon, there is a message from Jason.

Autumn — There's someone else in my life now — someone who truly loves me. I'll always remember our good times as kids, and I'll try to forget how much you hurt me. I'm looking forward now, not back, and I'd rather not talk with you. I'm sure you can understand that. — Jason

I read the message over and over, trying to take in what it says, what it means. Jason's finally stopped wanting to be with me. Why doesn't that feel like a wish come true? Why do I feel like crying?

Jason — Okay. I get it. You don't want to talk to me. But there's something you need to know.

I go to the kitchen and take an orange from the bowl of fruit Penny keeps on the counter. While I stand at the sink, peeling the orange, images of other times race through my head — Jason and Danni and I in the third grade, with our award-winning Native American village. Penny's laughter as she reassembled the baby crib. Jason's birthday and all that went with it. Underneath it all, like always, are fleeting glimpses of Dad, and Grams, and Casper.

The orange is sweet and juicy and the scent of orange peel fills the kitchen. I rinse my hands, go back to the computer and continue my message to Jason. I'm determined to sit here until I've sent him the whole story. Maybe it's best to be blunt.

*I'm pregnant. The baby is due in February. It's a girl. I
didn't tell you at first because I planned to have an abortion
and I was afraid you'd try to stop me. Then there was all of
that time after the accident when I was not thinking straight.
When I sort of woke up from that, it was too late to get an
abortion. No way do I want a baby right now, and even if I
did, I couldn't possibly give it a good life. I've already signed
the adoption release forms. Right now, I'm staying with the
people who will be adopting the baby. They're very nice people. Some time today or tomorrow you'll get some information from the adoption consultant, and there will be a release
form for you to sign. I wanted you to hear about all of this
from me, before the letter gets to you. I'm sorry I hurt you. I
never meant to. Your friend — Autumn.*

Minutes after I press "send" my cell phone rings. It's Jason.
"This is totally bizarre," he says. "I don't believe it!"
"It's true!"
"Well it can't be mine! The only time we ever did anything was
clear back in May. I saw you in September and you weren't preg-
nant then!"
"I was, too! You just didn't notice!"
"You were playing volleyball! How could you have been preg-
nant? I'm not buying it."
"So don't then! Just sign the paper that says you deny pater-
nity!"
"So whose is it, anyway? I'm just curious."
I hang up. The phone rings again. I turn it off. Gad I wish I could
go for a run — run off anger, and hurt, and frustration and loss! Instead I walk over to the park where Nikki and I went the other day.
   I watch from a distance as a woman, the mom I guess, helps her
little kid into one of the baby swings and straps her in. I decide it's
"her" because she's wearing a pink stocking cap and a pink sweater.
The mom squats down in front of the baby and gently pushes her
back and forth. Every time the swing comes forward, close to the
mom, the baby reaches out and laughs, which gets the mom laughing, too.

At school I hardly notice the babies at the infant center. I sort of keep to myself and get as much work done as possible, so even if I'm out of school for a few weeks when the baby's born, I'll still have enough credits to graduate on time. I can't help noticing now, though, that this mom is pretty happy with her baby. And I think about Gavin and Barry, how happy they seemed with little Dalton. But Gavin and Barry aren't kids. The mom over at the baby swings isn't a kid. I'm still a kid. I wouldn't be happy with a baby. Nikki and Penny will be happy with Nancy. I remind myself she's their baby.

"**C**old out?" Penny asks as I walk into the warm kitchen.

"A little," I admit, rubbing my hands together to warm them up.

She's washing a whole stack of Christmas plates and cups and saucers. The cups and saucers are white, with green and red trim around the edges. The plates have the same trim, but they also have big green Christmas trees in the middle.

Penny hands me a dishtowel.

"When I was home for Thanksgiving, my mother packed these up in an extra suitcase and sent them back with me as an early Christmas present," she says, rinsing a plate and putting it on the counter for me to dry.

"Growing up, I used to love seeing her get these dishes out in December. It meant Christmas was coming . . . You can just stack them on the table and I'll put them away later."

I dry carefully, looking at the perfectly balanced green tree centered in the middle of the plate, remembering the straggly tree Dad chose last year because he said it needed a home.

"I talked to Jason this afternoon," I say, picking up a cup to dry.

Penny puts another clean cup on the counter.

"You told him?"

"I told him everything except who I'm staying with and who the adoptive parents will be."

"And?"

"And he doesn't believe he's the father. I think he's going to sign that denial of paternity thing."

Penny breaks into a huge smile.

"Perfect!"

She attacks the dishwashing task with new energy, then sets the table with three Christmas plates and puts the rest away. She gets out red napkins, and puts a ceramic Santa Claus in the middle of the table.

"Christmas already?" Nikki says as she steps through the back door.

Penny laughs.

"You wouldn't be ready for Christmas until January if it weren't for me."

"I guess you're right," Nikki says, smiling.

At dinner I go through the whole Jason story again for Nikki. I tell her about the email, the telephone call, Jason's reaction. She's not as elated as Penny was.

"What if he changes his mind later? I'd rather have him admit he's the father and sign the consent form."

"What difference does it make?" Penny says. "Either way Baby Nancy is ours."

"I don't know. I want to talk to Audrey about it."

When Danni and I meet again at Jamba Juice, we order our drinks and go straight to the car.

"This is definitely not going to be a conversation for public consumption," I tell her.

I'm barely situated in the passenger seat with the door closed when Danni asks, "Who's the father?"

I take a deep breath.

"Jason."

"JASON!"

"Uh-huh."

"JASON GARCIA???"

"Uh-huh."

I tell her everything, starting with how he suddenly thought I was the one for him, and ending with how he doesn't believe he got me pregnant. She sits there, wide-eyed, through the whole story. Then I start apologizing all over the place, for not telling her in the very beginning that he was after me, for just going along with her schemes to get him to like her, for not telling her I was pregnant as soon as I knew, for not telling her right away when I got my period, for hitting her for scribbling on my pictures of a tree . . .

She starts laughing.

"What?"

She laughs harder.

"Danni? What???"

She wipes her eyes, shakes her head helplessly, and shrieks with laughter. I have no idea what she's laughing about but I dare anyone to witness one of Danni's laughing fits and not join in. Once I get started laughing, I'm as bad as she is — worse because . . .

I run from the car into the Jamba Juice restroom, almost in time. I'm drying my thighs and blotting my underwear with paper towels, when there's a loud banging on the door.

"Let me in!" Danni calls.

I open the door and she rushes to the toilet, which is the funniest thing ever. When our laughter finally subsides, and I'm as clean as I can get, we walk out of Jamba Juice, not looking at anyone at the tables, or the counter, and go straight down to Starbucks at the other end of the center.

"We can absolutely never go back to that place again," Danni says.

Even though it's chilly, we sit at an outside table. We want more privacy than we'd have inside where it's crowded with people. Besides, we're not buying anything.

"I was afraid . . . you know . . . when I told you about Jason, you'd hate me."

Danni shakes her head.

"I'm too happy with Evan to be mad over Jason."

"But if I'd told you months ago, before Evan? Like maybe I should have?"

"I don't know. On the way home last week, I started wondering how we could still be friends — especially the almost-sister kind of friends. It was like there was a whole huge part of you that I didn't even know — all of those secrets for so long. The more I thought about it, the angrier I got."

The baby does one of those somersault things and I shift around in the hard, metal chair trying to get comfortable.

"By the time I picked Hannah up from soccer practice, I was

fuming. But then she started talking about you, like she'd maybe sensed that you'd been in the car or something. Remember how she used to pretend she was a cat? And she could pick up our scent and follow us wherever we went?"

"Yeah, and she actually did find us once when we were trying to hide from her — like she'd sniffed us out."

Danni nods.

"Anyway, she started saying again that she missed you, and it wasn't as much fun having just one sister. . . so I told her maybe you weren't much of an almost-sister to us because you'd kept a lot of important secrets from us. She made her eyes go all squinty, like she does when she's mad, and she told me 'That's so stupid! She's still our almost-sister! She's still the essence of Autumn!' That's exactly what she said — the essence of Autumn."

"She's so cool. I really miss her."

"Well . . . I didn't admit it to her, but she was right. Whatever secrets you've had, you're still you and we're still almost-sisters."

"You're a better friend than I deserve," I tell her.

"How about you email that to me a thousand times," she laughs.

I stand and stretch my back.

"There's still more I have to tell you, but it's another really long story."

"C'mon. You can't just say that and then make me wait another week for the next installment!" she says, standing.

"No, really. It's too complicated."

We walk back to the car. On the way to the library she tells me more about Evan, how he used to be into drugs and then he found Christ. I glance at the picture of Jesus hanging from the mirror and wonder how Danni finds it so easy to believe and I don't.

When I get out at the library, I say to Danni, "I'm glad we're sure about being almost-sisters, but I don't think we'll ever share a mother again."

"Don't say that. I'm working on her."

"How?" I say, leaning back into the car.

Danni gives me a sort of condescending smile.

"You're not the only one with complicated stories," she says. "See you next week!"

She leans over, pulls the car door shut, and drives away with a wave. I call Penny to pick me up, then wait for her just inside the library doors, where it's warm.

In the evening I tell Nikki I don't want to keep any more secrets from Danni. I want to tell her where I'm living, and about our adoption plans.

"I've been thinking about that, too," she says. "We've got all of the legal stuff taken care of now — official foster placement for you, and the pre-adoption papers are all in order. Jason FAXED his denial of paternity to Audrey's office first thing this morning."

"It's a lie," I say.

"Well . . . that's between you and Jason, I guess. All it means to us is that he won't be getting in the way of adoption plans."

"What if he decides to tell the truth later on?"

"Yeah, I wondered about that, too. According to Audrey, he'd have to go through a big, expensive legal hassle to change things. He's essentially rescinded any paternal rights."

Nikki's quiet for a while, then she grins at me and says, "So . . . I guess we're getting a baby!"

"Does Penny know Jason sent the form in?"

"I left a message for her on her cell. She's been stuck in meetings all afternoon and half the night, but we'll probably be able to hear her shout for joy as soon as she picks up messages."

"So is it okay for me to tell Danni now?"

Nikki nods.

"I don't want to make a big announcement at school, but I'm sick of acting like we have something to be ashamed of. Tell whoever you want."

The phone rings and Nikki rushes to pick up. I hear her soft laughter and then she says, "It's true. We're going to be mommies."

She listens a while, then says "Love you, too," and hangs up.

Nikki comes back into the den and pulls a chair up next to where I sit working at the computer. She's got the kind of broad, beaming smile she gets when we win an especially tough game.

"Any kicks?" she asks, reaching tentatively toward my belly.

I slide my chair back.

"She was pretty active a few minutes ago," I say.

Nikki puts her hand gently on my belly.

"Come on, Nancy," she says. "Give Mommy a kick!"

We sit very quietly for a while, waiting. Nothing happens.

"She already questions authority," Nikki says with a grin.

"Goodnight, Autumn. And thank you."

It's funny. All along it's seemed like only Penny was interested in getting the baby, and Nikki was just doing it for Penny's sake. But now I'm thinking Nikki was just holding back, afraid to hope. And now that everything's signed, she can let herself be happy.

23

Saturday Penny and Nikki and I go to a tree lot back behind the Safeway market. Nikki and I find one we like right away, but Penny says it's too lopsided. We look up one row and down the next, looking at fir trees, pines, and spruces. I swear she's trying to find one that's as perfect as the picture on her plates. Finally, though, we settle on an almost perfect tree, tie it onto the Subaru, and drive it home at about fifteen miles an hour.

Nikki selects Christmas music from her iTunes library and hooks her iPod up to the living room speakers. Penny drags boxes of decorations from the hall closet, and we spend the afternoon decorating the tree, putting candles on every table, and draping garland over all the doorways. Nikki secures a giant red wreath to the front door and proclaims the task done.

"I think we need more lights on the tree," Penny says. "Don't you?"

"No! Stop!" Nikki says, smiling. "Already we're going to double our electricity bill this month!"

Penny steps back and assesses the tree.

"Okay, but next Christmas, for Nancy, we're going to have to add a lot more lights. Babies love lights."

"Okay, Mommy P," Nikki says.

That's what they've started calling each other, Mommy P. and Mommy J.

On Sunday, we decide to go to the big mall in Pasadena and get started on our Christmas shopping. Penny and Nikki give me $250.

"The state sends us a check each month to help pay for your food, and clothing, and other necessities," Nikki says. "But there's always extra."

"Thanks, but . . ."

"No buts," Penny says.

At the mall we go our separate ways, deciding to meet up again in an hour. Penny goes into a decorator shop to look for something for her parents, and Nikki goes down to the other end, to a kitchen shop, to look for something for Ella and Sandy. They are both carrying long lists of people to buy for. Earlier this morning I started a list, too. Compared to last year's, it's not very long.

I sit on a bench in front of the fountain, watching the water rise and fall, trying to decide where to start.

I'll get something for Danni, and Hannah, and Penny and Nikki. I'd like to get something for Madison, too, but what's the use? She can't keep anything personal.

Here are some of the people from last year's list that I won't be shopping for today. Carole and Donald — they're not exactly part of my life anymore. And Jason? Nope — guess not. And I won't need to buy a drawing gift for the party at Dad's work. And, of course, I won't be buying for Grams and Dad. I always got each of them something nice, and something funny. Last year, for a funny gift, I got Dad a fake toupee because I always liked to tease him that he was going bald. "Just wait and see," I'd say. "In two years you won't have a single hair left on your head." I wonder if that's going to be true. I heard somewhere that your hair and fingernails keep growing after you're dead, but . . . Shite! Why am I even thinking about that?

At the Discovery Store I find a very cool lava lamp for Hannah. At Banana Republic, for Danni, I choose a cream colored silk blouse that's fitted at the waist. Leaving the store, I realize I chose that style because it's what I wish I could be wearing. I take it out of the bag and look at it again. I'm pretty sure she'll like it. But I'll save the receipt, just in case.

I get a slow-cooker for Penny. She's been complaining that the one she uses now isn't big enough. Nikki? I don't know. Maybe a subscription to *Women's Sports.*

On my way to the kitchen shop I pass the Pet Boutique where every Christmas I used to buy a bag of gourmet dog biscuits for Casper, and breath sweetening chew bones. As a working dog, he didn't do toys, but he did love those special dog biscuits. I walk quickly past the little shop, trying not to think, or feel, or cry.

I'm remembering what the psychologist in *Ordinary People* told Conrad, that depression is a reduction of feeling. He's always pushing Conrad not to keep a lid on it, to cry, or vent, or whatever. I don't know about that. I feel safer keeping my awful sadness to myself.

Wednesday Danni and I meet at Starbucks, even though we don't like coffee.

"Maybe after the baby's born and my hair grows out, no one will recognize us back at Jamba Juice."

"Easy for you. I'll still look like the same old me."

"Well . . . Maybe you could get pregnant? That would definitely change your looks."

"Not funny," Danni says.

We each get bottled water and sit at a table that's kind of tucked behind a display rack.

"You tell me your complicated story first," I say.

Danni looks at me blankly.

"You know. You said you were working on your mother, and it was too complicated to tell right then."

"Oh, yeah. Well . . . when I found out what Mom'd really done . . . I mean, she didn't exactly lie about anything but she sure didn't tell the truth. Like, I could have been visiting you all that time you were in the home, or calling, or writing, whatever . . . Anyway, I was sooooo mad. And she started in on that stuff about what a terrible example it would be for Hannah to see you pregnant, and what it would do to my reputation for you to be pregnant, and then she started quoting all of this Bible stuff about unclean women, and plucking out your eye if it offends you . . . I swear it's like she's memorized the whole Bible and she's got this database in her head that lets her pull out whatever she needs to prove a point. She went into this whole long rant and then she said that was the end of it. She didn't want to hear another thing about it. Like she'd heard anything! I didn't get a chance to say one more word after I brought the subject up."

Finally, Danni pauses for breath.

"So how are you working on her?"

"Well, I was so mad, I told Evan what my mom had done . . ."

"You told Evan about me??"

"Not your name or anything. Just the situation."

"You said you wouldn't tell anyone . . ."

"No. Come on! He doesn't even know you!"

I wonder who else she's told, but then I think how tired I am of secrets and decide it doesn't matter.

"So he helped me find some better Bible verses, mostly from the New Testament. So I've been writing them out and leaving them places where I know she'll find them. Like this morning she found a note in the coffee cup that she got from the cupboard. It said, "Let whoever is without sin cast the first stone.""

"What did she say?"

"Nothing, but I'll wear her down eventually, you'll see. A few days ago she found "First remove the beam from your own eye. Then you will see clearly to cast the mote from the eye of another.""

"What's that mean?"

"I don't know. Evan said it would be a good one to use . . ."

"Be right back!" I say, rushing off to the restroom.

When I get back I apologize for leaving so fast, but sometimes it's just necessary.

"It's okay," Danni says. "So now your turn. What new secrets do I get to hear about today?"

"Maybe we should go back to your car," I say, anticipating some of the possible responses Danni will make when she hears first that I'm releasing the baby for adoption and then who the adoptive parents are going to be.

When we get in the car, Danni sits staring at the picture hanging from the mirror. Then she says,

"I'm totally Christian. I really am. And I agree with my mom about a lot of stuff. But I don't think Jesus would have kicked you out of our house. Jesus doesn't kick people out, no matter what."

I hope she'll still remember that by the time I finish telling her about my adoption plan. I talk as fast as I can, faster than Danni did just a few minutes ago when she talked about her mom. I spit out the details, racing to get it over with. Danni listens intently, her mouth half open.

"You're adopting your baby out?" she asks, as if she hasn't quite heard my whole speech.

"I'm giving her a good home. A good chance in life. No way can I take care of a baby."

"I could help," Danni says. "I'd be a good godmother."

"Where will you be next year?"

"College."

"Right. That's where I want to be, too. Not working at Pizza Hut to buy diapers."

"So . . . can she still be Genny with a G?"

"No. She won't be my baby. I won't name her."

"But did you tell them about Genny with a G? They might like that idea."

It's funny. I worried that Danni would give me a lot, I mean a lot, of shite about adoption, and I thought she might get really crazy when I told her who the adoptive parents would be. But all she's worried about is the name? So okay, that's easy to deal with.

"She's going to be Nancy, after Nancy Drew."

"Could she be Nancy Genny?"

"I guess you could suggest it."

When it's time to leave, Danni takes me back to Nikki and Penny's.

"Wow! Great tree!" she says, noticing the already lit tree in the corner windows.

"Do you want to come in and see it?"

She glances at the clock.

"Well, I guess it won't matter if I'm just a few minutes late."

Penny is at the table writing Christmas cards.

"Danni wants to see our tree up close," I say.

Penny looks up.

"Oh, hi. Danni is it? I think I saw you at a game a while back."

"Probably," Danni says.

She oohs and aahs over the tree, noticing each ornament and asking where it comes from. Penny happily explains the details.

"Come see if you think Hannah will like this," I say, walking down the hall to the pink room. Danni follows. I take the lava lamp from its box to show her, but she doesn't even look.

"Oh, this is sooooo sweet," she says, doing that high voiced sugary thing. "Oh, look at this!" She picks up a teddy bear and hugs it close. "And the pictures!"

"Uh, Danni? Can I show you this?"

She looks over at me like I'm the president of the anti-fun club or something.

"What?"

I show her the lamp.

"Do you think Hannah will like this?"

"Yeah. It's nice," she says, giving a quick glance before she takes the stuffed dog from the top of the dresser.

"Oh, I love this. Isn't it cute?"

I think about the silk blouse from Banana Republic. Maybe I should return it and get a stuffed dog instead.

On Christmas day a lot of the same people from Thanksgiving come to Nikki and Penny's house for dinner. Danni brings Hannah over later in the afternoon. While she's following Elvis around trying to get him to let her pet him, I ask Danni, in a whisper, if her mom knows they've come to see me.

"No, but what she doesn't know won't hurt her."

"Is that from the Bible, too?" I ask.

"I'm not sure. Maybe."

"Does Hannah know I'm having a baby?"

"No. I told her you got fat, and just to pretend not to notice so you wouldn't be embarrassed. That's not exactly a lie, is it?"

"Not exactly," I say.

I don't like to think of myself as fat, but one glance at my belly tells me to get off da Nile.

After she opens her gift, Hannah wants to set the lamp up right away, so she can watch what it does once it's warmed up.

The blouse looks great on Danni, and I suddenly feel even fatter, and awkward and dowdy and ugly and any other unflattering word you could find in the dictionary.

Hannah gives me a green and purple braided friendship bracelet that she made herself.

"It's for when you don't see me for a long time, you won't forget me," she says.

I give her a big hug, and even though she's been warned not to notice that I'm fat, she's noticing.

Danni gives me a gift certificate to Jamba Juice, which gets us both laughing hysterically. Hannah goes off to watch TV, mad because she doesn't know what we're laughing about.

"I have something else for you," Danni says, once we've calmed down. "Mom asked me to give this to you."

"I thought she didn't know you were here."

"She doesn't, exactly. But she knows we've been in touch. And she knows I wouldn't let the holidays pass without seeing you somewhere along the way."

Danni takes a package wrapped in silver paper from her purse and hands it to me.

"Open it."

I remove the paper and open the box. Inside is a white leather Bible with my name engraved in gold.

"Look inside," Danni says.

On the flyleaf, in Carole's flowery handwriting, it says, "To one who is always in my heart and in my prayers. Let this be your foundation. Yours in Christ, Carole Genevieve Hopkins."

"Isn't that sweet?"

I nod, not knowing what to say. Does it mean Carole cares? Or does it mean she'll only care if I read the Bible?

I run my hand over the soft leather.

"It's a pretty book," I say.

"I knew you'd like it."

I only said it was pretty. I didn't say I liked it. But I don't clarify that.

After Danni and Hannah leave I go back into the dining room, where people are having dessert.

"What did Danni give you?" Nikki asks.

I show her the gift certificate, and Hannah's bracelet, and the Bible from Carole.

"Are you religious?"

"Not really."

"Well, parts of the Bible are a good read, anyway," Glenn says.

"I thought you were an atheist?" Kim says.

"I am, but that doesn't mean I can't appreciate the Bible," he says.

That gets them all talking about religion.

"I'd be dead by now if I didn't have faith in a higher power," Sandy says.

"Or at least dead drunk," Ella says.

Gavin says he's a Buddhist. Barry's an ex-Baptist turned Episcopalian.

"I looked around for a long time and finally found a church where I felt welcome."

"What about Dalton?" Nikki asks. "Will you raise him to be Buddhist or Episcopalian?"

"Probably Episcopalian, with Buddhist leanings."

"Interesting combination," Sandy says.

"How about Baby Nancy?" Barry asks.

"Well . . . we're pretty welcome with the Unitarians," Penny says, "but we're not much for rushing out to church on Sunday mornings."

"We don't have to decide that just yet," Nikki says, laughing.

"She'll need something to rebel against when she's older," Ella says. "Why not start her out as a Catholic? That's what my parents did."

"Then she can morph into your kind of a Mother Mary Beatles Catholic?"

"Hey, it works for me," Ella says, then starts singing in a surprisingly beautiful voice:

"When I find myself in times of trouble, mother Mary comes to me, speaking words of wisdom, let it be. And in my hour of darkness

she is standing right in front of me, speaking words of wisdom, let it be."

The rest of the people at the table join in on the chorus, *"Let it be, let it be, let it be, let it be. Whisper words of wisdom, let it be."*

I am suddenly filled with a sense of overwhelming loneliness. I mutter an excuse and go back to the pink room where I lie on the bed, longing for my own family singing that other Beatles song, and for the scrawny tree. Longing for all that is lost.

Nikki comes to check on me.

"I just feel tired," I say. "The doctor said it's good to take an afternoon nap."

"Sure. We'll see you after you're rested."

Nikki closes the door gently behind her and I will myself to sleep.

In the morning I put the Bible in the bottom drawer, next to the photo album Carole made for me. Maybe someday I'll start reading it. Maybe not. If there's a God watching over us, like Carole says, why did He let my family die? Why does He let such horrible things happen in the world? But then I think of what Jason said about God that night under the stars, and what Sandy was saying about a "higher power," and I think maybe there's more to God than what I've heard from Carole.

Once Christmas is over and everyone's back in school, things move along pretty quickly. Penny goes with me to every doctor's visit. She listens to the baby's heartbeat and asks questions I'd never think to ask. She wants to know if the baby can hear music, or voices. She's read somewhere that it's good to play Mozart while babies are still in the womb, so we play Mozart at dinner every evening.

After dinner every night we do "kick counts." I lie down on my side, on the couch, and Penny holds her hands over my belly. We're supposed to see how long it takes the baby to move ten times. If it takes longer than two hours we're supposed to call the doctor. But usually she kicks ten times in less than an hour. It's a sign of good health.

Penny signs us up for a prepared childbirth class that starts on Janaury 14th and lasts for four weeks. Suddenly I'm scared. Not about the things I was scared about before, people finding out I was pregnant, or keeping other secrets, or losing Danni's friendship, or being stuck in the county home. Now I'm scared about the physical stuff. There's a baby inside me, and it's got to get out through a little, teeny, tiny opening.

They say — Karen, and the prepared childbirth leaders — that before the baby is born that little tiny hole gets bigger. I've looked at the diagrams in the childbirth book. Most of the girls at school who've already had their babies put their labor and delivery experiences somewhere along a scale from "not too bad" to "wonderful!" There is one girl who loves to talk about how horrible it was — excruciating pain that went on for days, but that's the same girl who just yesterday spent most of the morning crying and writhing in agony over a paper cut.

In our first childbirth class we go around the room and introduce ourselves. We tell our due dates, and what we hope to accomplish in the class. There's one other teenager in the group, a girl who's fourteen and whose mother is with her. Another woman brought her mother, and one is with her sister. The rest are with the babies' fathers. We're all pretty much here for the same reason, to know what to expect during labor and delivery, and to learn how to deal with it.

Every afternoon when Penny gets home from school, she coaches me in relaxation techniques and breathing rhythms. We practice a mad-cat exercise where I get on my hands and knees and arch my back and then push my stomach toward the floor. Yesterday when I was down on the floor arching my back, Elvis hissed at me. I guess I make a pretty convincing mad cat.

Monday morning there's a notice on the whiteboard:

Victor Munoz, 7 lbs. 6 oz., January 29, 3:13 a.m.

Proud Parents: Tiffany Sanchez and Hector Munoz

"Tiffany called me early this morning," Karen says. "Everything went well. She'll be home this afternoon."

Wednesday, at nutrition break, Tiffany stops by to show off the baby. Everyone hovers around and says how cute he is. I walk out to the parking lot with her, where Hector is waiting.

"I won't say it didn't hurt," she tells me, "but it was pretty easy. And look what I got for it!" she says, beaming down on baby Victor.

Hector gets out of the car and opens the door.

"It was harder on him," Tiffany says, nodding her head in his direction.

"Shit! I ain't never goin' through that again!" he says.

He takes the baby from Tiffany and carefully secures him in the infant seat. I watch them drive away thinking if I'd done things differently, that could have been me with Jason. I remind myself that I'm a kid. I remind myself that I didn't love Jason.

CHAPTER

24

With what I think of as nagging, and Penny refers to as encouragement, we finally complete my "Year After Birth Plan" to our adoption consultant's satisfaction.

For the month or so after delivery, while I'm "recovering," I'll be staying with Sandy and Ella. Both Penny and Audrey think that's best — so Penny and Nikki can bond with the baby, and I won't be trying to get in on the mommy act. That's fine with me. The more I'm around Sandy and Ella, the more I like them, plus I'll like being close to the beach.

I've talked with Wayne, Casper's trainer, and he's helped me get set up with a job at the training center. He said the main supervisor remembered me from my internship and is eager to have me back. I'll be there until school starts in August. Nikki's been talking with the recruiter at Cal Poly, and I may still be able to get the scholarship. That's the only part of my plan that Audrey's not satisfied with, because it's still not certain.

"We need a back-up plan," she keeps saying.

Nikki tells her she's sure things will work out. I'm not worried, because when Nikki thinks things will work out, they usually do.

Between the childbirth classes, and all I've learned in the TAPP program, and hearing all about Tiffany's experience when she had Victor, by the time I feel my first contraction, I'm pretty relaxed about the whole thing and ready to get it over with.

I've been so uncomfortable these last few weeks, I've had a hard time sleeping. And I'm hecka tired of feeling like a blimp. So when I realize the twinges I've been getting are probably the beginning of labor, I'm actually relieved.

Sometime around three-thirty in the morning, I turn on the bedside lamp and start timing things. A little before five I knock on Nikki and Penny's bedroom door.

"I think labor's starting," I say.

Penny opens the door, all smiles. Nikki sits up in bed, rubbing her eyes. We sit in the den, timing contractions. Penny calls Dr. Tully with a report, and the doctor says it's probably time to go to the hospital. Penny and Nikki both call for substitutes, and we're dressed and in the car within about ten minutes.

At the hospital, after a while of not much happening, things become more intense.

Penny sits on a stool, facing me, cueing me to take short, quick breaths, the way we practiced in birthing class.

"Inhale. In. In. Exhale. Ex. Ex."

"In. In. In. Ex. Ex. Ex."

I follow her lead, three quick gasps in, three quick puffs out. A nurse comes in and takes my chart from the folder at the end of the bed.

"Are you timing contractions?" she asks.

"About three minutes," Penny says, continuing to cue my breathing by raising her hand in three jerky motions for inhales and lowering it three jerky times for exhales.

"Keep it up. You're doing great," Penny tells me.

A pain starts low in my back, encircles my belly, moves lower, tighter, so tight the room turns bright blue. I reach for Penny's hand, gripping with all my might.

"In. In. In . . . " she chants.

The nurse steps to the other side of the bed and places her hand on my belly. I breathe fast and hard until the pain gradually subsides. I feel something warm and wet under my butt, like I've let loose with gallons of pee.

"I think I wet the bed," I say, all embarrassed.

The nurse checks the bed pad and smiles at me.

"You didn't wet the bed. Your amniotic sac broke. That's good," she says. "Things will go faster now."

She fusses around under my back and butt, getting rid of the soaked pad and putting a clean one under me.

Penny wipes my face with a cool, damp washcloth. The nurse jots some notes on my chart and says she'll be back to check on me in a few minutes.

"When can we expect to see Doctor Tully?" Penny asks.

"She should be here within the next hour or so."

"Do you want to walk around some?" Penny says. "It might help."

I nod and lean forward. Penny puts her arm around me and helps me up. We walk down the hall to where Nikki sits reading the newspaper.

"How're you doing?"

"We're thinking a little walk might help," Penny says.

Nikki offers to walk with me so Penny can go for a bite to eat, but she doesn't want to leave. The three of us walk down the long hallway, past the nursery with babies lined up in little plastic crib things, then back around to the waiting room. I have to keep stopping so often to breathe through contractions, I decide to go back to the room and lie down.

Moments after Penny helps me back on the bed, my whole lower body tightens in a pushing cramp. Sweat pours from my face and chest.

Penny prompts me back to my breathing pattern, then has me try a relaxation technique we learned in the childbirth class. It helps a little.

Dr. Tully comes in and checks my chart. She puts her hand on my belly to feel the contraction.

"Let's take a look," she says, moving to the foot of the bed and taking sterile gloves from the nurse.

Dr. T. pokes around, then stands up, trashes the gloves and

washes her hands.

"Getting close," she says.

Another sharp pain! I grab Penny's hand and squeeze with all my might, panting hard and fast.

"We'll give you a shot of demerol," Dr. T. says. "You'll still feel the pains, but it won't be as intense."

"Turn on your side," the nurse says.

I feel a quick stab on my butt just as another contraction begins.

"Not long now," Dr. T. says.

I'm panting, breathing, sweating, pushing. It feels like a thick, tough elastic band is squeezing my belly and back, tightening, compressing.

Pressure — starting above my belly button and gathering force — an internal tidal wave. My body, no longer mine to control, gathers force and pushes.

The nurse leans with full force on my upper abdomen.

"That's it! Push!"

"GOD!"

"We're getting there, Honey. Push!"

I push. The nurse leans.

Penny wipes my forehead.

A moment's relief and then here comes another one, bearing down, bearing down, bearing down and then — a cry, and Penny, sobbing.

"She's here, Autumn. It's baby Nancy. And oh, she's beautiful. She's so beautiful."

Doctor T. lays the wet, red slippery baby on my belly. I reach up and touch her fresh, new skin. She's crying — not hard, just enough to show that her lungs are working. I run my thumb gently over the top of her toes, first one foot and then the other. Her second and third toes are joined together. "She's one of us," I think, and I'm filled with love for this tiny baby, this part of me, and Dad, and Grams.

Penny cuts the umbilical cord, just like we planned. A nurse takes the baby away for a few minutes, then brings her back all clean and wrapped tightly in a soft white blanket. She places the baby close beside me in the bed. I put my arm around the tiny baby and feel her warm, soft body next to mine.

"Can I see her feet?"

"Of course," the nurse says, laughing. "That's what moms always want to do first off. Count fingers and toes."

Penny hovers over us as the nurse unwraps the blanket.

"Look at these precious little hands," the nurse says. "And all ten fingers, too."

I look at her feet, her tiny toes, the unseparated second and third toes on each foot.

"Oh," the nurse says. "Well . . . you'll want to talk with your pediatrician about that, but it's nothing to worry about."

I lean down and kiss the baby's little feet.

"I'd like to hold her now," Penny says.

The nurse rewraps the baby and hands her to Penny.

"Darling Baby," Penny says. "Darling little Nancy."

Penny looks at me, her eyes shining with happiness.

"Thank you, Autumn. Thank you for this most precious gift."

The nurse takes the baby back to the nursery and Penny goes out to the waiting room to tell Nikki the news.

Another nurse, Henry, comes in with fresh water. I tell him I'm cold and he returns quickly with another blanket. He fluffs my pillows and tucks the added blanket around me.

"There. You get some rest now, Girl! You've worked hard today," he says.

It's been so long since I've slept, I mean really slept, not just the half-sleep that came with the last month of pregnancy.

" . . . and our friends are all aboard, many more of them live next door . . ."

It's Dad's Saturday morning breakfast song! He's singing in his soft, off-key voice and mixing pancake batter in a fish-bowl.

" . . . and the band begins to play . . ." Grams comes riding in on Casper, playing her pretend trombone at full volume. Casper joins us on the chorus, and it turns out he sings better than Dad. Who would have thought Casper would have an English accent and sound a lot like Paul McCartney?

"We all live in a yellow submarine, yellow submarine, yellow submarine . . . "

"Autumn?"

A voice intrudes into my world.

"Time for your meds."

I struggle to stay below, with my family.

A gentle nudge of my shoulder draws me slowly away from the sea of green.

The yellow submarine sinks far below me. I try to stay with it, to go deeper, but instead, I float to the surface against all force of my will.

"You are one sound sleeper," the nurse says, holding a glass of water in one hand and a tiny paper cup with three pills in the other.

"I wanted to stay through breakfast," I say, still groggy.

"Oh, you will, Baby. You're not leaving until tomorrow afternoon."

"No . . . I mean . . . a different breakfast."

He gives me a puzzled look.

"You'll get to fill out your breakfast menu later. There'll be lots to choose from."

He watches as I swallow all three pills, then wheels his cart out of the room.

I've just snuggled down under the covers, ready to close my eyes again, when Audrey comes into the room.

"Hey, Autumn, how do you feel?"

"Tired," I say.

"I hear you did a great job," she says, smiling and pulling the chair up beside my bed. She opens her briefcase and gets some papers from it.

"This won't take long," she says, arranging the papers on a clipboard and putting yellow sticky tabs by signature lines.

"They say exactly the same thing as the forms you signed back in December, but for a release to be legal and binding, the birthmother has to sign after she's given birth."

"So I could change my mind?"

Audrey looks up from the papers.

"Legally? Yes, you can change your mind."

She hands me the clipboard and a pen, frowning.

"Of course, you'd break two kind hearts, but it is a choice you have."

"Come back in ten minutes," I tell her.

"Oh, Autumn! You have a well thought out plan. Don't let the emotion of birth cause you to do something foolish."

"I just want to think. I can't think with you sitting there watching me."

Audrey walks out of the room, her high heels clicking against the hard, tile floor.

I didn't know how much I'd love my baby! But where would we go? What would we do? What's best for her? What's best for me?

I pick up the forms. They're exact copies of the ones I signed before. I change some things. I say that I do want to spend some time alone in the hospital with the baby, and that I want a picture of her once a month. Not just on her birthday or Christmas. I say I want to see her four times a year, and I want to be with her for one week, twice a year, after she gets to be five years old. I initial all of the changes and sign the papers with tomorrow's date. Then I lean back and close my eyes, waiting for Audrey.

She smiles when she sees the signatures.

"I'm sure you're doing the right thing," she says.

Her smile fades as she notices the changes.

"This is quite a different plan than the first one," she says. "Have you talked this over with Penny and Jean?"

"I just decided," I say.

"They may not like these changes. It implies a much greater involvement in the child's life."

She scans down to the signature line. "Oh, and you made a mistake on the date. This is the 14th, not the 15th."

"I want her to be my baby for the rest of today."

Audrey looks back over the papers one more time. She leaves copies with me, and puts the originals back in her briefcase.

"Well . . . good luck to you, Autumn. I'm sure this is all going to work out."

"I'm sure it will," I tell her, eager to hear the clickety-clack of her high heels fading down the hallway.

I turn the call light on and wait, watching the door. I'm relieved to see that the one answering my call is Henry.

"What can I do for you, Love?"

"I want my baby in my room tonight."

He takes my chart from the holder at the foot of the bed.

"It says here the baby's going to stay in the nursery."

"I changed my mind," I tell him. "I just want one night with her."

Henry looks at me strangely, then looks at the chart again.

"Oh, I get it. But . . . the baby is now, officially, in the custody of the adoptive parents. Am I right?"

I show him the newly signed papers with tomorrow's date.

"Okay, Love. One baby coming right up."

He's back in minutes, wheeling her crib in. He checks the baby's bracelet, and mine, raises my bed to a sitting position, takes her from the crib and places her in my arms. He bunches up a pillow and puts it under my arm for support.

"She may need a bottle pretty soon," he says. "She'll let you know. Just turn on your light and I'll come set you up."

I hold her for a long time, looking down at her face. She squirms now and then, and fusses just a little, but mostly she sleeps.

"Listen, Baby. I want you to know that I love you with all of my heart and soul, and that I'll always love you, no matter what happens. That letter that I wrote to you back before I knew you? When I said I didn't love you? That's a lie. I hope you never see that letter. As soon as I find it I'll tear it up. But in case I don't find it, and you do, I want you to know that letter is a really terrible lie. When I wrote it I didn't know I was lying, but I was — big time."

She squirms a little and makes a funny sound, and I wonder if she needs a diaper change. Her eyes flutter open and then close again.

"I'm going to be part of your life. Maybe not an everyday part, but I'm going to be checking in with you. You'll like Nikki and Penny. I chose two really good parents for you. That's one way I'm doing right by you . . ."

She starts fussing again, and then works into a cry. Her face gets red and I can feel her chest heaving with every breath. I turn on the call light and hope Henry hurries. What if there's something really terribly wrong with her? What if she cries herself to death? She's so little . . .

Henry comes in and takes her from me, cooing to her as he puts her back down in the crib. He changes her diaper, then goes to the nursery for a bottle. She's still crying and I'm rocking her crib back and forth, hoping to comfort her. He puts her back in my arms, hands me the bottle, and shows me the best feeding position.

"They don't eat much the first day or so, but it's worth a try," he says.

I hold the bottle to her mouth. She turns her head away. After a while I try again. This time she lets the nipple stay in her mouth and sucks at it from time to time. She opens her eyes and looks up at me.

"I love you," I say to her. "I love you forever."

It seems like she's listening. I tell her over and over that I love her. She drops off to sleep again, and when my arm is so tired it hurts, I put her back in the crib. I'm still watching her sleep when Henry comes in a little after midnight.

"Time's up," he says. "Do you want to hold her again one more time?"

I nod, and he places her in my arms.

"I'll be back in about five," he says, walking out the door.

"This isn't a sad goodbye," I tell the sleeping baby. "I'll see you again pretty soon."

She opens her eyes and looks straight into mine.

"I've had to say some sad goodbyes to my family — goodbyes that can't be followed by hellos. But you, Baby, before you know it, we'll be saying hello again. We've got goodbyes, but we've got plenty more hellos coming up. I'm going to be happy about that. You can be happy about that, too."

Henry sticks his head in the doorway. I kiss my baby's soft, sweet forehead.

"Bye for now," I tell her. "I love you."

Henry puts her back in the crib and wheels her away.

25

I spend five weeks in Long Beach with Sandy and Ella and the first week, all I want to do is sleep. Then I start doing a short walk in the morning and a short walk in the afternoon. Nikki comes to visit on Saturday, bringing the rest of my stuff. We drive the two miles or so to the beach and sit on a bench along the boardwalk.

"Want one?" Nikki says, pulling a couple of power bars from her pocket.

"Thanks," I say, tearing open the wrapper and taking a bite of the granola/raspberry bar.

"I suppose you're going to need some new clothes pretty soon," Nikki says.

"I hope so, but look!"

I pull my sweatshirt up, showing how I still can't button my jeans.

"You'll get rid of that as soon as you're able to exercise," she laughs.

"Did you bring pictures of Nancy?"

Nikki shakes her head.

"She's okay, isn't she?"

"She's great. Wonderful," Nikki laughs. "She sleeps all day and keeps us up all night."

"I want to see her before I leave."

"Well, sure. We can work that out. It's just . . ."

"Penny doesn't want me to, does she?"

Nikki doesn't say anything.

"I was just a baby carrier for her and now that's over she doesn't give a shite about me anymore."

"It's not that, Autumn. She's crazy about the baby. We both are. But . . . Penny's afraid that if you see the baby, you'll want to take her away with you."

"I will want to take the baby away. But I'm not going to do it! How stupid does she think I am? I'm going to take a baby to the guide dog training center? And what, leave her locked up in a bedroom all day? Tell Penny to get a grip!"

"You know, there are horror stories out there, about birthparents coming back for kids when they're three, or four, or whatever, and ripping them out of secure, loving homes . . ."

"I'm not a horror story. I love the baby and I wouldn't do anything to hurt her. I wouldn't do anything to hurt you or Penny either, but Penny doesn't mind hurting me."

Nikki tosses a chunk of her power bar out on the sand and two seagulls swoop down to get it. I toss a chunk of my bar close to the seagull that lost out on the first piece, but the other one manages to snatch it up.

I try again, and again the aggressive gull wins the toss. Nikki laughs. I give up and eat the last bit of food myself.

"I just want to see her for a little while."

"Of course. We'll work it out."

By the end of March I'm jogging two miles a day and working out with weights at the Y. I call Wayne at the guide dog training center.

"Sounds like you're ready," he says. "Come anytime next week. Just say when and I'll pick you up at the bus depot."

I call Nikki to tell her when I'm leaving for the training center in northern California, and to remind her that I still want to see the baby before I go. The next morning, Penny calls. After we get through the awkward how've you been chit-chat, including long pauses, she gets to the point.

"I just needed some time," she says. "I thought you might, too."

There's another long pause.

"I do care about you, Autumn. And I want you to be a part of Nancy's life. I'm sorry if you felt shut out . . . Do you have plans for next Sunday?"

"No."

"Maybe you'd like to come over and have dinner with us? You could invite your friend Danni, too, if you want to."

"And see Nancy?"

"Yes, and see Nancy."

I spend the rest of the week taking care of details. One day, Ella lets me borrow her car and I drive over to the county home to see Miss F. and Ms. Lee.

"You look wonderful!" Ms. Lee says. "Not at all like the anemic, discouraged girl I first met."

They are full of questions about what's next for me and want to hear all about my job with the guide dogs and my college plans. Before I leave, Miss F. reaches into a pile of papers and pulls out the card I sent to Madison at Christmas time.

"She's back with her mother for a while," Miss F. says.

"Do you know her new address?"

"No . . . They moved just a few weeks after we released Madison back to her mother's custody and we've not been able to locate them."

As I reach for the card, Ms. Lee suggests I leave it here.

"She'll be back," she says.

I write my new return address on the Christmas envelope and hand it back to Miss F.

Walking out the door of the county home, I think about all of the girls I met while I was there. As unlucky as I've been, first my mom dying, then losing the rest of my family, at least for most of my life I had a family that loved me, and took good care of me, and helped me learn how to live in the world. I wish Madison, and

Dericia, and all the other kids inside could have had that. I know Baby Nancy will.

On Sunday, Ella and Sandy are already out for their walk along the beach when Nikki comes to get me.

"I don't think they'd mind if we had a quick game of air hockey before we leave, do you?" Nikki asks. "I hate to have you leave town before I can regain my championship."

I win the first game.

"Two out of three?" Nikki asks.

"Sure."

She wins the second game, and I win the third.

"I hope I'm not losing my touch," she says with a smile.

I admit to her that I've had plenty of practice since I've been staying here.

"I'm being groomed for the Thanksgiving tournament," I say.

She looks puzzled, then breaks into a huge smile.

"Well, then, I'd better start practicing."

Penny meets us at the door, holding Baby Nancy.

"Can I hold her?" I ask.

"Why don't you have a seat first?"

I sit in the big recliner, the only chair that offered comfort during my last month of pregnancy.

"Just be careful with her little head," Penny says, placing the baby in my arms.

"Hello," I whisper to her. "A happy hello to you."

Her eyes fix on mine and I wonder if she somehow remembers me from our one night together. Or maybe she senses that my body is the one that housed and nourished her for nine months.

I hold her close, remembering the scrawny little red-faced infant I first held in my arms.

"She's grown," I say.

"She's already gained over a pound since she came home from the hospital," Nikki says.

The three of us sit watching Baby Nancy until she starts fussing. Penny goes into the kitchen to fix a bottle.

"Our lives have changed drastically," Nikki says, smiling down at the baby. "Only a little over eight pounds, and Nancy's already the one in charge."

"Like her namesake," I say.

"Yep. Pretty soon she'll be wanting a roadster."

"If only we had Hannah for a housekeeper," Penny says, coming in with a bottle.

"Here we go, Sweetheart," she says, easing the baby from my arms.

"Maybe Autumn would like to feed her," Nikki says.

"Oh, that's okay," Penny says, sitting down with the baby and holding the bottle to her mouth.

The baby sucks steadily at the bottle, looking up into Penny's eyes. After she's been fed and burped, Penny carries her back to the pink room.

"Let's change you and see if you're ready for a little nap," she says.

I follow her back to the pink room and watch as Penny takes off the wet diaper, cleans her little parts with a baby wipe, puts on a fresh diaper and lays her gently in the crib. She winds up the teddy bear that plays "You Are My Sunshine," and pauses in the doorway, waiting for me to follow.

"I'd like to stay in here with her for just a few minutes," I whisper.

Penny looks hesitant, then nods her head and leaves the room. I stand over the crib looking down on the baby.

"See, it's just like I told you," I say softly. "We'll get lots of happy hellos, so we don't need to be sad about our goodbyes. I love you, little Nancy."

I stand watching her until the song winds down, then tiptoe out.

Danni arrives at the same time the pizza's delivered.

"Where's the little baby?" she says, her voice going high and squeaky with anticipation.

"She's sleeping," Penny says in a whisper.

"Oh," Danni whispers back, "Can I see her?"

"Well . . . just be very quiet."

I walk with Danni back to the pink room.

"Oh, she's adorable," she whispers.

Danni moves closer to the crib and the baby stirs. We both tiptoe out and join Nikki and Penny at the table. Over pizza and salad, Nikki and Danni talk about the last track meet which was, in Nikki's words, a disaster. Danni talks about plans for Grad Nite at Disneyland, and how because Evan isn't a student at Hamilton High, he has to get special permission from the school to be her date.

"Will you be coming back for graduation?" Danni asks.

I shake my head.

"My diploma's from San Remo TAPP, not Hamilton High. I can't go through any of Hamilton's graduation ceremonies."

"That sucks! Almost your whole time in high school has been at Hamilton! And after all you've done? No way would we have won C.I.F. without you! You should be walking across the stage with everybody else!!"

"It's okay," I say, surprised to know that I mean it.

After dinner we look in on Baby Nancy one more time. When we get ready to leave, Nikki draws both me and Danni into a broad hug.

"It won't be half the team without you two," she says. "I'll miss you."

At the door, Penny hugs me tight.

"Call or email anytime. Come see us when you can."

They stand at the door, waving, as we drive away.

"They're very good people," I say to Danni.

"I know," she says.

On the way back to Long Beach we talk about the funny old times, the scary times, the changes in our lives. Parked in front of Ella and Sandy's house, Danni says, "I may not be going to Cal Poly after all."

"Why not?"

"I may go to Bible College with Evan."

"But you'll lose your scholarship, won't you?"

"My parents say it's worth the money to have me in a Christian school. Besides, I don't want to be so far away from Evan."

I sit staring out the window, not knowing what to say. All through high school we planned on going to college together. Of course, we'd planned on double dating to Grad Night, and walking across the Hamilton High stage with our whole class, too. I have to admit, Danni's not the only one who's changed our plans.

"Nobody else knows this yet, but . . . Evan and I are getting married next year."

"Married? You and Evan?"

"Yes. And I want you to be my maid of honor. June 25. Save the date!"

"Yeah. Okay," I say, still thinking about how we won't be roommates at Cal Poly, and, worse yet, we won't be teammates.

"Do you think Nikki and Penny will let Nancy be our flower girl?"

I laugh.

"I'm going to miss your airheadedness!"

"What? You don't think they'll let her??"

"Well . . . She may not be walking yet. Would you mind if she has to crawl down the aisle?"

That gets us laughing.

Danni pesters me to come back for graduation, just to be there and to see everyone. She's very insistent and I tell her maybe I will, just because I don't want to argue with her. But in my heart, I know I won't do that. My life has already moved far away from the old Hamilton High life, and as Grams used to say, I would be a "fish out of water."

After a teary promise to keep in touch, we say goodbye. I can't help wondering if we'll stay sister-close with all of the coming changes, but I know we'll always care.

It turns out I'm a "natural" at working with the dogs at the training center, at least that's what my supervising instructors say. One of the dogs I help take care of, Sheba, is a retired guide. When I first saw her she reminded me so much of Casper I decided to check her records. Sure enough, she has the same parents. She's older than Casper would have been, so they weren't from the same litter, but her markings are identical to his. Sometimes I get to take her home with me at night, to the apartment I share with three other girls. It's comforting to have a Casper look-alike sleeping at the foot of my bed.

I often walk with Jerry, one of the other dog care assistants, when we're exercising the dogs. With the dogs-in-training, we walk along the sidewalks, and across busy streets, getting them used to traffic noises and to crowds of people. With the retired dogs, though, we like to take them along the quiet, wooded pathways on the other side of town. Jerry grew up near here, so he knows where to find all of the half-hidden paths.

On our last walk together, Jerry asked if I'd like to go to a movie Friday night. I said yes. I can tell he likes me, and I think I could like him, too. One thing I know for certain, though. If he's got any of those little bottles of champagne in his car Friday night, I'm out of there.

Speaking of little bottles of champagne, I got a package in the mail last week — from Jason! He said he got my address from Danni, and he hoped things were going well for me. He said he didn't want to change anything with the adoption papers, but he'd been thinking about things. He said:

> *I want your baby's family to have this information. Would you please pass these papers along for me?*

Stapled together were Jason's health records for his whole life, from a copy of his first pediatrician's report to the results of his pre-entrance physical exam for University of Iowa. In the family history section it said one of his grandparents had diabetes, one had heart problems and high blood pressure, and his mother had once been treated for seizures. It was a very thorough history and included Jason's full name, blood type, and place and date of birth.

I don't know if he's hoping Nancy will make contact some time, when she's older, or if he just wants them to know what the genetic tendencies could be. Either way, I emailed him a very brief thank you and sent the packet on to Nikki and Penny.

The scholarship finally came through, and I'm eager to start college in August. Even though Danni won't be at Cal Poly, Krystal will. I haven't seen her since last October. I'm looking forward to that happy hello. Also, Krystal loves to talk about dreams, and I want to get back to a dream routine.

In a few months, when I turn eighteen, I'll be getting whatever money my dad and Grams had in their bank accounts, and money from Dad's insurance policy. It won't be much, but enough to see me through college if I'm careful, and if I continue to get a scholarship each year.

I still miss my family something awful, but like Conrad, from *Ordinary People*, I'm starting to feel alive again. It's a good feeling.

Early Thursday, before I have to catch the afternoon bus for San Luis Obispo, I take Sheba for an easy walk along one of the paths at the edge of the woods. Sheba tires quickly now, so we stop to rest about halfway into our walk. I sit on a tree stump and Sheba sits beside me, tall and straight, as if she were still on the job.

I catch a shimmer of light from something near Sheba's front paw, and stoop to pick it up. It's a dirt-encrusted rock with a tiny speck of fool's gold showing — just enough to catch the light. I scrape at the dirt with my fingernail, wondering if there's more fool's gold than just that little speck. There isn't, but as I scrape, the shape of the rock becomes more obvious. It's a heart, smaller than the one in my pocket, but definitely a heart.

On the way back to the training center, holding Sheba's leash with one hand and the new-found rock in the other, I continue rubbing the dirt away. Someday, twelve or thirteen years from now, I'll give Nancy this rock. I'll remind her that I'll always love her, no matter what mistakes she may make, and that I'm sure she'll always be part of the solution, like she has been since the day she was born.

ABOUT

THE

AUTHOR

In addition to *No More Sad Goodbyes,* Marilyn Reynolds is the author of seven other young adult novels: *If You Loved Me, Love Rules, Baby Help, But What About Me? Too Soon for Jeff, Detour for Emmy,* and *Telling,* and a book of short stories, *Beyond Dreams,* all part of the popular **True-to-Life Series from Hamilton High.** She is also the author of *I Won't Read and You Can't Make Me: Reaching Reluctant Teen Readers.*

Besides her books for teens, Reynolds has a variety of published personal essays to her credit, and was nominated for an Emmy Award for the ABC Afterschool Special teleplay of *Too Soon for Jeff.*

Reynolds is a seasoned educator who has worked for more than twenty-five years with teenagers facing a multitude of crises. Her extensive background with young adults includes teaching reluctant learners and at-risk teens at an alternative high school in Southern California. She often is a guest speaker and seminar leader for programs and organizations that serve teens, parents, teachers, and writers.

When she is not reading, writing novels, or participating in conferences, Reynolds enjoys walks along the American River, visits from children and grandchildren, and movies and dinners out. She and her husband, Mike, live in northern California.

NOVELS BY MARILYN REYNOLDS
True to Life Series from Hamilton High

LOVE RULES — A testament to the power of love — in family, in friendships, and in teen couples, whether gay or straight, of the same ethnicity or not. It is a testament to the power of gay/straight alliances in working toward the safety of all students.

IF YOU LOVED ME — Are love and sex synonymous? Must Lauren break her promise to herself in order to keep Tyler's love? ". . . an engaging, thought-provoking read, recommended for reluctant readers." BookList.

BABY HELP — Melissa doesn't consider herself abused — after all, Rudy only hits her occasionally when he's drinking . . . until she realizes the effect his abuse is having on their child.

DETOUR FOR EMMY — Novel about Emmy, pregnant at 15. American Library Association Best Books for Young Adults List; South Carolina Young Adult Book Award.

TOO SOON FOR JEFF — The story of Jeff Browning, a senior at Hamilton High School, a nationally ranked debater, and reluctant father of Christy Calderon's unborn baby. Best Books for Young Adults List; Quick Pick Recommendation for Young Adult Reluctant Readers; ABC After-School TV Special.

BUT WHAT ABOUT ME? — Erica pours more and more of her heart and soul into helping boyfriend Danny get his life back on track. But the more she tries to help him, the more she loses sight of her own dreams. It takes a tragic turn of events to show Erica that she can't "save" Danny, and that she is losing herself in the process of trying.

TELLING — When twelve-year-old Cassie is accosted and fondled by the father of the children for whom she babysits, she feels dirty and confused. "A sad, frightening, ultimately hopeful, and definitely worthwhile purchase." BookList.

BEYOND DREAMS — Six short stories dealing with situations faced by teenagers — drinking and driving, racism, school failure, abortion, partner abuse, aging relative. ". . . book will hit home with teens." VOYA

Visit your bookstore — or order directly from Morning Glory Press
6595 San Haroldo Way, Buena Park, CA 90620. 1.888.612.8254.
Free catalog on request.
Visit our web site at **www.morningglorypress.com**

ORDER FORM
Morning Glory Press
6595 San Haroldo Way, Buena Park, CA 90620
714.828.1998; 1.888.612.8254   Fax 714.828.2049
For complete catalog, contact Morning Glory Press

			Price	Total
Novels by Marilyn Reynolds:				
___	*No More Sad Goodbye*	978-1-932538-71-7	9.95	_____
___	Hardcover	978-1-932538-72-4	15.95	_____
___	*Love Rules*	1-885356-76-5	9.95	_____
___	*If You Loved Me*	1-885356-55-2	8.95	_____
___	*Baby Help*	1-885356-27-7	8.95	_____
___	*But What About Me?*	1-885356-10-2	8.95	_____
___	*Too Soon for Jeff*	0-930934-91-1	8.95	_____
___	*Detour for Emmy*	0-930934-76-8	8.95	_____
___	*Telling*	1-885356-03-x	8.95	_____
___	*Beyond Dreams*	1-885356-00-5	8.95	_____

Also by Marilyn Reynolds

___ *I Won't Read and You Can't Make Me*

0-325-00605-9   17.00   _____

Other titles (non-fiction) for Young Adults

		Price	Total
___ *Breaking Free from Partner Abuse*	1-885356-53-6	8.95	_____
___ *Moving On*		4.95	_____
___ *Will the Dollars Stretch?*	1-885356-78-1	7.95	_____
___ *Dreams to Reality*	978-1-932538-36-6	14.95	_____
___ *Mommy, I'm Hungry!*	978-1-932538-51-9	12.95	_____
___ *Mami, tengo hambre!*	978-1-932538-75-5	12.95	_____
___ *Your Pregnancy/Newborn Journey*	1-932538-00-3	12.95	_____
___ *Your Baby's First Year*	1-932538-03-8	12.95	_____
___ *The Challenge of Toddlers*	1-932538-06-2	12.95	_____
___ *Discipline from Birth to Three*	1-932538-09-7	12.95	_____
Teen Dads: Rights, Responsibilities and Joys	1-885356-68-4	12.95	_____

TOTAL   _____

Add postage: 10% of total—Min., $3.50; 30%, Canada   _____
California residents add 7.75% sales tax   _____

TOTAL   _____

Ask about quantity discounts, Teacher, Student Guides.
Prepayment requested. School/library purchase orders accepted.
If not satisfied, return in 15 days for refund.

NAME _____ PHONE_____

ADDRESS _____